magnolia

ALSO BY KRISTI COOK

magnolia

kristi cook

SIMON PULSE
New York   London   Toronto   Sydney   New Delhi

SIMON PULSE

An imprint of Simon & Schuster Children's Publishing Division

1230 Avenue of the Americas, New York, NY 10020

This Simon Pulse edition August 2014

Text copyright © 2014 by Kristina Cook Hort

Cover photograph copyright © 2014 by Stephen Carroll/Trevillion Images

All rights reserved, including the right of reproduction in whole or in part in any form.

SIMON PULSE and colophon are registered trademarks of Simon & Schuster, Inc.

For information about special discounts for bulk purchases, please contact Simon & Schuster Special Sales at 1-866-506-1949 or business@simonandschuster.com.

The Simon & Schuster Speakers Bureau can bring authors to your live event. For more information or to book an event contact the Simon & Schuster Speakers Bureau at 1-866-248-3049 or visit our website at www.simonspeakers.com.

Book design by Regina Flath

The text of this book was set in Adobe Caslon Pro.

Manufactured in the United States of America

10 9 8 7 6 5 4 3 2 1

Library of Congress Cataloging-in-Publication Data

Cook, Kristi.

Magnolia / by Kristi Cook. — 1st Simon Pulse hardcover edition.

p. cm.

Summary: High school seniors Ryder and Jemma have been at odds for four years, despite their mothers' lifelong plan that they will marry one day, but when a storm ravages their small Mississippi town, the pair's true feelings are revealed.

[1. Family life—Mississippi—Fiction. 2. Interpersonal relations—Fiction. 3. College choice—Fiction. 4. Love—Fiction. 5. High schools—Fiction. 6. Schools—Fiction. 7. Mississippi—Fiction.] I. Title.

PZ7.C76984Mag 2014

[Fic]—dc23

2013050999

ISBN 978-1-4424-8535-8 (hc)

ISBN 978-1-4424-8534-1 (pbk)

ISBN 978-1-4424-8536-5 (eBook)

For my University of Southern Mississippi Phi Mu sisters,
who know all too well that you can take the girl out of Mississippi
but you can't take the Mississippi out of the girl

ACKNOWLEDGMENTS

Enormous thanks to:

Jennifer Klonsky, who somehow saw the potential in this book in just a few scant pages.

Nicole Ellul, whose editorial brilliance made it a much stronger book. A million thank-yous and a hearty round of applause.

Amalie Howard, BFF and critique partner extraordinaire. I couldn't do it without you! Seriously. I mean *seriously* seriously.

Cindy Thomas, for patiently listening to me moan and groan, and then cracking that whip and making me Just. Do. It. What would I do without you?

Melinda Rayner Courtney, for being my sounding board for all things Mississippi, and for sending me pictures of *real* Mississippi. I'm proud to call you sister!

The HB&K society (you know who you are!) for helping me figure out my plot, and for listening to me wax poetic about AJ McCarron.

My agent, Marcy Posner, for everything, all these years.

Ella, for reading all the dialogue in that super-authentic (ha!) southern accent. You made it fun!

Lastly, to my family—Dan, Vivian, and Ella (yes, again)—for keeping me sane. Love you!

ACT I

For never was a story of more woe
Than this of Juliet and her Romeo.

—William Shakespeare, *Romeo and Juliet*

ACT I

Scene 1

Glancing out my window, I hold up my finger and thumb, creating a little frame around Ryder Marsden, who stands outside on the lawn below. I close one eye to get the illusion just right and then pretend to squash him.

Take *that*.

I let the curtains fall back against the glass, effectively blocking the view of my nemesis standing there beneath the twinkle lights, looking way too hot in his charcoal-colored suit. It would be *so* much easier to hate him if he didn't look so good. And I want to hate him; I really do.

You know those tragic stories where two kids from feuding families fall in love? Okay, flip that inside out and turn it on its head and you've got *our* story, Ryder's and mine.

It all began like this: On April 6, 1862, at the Battle of Shiloh, Captain Jeremiah D. Marsden—that's Ryder's ancestor—took a minié ball in the left kneecap. Corporal Lewiston G. Cafferty—that's mine—picked up Captain Marsden and carried him off the field of battle to safety.

On his back. More than a mile. Barefoot.

At least, that's how the story goes. Frankly, I'm a little skeptical, but whatever. The point is, the Marsdens and the Caffertys have been like *this* ever since.

And when I say like *this*, I'm talking complete and utter familial devotion. Our families' lives are so intertwined it's sometimes hard to remember who belongs where and with whom. We do everything together—church, backyard barbeques, even vacations. One of my favorite stories is about the time my uncle Don was somehow left behind with the Marsdens after a trip to the coast and no one noticed for two weeks. Seriously.

The Marsdens and the Caffertys play out their drama right here in Magnolia Branch, Mississippi, population 2,190. This little slice of heaven boasts one traffic light, six churches, a library, and a picturesque town square. The only nod to civilization is a Ward's just off the highway, and you wouldn't believe how hard some of the locals fought it when they first proposed it, back before I was born.

If you're wondering what it's like to grow up here, just

consider this—there are *six* choices when it comes to places of worship, but only *one* when it comes to fast food (the aforementioned Ward's). Need I say more? By the way, if you want to see some real Shakespearean-style feuding, look no farther than First Methodist and Cavalry Baptist—they've been going at it for years.

Truth be told, not much has changed here in Magnolia Branch since the war—and when anyone around here says "the war," they mean the Civil War. Yeah, a hundred and fifty years and several other wars later.

The Marsdens still live at Magnolia Landing, an old, antebellum-era plantation house on two-hundred-plus acres down by Flint Creek. It looks just like you'd imagine—pristine white and perfectly symmetrical, with huge columns and a half-mile-long drive shaded by a canopy of ancient oaks dripping Spanish moss.

And we Caffertys still live just down the road in a house that once served as Magnolia Landing's overseer's cottage. The house has been added on to several times throughout the years, giving it a haphazard, rambling look. Even so, I think it's perfect—whitewashed brick and clapboard with wide plank floors and sleeping porches. Unlike Magnolia Landing, our house looks comfortable and lived in. Visiting the Marsdens is like visiting a museum—and really, who wants to live in a museum?

Anyway, our families have been desperate to unite through matrimonial bliss for as long as anyone can remember. But as fate would have it, they were always out of sync. Or totally *in* sync, depending on how you look at it. Either way, in all these years, there hasn't been a single eligible male-female pair who could get the job done.

Until Ryder and me, that is.

We were born exactly six weeks apart, a perfect match, age-wise. You can imagine what it's been like since our mothers first plopped us into a crib together, rubbing their hands in conspiratorial glee as they planned our wedding. Playdates followed where the adults smiled and cooed as they watched us dig in the sandbox, where Ryder tugging on my pigtails was a sure sign of his adoration, where me throwing sand in his face only proved my devotion.

Star-crossed love? Ha! Not even close. Mostly, I try to avoid him whenever possible. I'm not sure how I'm going to accomplish that tonight, though.

Because tonight is the annual Magnolia Branch Historical Society Gala. Think huge, formal party where the who's who of Magnolia Branch gather to rub shoulders and gossip while they sip champagne and eat fancy food. My mom is this year's chair and hostess, which means I have to smile and make nice and mingle with the guests. And yes, Ryder Marsden is one of the guests.

"Ugh," I groan, peering out the window at the growing crowd. The party is in full swing out on the lawn, and I'm sure my mom is wondering where I am. Reluctantly, I leave behind the comfortable cocoon of my bedroom and hurry down the stairs and through the front hall. Smoothing down my pale blue dress with damp palms, I step out onto the front porch and take a deep, calming breath.

The first thing I notice is the oppressive heat. It must be close to ninety degrees, the air warm and heavy even though the sun set a half hour ago. The full moon has risen over the horizon, casting a silvery glow on the scene before me. The effect is magical, and I shiver despite the heat.

The yard has been completely transformed, every tree wrapped with bright twinkle lights, colorful paper lanterns strung between them. There's a wooden dance floor out in the middle of the lawn, the band set just behind it. The strings are playing something slow and pretty while the rest of the musicians ready their instruments.

My mom has set up the buffet beneath the tallest, broadest magnolia tree, long tables filled with silver chafing dishes and manned by servers wearing crisp white aprons. She's rented real china dishes for tonight—I'd helped her pick out the pattern, plain ivory with a bamboolike border.

Round tables are grouped around the dance floor, all draped in cream linens. Each table is lit by an ivory pillar candle in a hurricane vase, colorful hydrangeas arranged artfully around the base. It's beautiful, all of it.

I search for my mom and find her standing beside the buffet with Laura Grace Marsden, Ryder's mom. They are BFFs, of course—sorority sisters at Ole Miss, mutual maids of honor. Mama spies me and waves, gesturing for me to join them.

"Jemma!" Laura Grace calls out as I make my way toward them, my silver flats silent on the thick grass. "You look like a princess, honey. Come here and give me some sugar."

I hurry to her side and allow her to wrap me in a Shalimar-scented hug. "You like the dress?" I ask her.

She grasps my shoulders and eyes me at arm's length, her gaze scanning me from head to toe. "It's gorgeous! Vintage?"

Grinning, I nod. "From 1960-something. Lucy helped me fix it up."

We'd had to cut away most of the ratty blue tulle and replace the skirt, along with adding a new zipper. But the original satin bodice was intact, and it's beyond gorgeous.

Laura Grace touches one of the pale pink rosettes at my hip. "You and Lucy should go into business together. Folks'd pay a fortune for a dress like this."

Mama smiles archly. "I told you so."

I ignore that. "Have you seen Morgan and Lucy?"

She points to her left. "Down by the creek with the boys. If you find Daddy, send him over here, okay? I think that strand of lights is coming loose." She glances up at the twinkling limb overhead.

"Sure," I say, though the lights in question look fine to me. Good thing, since my dad is a doctor, not an electrician, as he likes to say. Apparently, it's a Star Trek thing.

And by "doctor" he means the PhD kind—he's a physics professor over at the university.

"Oh, and, Jemma?" Laura Grace offers me a dazzling smile. "You make sure to save a dance for my son."

I can't help but roll my eyes. Yeah, as if *that's* going to happen.

As I set off to find my friends I actually hear the two of them giggling behind me.

Unbelievable. What are they, twelve?

As I round the dance floor I spot my dad over by the bar. "Hey," I call out, hooking a thumb in my mom's direction. "You're wanted over by the buffet. Something about loose lights."

He picks up his drink with a sigh. "On my way."

I hurry my pace, eager to find my friends. The moon illuminates the sandy, moss-strewn path that leads down to the creek, but I could easily find my way in the dark. I love to come down here at night and listen to the symphony of sounds—frogs croaking, katydids singing, owls hooting. The Mississippi Moonlight Sonata, as I like to call it.

When my sister, Nan, and I were kids, we would sneak down here on hot summer nights. We'd hike up our nightgowns and wade in the shallows to cool off and then lie down on the hard, scratchy picnic tables, staring up at the sky.

I miss my sister. None of us could understand why she chose Southern Miss—a good four-hour drive from home—when she could've gone to school in Oxford. But that's Nan, always unpredictable, always rebelling against my parents' expectations.

Not like me.

I can't help but sigh as I follow the path down the slope and around the bend to the sandy clearing on the edge of the flat, black water.

"Fashionably late, as always," Morgan calls out in greeting, her body a dark silhouette against the night sky. She's perched on one of the picnic tables, her strappy-sandaled feet resting on the bench below.

"Hey, I've got a rep to uphold," I shoot back. "Wouldn't want to disappoint my fans. What are y'all doing down here?"

"The guys are sneaking in a case of beer. By boat," she adds with a grin. "Me, I'm just watching."

I can just make out a handful of boys down by the water's edge, hauling in a sleek canoe.

"Very clever," I say. "Let me guess—Mason's idea?"

"Probably." Morgan unfolds her long legs and steps gracefully down to the ground, coming around the table to stand beside me.

"You look great!" I say, taking in her simple pink silk sheath dress. Her pale blond hair is twisted into a knot at the back of her head, and a strand of creamy pearls encircles her throat. Morgan is the reigning Miss Teen Lafayette County, and she looks every bit the part tonight.

Her mouth curves into a pageant-perfected smile. "You look great too. Love the dress."

"What, this ol' thing?" I quip.

"No camera? I figured you'd be filming the party for sure."

I carry my video camera with me everywhere. It's a hobby of mine. I like to make movies. And, okay . . . I'd love to go to film school next year, but that's a whole nother story. "Mama made me promise to leave it in my room tonight—said it would make the guests feel uncomfortable or something," I say with a shrug. "Where's Lucy, by the way?"

"I sent her off to find you ten minutes ago. She must have gotten lost." She shifts her gaze to the spot just above my left shoulder. "Wait, here she comes."

I swat at a mosquito as I turn to watch Lucy make her way toward us with a murderous scowl on her face. "I just got stuck talking to Mr. Donaldson for, like, fifteen minutes," she calls out. "I'm all hoarse now. Where the hell *were* you?"

Mr. Donaldson is our AP European History teacher. He's

starting to go deaf in one ear but refuses to acknowledge it, so you have to yell at him. Loudly.

"We must have crossed paths or something," I say with a shrug.

"So, what do you think?" Lucy strikes a runway pose, right down to the purposefully blank expression. The white halter neckline sets off her dark, bronze-brown skin, the easy drape of fabric highlighting her curves. She's had her hair relaxed, and soft, glamorous-looking waves fall just past her shoulders.

"Perfect," I reply. "As always." She looks sophisticated, far beyond her seventeen years.

The boys have reached the picnic tables now, hooting triumphantly as they pass around the contraband cans of Schaefer Light.

"Y'all better take it easy," I call out. "No ruining Mama's party, okay?"

A grinning Ben salutes me with his beer. "Yes'm."

Ben is Ryder's cousin—second cousin, to be specific—and one of his best friends, even though they couldn't be any more different. Ben is sweet, thoughtful. Kind.

Whereas Ryder, well . . . I'll tell you about Ryder. He's the star quarterback of our Division 1A state-championship football team. Top student in our class, and he doesn't even have to work at it. He plays the piano like some kind of freaking prodigy, and I wouldn't be surprised if he composed sonatas or something in his spare time.

Oh, and did I mention that he's gorgeous? Of course he is. Six foot four, two hundred ten pounds of swoon-worthy good looks. Spiky dark hair, chocolate brown eyes, and full-on dimples.

And his future? Right now half the SEC is courting him hard, and the other half is wishing they were. It's a foregone conclusion that he'll play for Ole Miss—Mississippi's golden boy, kept right here at home.

Ryder brushes past me and my friends as if we don't exist, unworthy of his notice, as he follows Ben and the rest of the guys—Mason, Tanner, and Patrick—to the picnic table behind us.

Tonight, the guys are wearing the standard dress uniform of khakis with a white oxford-cloth shirt and colorful tie. Their jackets—navy blue, of course—have long since been discarded, their ties loosened and hanging untidily against their shirtfronts.

Only Ryder, discordant in his charcoal suit and French-blue tie, remains jacketed and fully buttoned up, not even appearing to break a sweat despite the oppressive heat. He's also the only one without a beer, I notice.

That doesn't mean he's quiet, though. They're loud and raucous, all of them, shouting and cursing at each other as they discuss—what else?—football.

"You've gotta see this dude's arm to believe it," Tanner is saying. "I'm talking perfect spiral." He mimes a throw.

"So? You need receivers who don't suck ass for it to make any difference." Mason tips back his beer and downs nearly half its contents in a single, long gulp. Mason is Ryder's other best friend. He also happens to be Morgan's twin brother. Back in elementary school, he wore his hair so long that people often mistook them for identical twin girls—a little factoid I like to revisit whenever he gets too annoying, which is often. He can be a jerk sometimes—hot-tempered and a little crude.

"Let's see if you're still singing the same song in two weeks, after we kick your sorry asses," Tanner says sourly.

"Just thinking it ain't gonna make it so, bro. Where'd you say this kid transferred from? Holy Cross?" Mason shakes his head, chuckling. "Yeah, I'm not worried. You worried, Ryder?"

All the guys' heads swivel toward Ryder. He tosses the football he's holding into the air and catches it. "Nope," he says with a cocky grin.

"Maybe you should be." Tanner is glaring now, his arms folded across his scrawny chest. Tanner is *my* cousin, on my mom's side. He goes to West Lafayette High, our big football rival. It's some kind of weird districting thing, because he went to elementary and middle school with us. He probably could've applied for a waiver or something, but he didn't. Mason claims it's because Tanner knew he wasn't good enough to play ball for

Magnolia Branch, and who knows? Maybe he's right. Either way, things have a habit of getting pretty heated whenever he's around nowadays.

"Hey, did y'all catch the Alabama-LSU game this afternoon?" Ben asks, obviously trying to defuse the situation.

"They're such morons," Lucy mutters as the boys' conversation steers toward more neutral ground.

Morgan nods. "Mason brought his shotgun, by the way. In the boat with the beer. They'll probably go off and shoot stuff before the night is over."

"So long as Jemma doesn't go with them." Lucy directs a stern glare in my direction.

Because I'm the best shot in all of Magnolia Branch—an indisputable fact. I've got trophies to show for it. Not that I would ever shoot a living thing—it's just targets and skeet for me, thank you very much. But yeah, Mama taught me to sew, Daddy to shoot. That's the way we roll here in Magnolia Branch.

"Not in this dress and not with boys who've been drinking," I say, stealing a glance over my shoulder at the boys in question.

At that exact moment, Patrick turns toward me and our gazes collide. He smiles at me—a goofy, mischievous grin.

Inexplicably, my stomach flutters in response. I swallow hard, my pulse racing.

Oh, no.

If there's one thing I know about Patrick Hughes, it's that he's trouble. *Big* trouble. The Hugheses are old money—and I mean *way* old money—and Patrick is their little prince. Like Mason, he's prone to having *too* good of a time, as evidenced by not one but *two* DUIs in the past year alone. Lucky for him, his daddy's a lawyer, a partner at Marsden, Hughes & Fogarty, along with Ryder's dad.

Nope, my parents would definitely *not* approve, despite his wealth and pedigree.

Who knows? Maybe that's why I smile back.

ACT I
Scene 2

Something seems to have shifted inside me since that shared glance with Patrick down by the creek. It's not like he hasn't smiled at me before—he has, plenty of times. But this was somehow different. It was almost like . . . like he was really noticing me for the first time. Which is ridiculous, since we've known each other since forever. We even took a film class together at the Y last summer. He's actually pretty sweet when you get him away from the pack, despite his bad-boy image.

I'm hyperaware of his presence now, involuntarily searching for him in the crowd as we join the party. Several times I think I catch him watching me, staring at me intently as I sit at one of the round tables eating dinner. And later, when I'm out on the dance floor with Lucy and Morgan.

So it's not a total surprise when he intercepts me on my way to the punch table and asks me to dance. The musicians have just begun to play a slow song—something that sounds like an old-fashioned waltz. I say yes, allowing him to take my hand and lead me back out to the center of the dance floor. I feel strangely conspicuous as Patrick wraps his arms around my waist and pulls me close, as if everyone is watching us.

And they are, I realize.

I clasp my hands around his neck, steadying him as he sways dangerously against me, threatening to topple us both right there in the middle of the dance floor.

"You look pretty," he whispers, his breath hot against my ear.

"Yeah, I think that's the beer talking."

"No, seriously. I mean it. You're really, really pretty."

Over his shoulder, I see my mom watching us with a scowl. This is probably a mistake, I realize, but I feel reckless tonight. Bold. Like I want to break some rules or something.

Which is totally out of character for me. I've always played by the rules, performed my role to perfection—dutiful daughter, devoted sister, straight-A student, cocaptain of the cheerleading squad. I do exactly what's expected of me, live the life my parents have imagined for me. Sometimes I wonder who the *real* Jemma Cafferty is—if I'll ever find her.

If I want to.

"Thanks," I murmur. "You don't look so bad yourself."

"Let's go somewhere and talk," he says, his voice low. Releasing my waist, he reaches for my hand and tugs me toward the edge of the dance floor.

"I don't think that's such a good idea," I say. Still, I follow him. My heart is pounding against my ribs as we weave our way through the crowd, toward the back of the house.

"I meant what I said," he tells me as soon as we find ourselves alone. "You really do look pretty tonight. I mean, you always do. But especially now." He sways a little, and I reach out to steady him.

"You okay?" I ask. He's definitely a little drunk.

"Yeah. I really, really wanna kiss you right now."

"Oh yeah?" I ask.

He nods. "Yeah." He reaches for my hand and pulls me into the shadows, pressing me roughly against the trunk of a tree. I don't resist, not even when his lips find mine.

His kiss is surprisingly gentle—almost tentative. I want more. *Need* more. I open my mouth against his, feeling dangerously light-headed as his hands skim up my sides, drawing gooseflesh in their wake.

I draw him closer, till the entire length of his body is pressed against mine. It's been so long since I've been kissed, I realize with a start. *Too* long.

And now Patrick is here, and he smells so good—like

cologne and the outdoors. His breath is warm against my skin, his kisses featherlight. I hardly notice it when he hooks his thumbs under my dress straps and slides them down, baring my shoulders.

"Dude, there you are!" a voice calls out. Mason. *Shit.*

I duck out from under Patrick's arms.

"Oh, hey, Jemma," Mason says with a knowing grin. "Didn't mean to interrupt."

"Great timing, man," Patrick mutters.

Mason holds both hands up in surrender. "Sorry. I'll just let you two get back to—"

"No, we're done." My cheeks are flaming as I tug up my straps and brush off my backside, hoping the bark didn't rip the delicate tulle.

"Aww, c'mon, Jem," Patrick says. "Don't run off like this." He looks genuinely hurt, his hazel eyes slightly unfocused.

I shake my head. "I've got to go find Morgan and Lucy. I'll catch you later, okay?" I add, feeling guilty now. I hurry off, trying to ignore what sounds like the two guys slapping a high five behind me.

Great. Just great.

"What the hell?" Lucy asks, as soon as I find her and Morgan back by the buffet, piling dessert onto their plates. "Did you really just run off to hook up with Patrick? Because that's what it looked like."

"What's this in your hair?" Morgan's fingers brush against the back of my head. She pulls out a prickly twig and holds it up, examining it with drawn brows.

"There was no hooking up," I protest, taking the twig and dropping it to the ground. "We . . . kissed, that's all. And Mason caught us, so give it about five minutes and everyone here will know. Shit."

"Seriously?" Lucy asks, her voice laced with incredulity. "Why on earth would you kiss Patrick Hughes?"

"I have no idea. I just . . . I don't know. He's cute," I add lamely. He *is* cute. Why hadn't I noticed it before tonight?

Lucy shrugs. "I guess if you like skinny white boys."

"I'm getting a headache," I say, massaging my temples. "I think I might be about ready to call it a night."

Lucy eyes me sharply. "Coward."

"Yeah, the party's at *your* house," Morgan reminds me. "Where are you going to go? At least have some dessert first." She puts two mini éclairs and a cream puff on a plate and hands it to me.

I take it with a sigh and follow them to a table. Just as we sit down, Tanner sidles up and waggles his brows at me suggestively. "Hey, heard you were having some fun tonight, Jemma. You and the Pat Man, huh?"

Heat floods my cheeks. "Oh my God. Shut up, okay? There's no me and anyone."

He folds his arms across his chest. "That's not what Mason says."

"My brother is an idiot," Morgan says around a mouthful of pastry. "You know, in case you didn't notice. By the way, your fly's unzipped."

Tanner glances down at his gaping fly with a shrug.

"Real classy," Lucy says. "Your mom must be *so* proud."

Grinning, he makes a show of zipping up. "Aw, you know you want some of this, Luce."

"You're delusional," she says, rolling her eyes. "Go away, Tanner."

"Yeah, before I puke," Morgan adds.

Tanner lets the insults roll off, unaffected. "Before I go, just a heads-up. It looks like Patrick is over there talking to your dad, Jemma. I wonder what they're talking about." He winks at me. "Later, cuz."

I choke on a lump of custard. "Wha—?" I manage, rising on unsteady legs. I spot Patrick and my dad standing by the bar, their heads bent together in conversation.

Lucy reaches for my hand and pulls me back into my seat. "Chill, okay? I'm sure they're just talking. About, you know"— she waves one hand dismissively—"something."

I drop my head my head into my hands. "Easy for you to say."

Lucy's dark eyes narrow a fraction. "Ugh, I can't believe your mom invited *her*."

I follow her gaze to find Cheryl Jackson standing beside the punch bowl, filling her cup.

"She volunteers at the library," I say. "Mama didn't have a choice. Trust me, she wasn't happy about it. She was hoping she wouldn't show."

Morgan wrinkles her nose. "And miss an opportunity to hobnob with Magnolia Branch's finest? Not a chance."

"Well, she can kiss my ass," Lucy says with a scowl.

Lucy's mother, Dr. Parrish, is a pediatrician—the best in town, by a long shot. Most everyone adores Dr. Parrish, except for Cheryl Jackson, who'd been very vocal about taking her children elsewhere because she couldn't possibly trust her precious babies to one of "those" people. And by "those" people, she means black people. Of course, her son is a complete tool, and her daughter spent half of last semester in rehab, so there you go.

Morgan nudges me in the ribs. "You should go tell her that Dr. Parrish made the punch. See how fast she spits it out."

We all laugh a bit uneasily, because it's probably true. Ignorant beyotch.

My gaze is involuntarily drawn back toward my dad and Patrick, who are still standing together, discussing . . . something. My stomach lurches uncomfortably, and I push away my plate of sweets. "What could they possibly have to talk about?"

"There's no telling," Morgan says. "I still can't believe you kissed him."

"Speaking of," Lucy says coyly, "on a scale of one to ten . . . ?"

I just stare at her, mouth agape. "What, you want me to *rate* him?"

"Uh, yeah," Lucy answers, smiling wickedly. "Don't leave us hanging."

"Fine." I let out my breath in a huff. "He was a perfectly competent kisser."

"Perfectly competent? Yeah, I don't think so. C'mon, you gotta dish, girlfriend."

I fold my arms across my chest. "Don't you think I'm in enough trouble as it is?"

Her response is a pointed stare.

"Okay, fine. He was a good kisser. *Really* good. A seven, maybe an eight. There, are you satisfied?"

Her lips twitch with a smile. "I figured he would be."

Morgan mimes sticking her finger down her throat and gagging.

"Your mama's going to be brokenhearted, you know," Lucy says, reaching for my abandoned plate and pulling it toward her. She picks up a half-eaten éclair and examines it, then sets it back down. "Hasn't she already picked out a china pattern for you and Ryder?"

"Ha-ha, very funny." But truth be told, she probably has.

Ugh. "Seriously, y'all, my head is killing me. I'm ready for bed."

Morgan brushes crumbs from her lap and stands. "Okay, fine. Ditch us. You ready to go, Luce, or are you going to wait around for your parents?"

"Nah, I'm ready." Lucy stands and smoothes down her dress. "If I eat one more bite, I'm going to bust. Better quit while I'm ahead."

In the distance, a single shot rings out. From the treetops down by the creek, birds scatter noisily into the sky.

"There go the boys," Morgan says with a sigh.

I shake my head. "Mama's going to have their hides for making such a racket."

A half hour later, I've changed into my pj's and made myself a cup of chamomile-jasmine tea. Despite the lingering heat, I throw open the pair of French doors and step out onto my narrow little balcony—a Juliet balcony, Mama calls it. Leaning against the cool metal balustrade, I sip my tea, hoping it will soothe my nerves. My bedroom is on the second floor, facing the creek, on the opposite side of the house from the party. Still, I can hear the strains of the band floating on the warm, quiet breeze, mingling with the sounds of laughter. I feel bad for ducking out early, but I'd known that Tanner's taunts weren't going to be the end of it. Even worse, I knew I'd probably have to face Patrick again if I'd stayed.

And I can't face him, not yet. I mean, I've known Patrick my whole life, and I've never even *thought* about kissing him before tonight. I'm still trying to wrap my head around it, to figure out what has changed between us—if I even *want* things to change.

Sighing heavily, I glance up at the full moon. Here I am, obsessing over it, while Patrick probably hasn't given it a second thought. For all I know, he's already forgotten about it. He'd been drinking, after all. Then again, they had twelve beers between the five of them—well, four, if you don't count Ryder. At most, Patrick had a little buzz going on. Not enough to account for a full-on memory loss.

"Hey, Patrick is looking for you."

The voice startles me so badly that I slosh tea on myself. I look down to find Ryder standing below, his hands thrust into his pants pockets as he stares up at me, his mouth drawn into a tight line.

"Tell him I went to bed," I say. "And thanks a lot for scaring me half to death." Scowling, I swipe futilely at the wet splotch on the front of my tank top. He's lucky the tea wasn't hot.

Ryder takes a step closer, till he's standing just beneath the balcony. He tilts his face upward, and I can see the contempt there in his features. "So now you're just going to blow him off?"

"Why don't you do me a favor and mind your own business," I shoot back.

"Patrick is my friend; therefore, it *is* my business. By the way, you *do* know he's one to kiss and tell, right?"

"You just said he was your friend."

He shrugs. "Hey, it's *your* reputation."

"Since when do you care about my reputation, Ryder? Anyway, we were just kissing, if you must know. I've heard worse tales about you and Rosie. Maybe it's *her* reputation you should be worried about."

Rosie is my cousin—a distant one, on my dad's side. She's had a thing for Ryder for as long as anyone can remember, and rumor has it she finally made her move at a party last weekend. Apparently, he was *very* receptive—like, feeling-her-up-in-a-dark-corner receptive. At least, that's what Morgan heard.

"What are people saying about me and Rosie?" Ryder asks, his brows drawn.

I throw one hand up in the air. "Never mind. It's not like I care, anyway."

"No, 'course you don't," he snaps back.

"What's that supposed to mean?"

He shakes his head. "Nothing, Jemma. Just . . . go to bed, why don't you?"

"What, are you my dad now? How about this? I'll go to bed when I'm ready to go to bed."

"Wow, that's real mature."

"You're such a jerk, Ryder."

"A jerk? That's the best you've got? You're really off your game tonight."

"You are *really* getting on my nerves," I say, my skin flushing hotly.

He just shrugs, looking entirely unmoved. "What else is new? I've always gotten on your nerves."

"Not always," I say, and my heart catches a little. I squeeze my eyes shut, forcing back the memories. When I open them again, he's still standing there, glowering at me.

"Great, here we go again." He starts to walk away and then turns back to face me. "You know what? I have no idea what I did to piss you off, but—"

"Seriously?" I sputter. "I'll give you a hint—eighth grade."

"You're mad at me about something I did in *eighth* grade, Jem? That was four fucking years ago. Whatever it was, why don't you grow up and get over it?"

"Why don't you go to hell," I shoot back.

"I'm leaving now," he says, turning to stalk away.

"Good!" I shout, tears burning behind my eyelids. "Go. I hate you, Ryder Marsden!"

"Yeah, well . . . the feeling's mutual," he throws back over one shoulder.

Even though I know it's childish of me, I storm back inside and slam the French doors with as much force as I can muster, nearly rattling them off their hinges.

Charming, right?

ACT I
Scene 3

My mom lets me sleep in the next day. When I finally rouse myself enough to check the time, the bright, midday sun is already streaming through the windows, casting yellow stripes across the fluffy white duvet.

I vaguely remember my mom knocking on my door around ten to tell me she was going to church, but I'd fallen right back asleep the moment I'd heard the front door shut. I know she's biding her time, eager to ask me what's going on with Patrick. Since I'm not quite ready for that conversation, I hustle out of bed. Church ended five minutes ago, which means she'll be home any minute now.

Moving quickly, I throw on a pair of cutoffs. I ignore my growling stomach as I hurry down the stairs and out the front door. Yes, I'm a coward—especially when it comes to Mama.

I pause on the front porch only long enough to give Beau and Sadie a quick scratch behind the ear. It's impossible not to smile at the mismatched pair—Beau's a chocolate Lab mix, Sadie some sort of silver-blond terrier mash-up. They're rescues, just like the three cats lying indolently in the grass, sunning themselves. Kirk, Spock, and Sulu—Daddy named them. 'Course, Sulu turned out to be a she and thus should have been named Uhura instead, but whatever.

Embarrassed that I even *know* this, I make my way down the porch steps and across the yard, trying to get away from the house as fast as I can. Beau and Sadie join me, their tongues lolling happily as they race ahead of me and then circle back to my side, rubbing against my legs before racing off again.

I head toward the barn, thinking I'll get some target practice in. Since we don't have horses, my dad has turned the barn into a workshop for him and a makeshift shooting range for me. It's my favorite place to blow off steam and get my head on straight—two things I'm in desperate need of right now. Between this whole crazy thing with Patrick and last night's argument with Ryder, well . . .

I pick up my pace, my bare feet slapping against the packed-dirt path, sending up puffs of dust in my wake. I don't slow down until I reach the enormous oak tree—the largest on our property. A swing still hangs from one of the wide limbs, swaying gently on the breeze. The barn lies just beyond, its peaked tin roof reflecting the sun. The doors are thrown open, and I can hear music drifting out—Jimmy Buffett—which means my dad is inside, probably working on one of his pieces of furniture.

Which is fine—Daddy doesn't ask embarrassing questions or force me to talk about things I don't want to talk about, like Mama does.

"Sorry," I say, shooing the dogs out. "You know the rules." I close and latch the lower doors, leaving the upper panels open to take advantage of the cooling breeze. "Hey," I call out to my dad, who's standing over by the gun safe with his back to me. "You didn't go to church with Mama?"

He turns to face me. "Oh, hey, half-pint." Yeah, it's a *Little House on the Prairie* thing. Embarrassing, I know. "Nah, she went with Laura Grace. I figured the pair of them would be yammering on nonstop about the party, so . . ." He trails off with a shrug. "You want Delilah?"

"Yeah, thanks." I watch as he reaches inside the gun safe and retrieves my pistol—a .22 caliber Ruger Mark III with a five-point-five-inch barrel. Daddy bought it for me for my thirteenth birthday, despite my mom's protests. She wanted to buy me a sewing machine instead. For some unknown reason, I named the pistol "Delilah," which I thought sounded kind of badass. I know it's silly, but the name stuck.

He hands me the pistol, along with my noise-canceling headset—a lavender set with swirly silver designs on each earpiece. "Mind if I stick around and watch you for a bit?" he asks.

"Nah, go ahead." I loop the headset around my neck. "Maybe you could change the music to something from this century, though?"

He pulls a frown. "What's wrong with Buffett? He's a Mississippi boy."

"Yeah, I know. You've told me, like, a million times," I say with a grin. "Anyway, you know I like Buffett just fine."

"That's because I've raised you well. But, here, I'll change it." He fiddles with the stereo, switching it over to the radio. "Hey, don't forget we're having an early dinner at Magnolia Landing tonight. They're expecting us at six."

My heart sinks—the last thing I want to do is hang out with Ryder tonight. Or *any* night, for that matter. "Aww, do I have to go?"

He looks taken aback. "Of course you do." He watches me thoughtfully for a second. "I don't understand what's going on with you and Ryder these days. The two of you used to get along so well."

"Oh no," I say with a groan. "Not you, too."

"I'm not saying you have to be best buddies, or whatever the heck your mom and Laura Grace think you two should be." He winces, and I realize with a start that maybe he's on my side, after all. "But you could at least be civil to each other, couldn't you?"

"Dad, stop. Please? I don't want to talk about Ryder, okay?"

He holds up both hands in surrender. "Okay, okay. Just make sure you're ready to go at quarter to six."

I nod. "Fine." I reach for my headset, then stop myself. "Oh, wait, I meant to ask . . . What were you and Patrick Hughes talking about last night?"

"Oh. That. Patrick was 'jokingly'"—he makes air quotes around the word—"asking for your hand in marriage. I 'jokingly'"—those air quotes again—"told him that he better get his act together or stay the hell away from my daughter."

I just stare at him, my mouth agape in horror.

"He assured me that he's seen the error in his ways and is on the straight and narrow now."

"Please tell me you're joking," I say with a grimace.

He shakes his head. "I wish I were. Your mama's not happy, by the way. Seems to think the two of you were way too cozy last night. Apparently, Cheryl Jackson said something to her."

"Oh my God! Cheryl Jackson?"

He shrugs. "You know how she is."

"Oh, I know, all right." That woman needs to learn to mind her own damn business.

"Anyway, I'll let you get to it," Daddy says, pointing to Delilah.

I nod, slipping the headset over my ears, effectively ending the conversation. Delilah is heavy and cool in my hand, the familiar weight comforting. It takes me only a couple of minutes to get her locked and loaded, and then I move toward one of the stalls and pick up a pair of goggles.

I shoot for close to an hour. At some point, my dad slips out with a wave, but I barely notice. I'm too focused on the target in front of me, the center bull's-eye blown to bits. Daddy thinks I'm good enough for the Olympic trials, but for women it's just air pistols or skeet, which isn't nearly as fun. Air pistols seem like playing with toys, whereas .22 calibers like Delilah are the real deal, you know? Anyway, I've got enough on my plate as it is, what with college applications and senior year in general. Which reminds me . . .

I need to sit down and talk to my parents. I can't put it off any longer. With a sigh, I set down Delilah, then slip off my goggles and headset, swiping at the sweat on my brow with the back of one hand.

Here's the thing. My parents expect me to go to Ole Miss. They talk about it as if it's a done deal. "Next year, when you're in Oxford . . ." and "You'll probably live at the sorority house, but . . ." They've got it all planned out. I'll pledge Phi Delta, just like Mama and Laura Grace did, date frat boys, cheer for the Rebels if I'm lucky enough to make the squad. It doesn't really matter what I major in. All that matters is that I get a degree, marry a good ol' southern boy—you know, someone like Ryder—and raise my family right here in Magnolia Branch. That's the only future they've imagined for me, the only thing that makes any sense to them.

But . . . I'm not sure that's what *I* want.

Ever since that film class last year, it's all I've been thinking about. I'd requested information packets from several film schools, ruthlessly checking the mail each day before my parents got home from work and stashing the brochures in my desk drawer. Late at night, after my parents went to bed, I'd read them cover to cover and then check their websites for additional information. Ultimately, I'd narrowed it down to NYU's Tisch School of the Arts. Only problem is, I haven't discussed it with my parents yet, and I'm running out of time.

The deadline for early decision is November first, less than two months away. I've already completed most of the application package, everything except the final two elements of a four-part portfolio that includes a ten-minute film. But, obviously, I'm going to need my parents' support or it's never going to happen. New York is a long way away, and NYU is expensive. *Really* expensive.

Who knows? Maybe it's just a pipe dream. Still, I'm not quite ready to give it up.

I head over to the gun safe to put Delilah away, thinking that maybe I can talk to them now, before I lose my nerve.

It's not like it's going to get any easier the longer I wait, and if they say no, well . . . I guess I won't bother with the rest of the portfolio.

When I return to the house fifteen minutes later with Beau and Sadie in tow, I find both my parents sitting together at the kitchen table, drinking coffee. My dad has obviously just showered—his hair is damp—and my mom has changed from her church clothes into a pair of bleach-stained shorts and an old T-shirt, her usual Sunday-afternoon attire. Her blond hair is pulled back into a ponytail, and she smells like sunscreen and bug repellant.

I realize I better catch her now before she heads out to her gardens—a vegetable plot just off the kitchen and a larger, fenced-in space out back where she grows Old World roses along with other colorful flowers that I can't name.

"Hey, can I talk to y'all for a sec?" I ask, sliding into the chair opposite them.

My mom raises one brow quizzically. "Is this about Patrick? Because I'm not sure I like—"

"It's not about Patrick." I take a deep, calming breath. *I can do this.* "It's about my college apps."

Daddy sets down his mug. "How's that coming, hon? You need help with your essays?"

"No, nothing like that. It's just . . . I know we talked about applying to just the state schools, but I was thinking . . . I mean, you know how I like to make movies and all. I was hoping that I could apply to a film school, too."

My mom's blue eyes narrow a fraction. "Film school?"

I swallow hard. "NYU, actually. You know . . . in New York City," I add lamely.

"New York City?" my dad parrots back, somehow making it sound like Mars or something.

I plow on recklessly. "Yeah, I've read over their materials, and I think their program sounds awesome. It's a good school, too. And . . . well, I'd like to at least apply and see what happens. I know it's a long shot, but—"

"We're not sending you off to New York City, Jemma," Daddy says, shaking his head. "That's all there is to it."

My parents exchange a glance, and then Mama nods. "Besides," she says, "all your friends are going to Ole Miss. What would you do in New York? Alone? And film school . . ." She trails off with a shrug. "You're a straight-A student, Jem. Why would you throw that all away for some crazy idea—"

"I wouldn't be throwing anything away. They have academic programs at NYU, too, you know. Maybe I could . . . I don't know, double major in film and English lit or something like that."

"Where did you even come up with this idea?" Daddy asks, sounding a little dazed.

I fold my arms across my chest, trying not to look *too* defiant. "That class I took last summer. You know, the one at the Y? The teacher said I had a cinematic eye. I know it's hard to believe, but she actually thought I had talent. *Real* talent."

My mom eyes me suspiciously. "Are you sure this doesn't have something to do with Patrick? He took that class with you, didn't he?"

I can't help but roll my eyes. "This has *nothing* to do with him. We've never even talked about it. This is just something that I really, really want to do."

Daddy rakes a hand through his hair. "Look, Jemma, if you're serious about this, then let me and your mom look over the application materials, okay?"

Mama shoots him a glare, and a little breath of triumph makes me sit up straight in my seat. I nod, barely able to believe what I'm hearing.

"Let's give her a chance to make her case, Shelby," he tells her. "If she's really interested in film—"

"This is New York City we're talking about, Brad," Mama shoots back. "I mean, maybe Atlanta or even Houston . . ." She trails off, shaking her head. "But I am *not* sending my baby girl off to New York, away from everyone and everything she knows."

Daddy lays a gentle hand on her wrist and then looks back at me, his green gaze steady and serious. "Your mom and I will discuss it more later, okay, hon? In private. I don't want you to get your hopes up, though," he warns. "NYU is a private university. I'm not even sure we could afford it." He glances over at my mom apologetically, but she remains silent, her mouth set in a hard line. "Now, how 'bout some lunch? You hungry?"

As if on cue, my stomach growls. "Starved," I say, suppressing a grin. Because, okay, I know he warned me not to get my hopes up and all, but that went better than I expected. *Way* better.

Maybe there's a chance I'll get that other life I imagined, after all.

ACT I
Scene 4

T he roast is delicious, Laura Grace," Daddy says as he
sets down his silver—*real* silver—and reaches for his
crystal water goblet.

Laura Grace beams at him, her pale blond hair perfectly
coiffed, not a strand out of place. "Why, thank you, Bradley. I
wish I could take credit for the meal, but it all belongs to Lou.
I don't know what I'd do without that woman. We might just
starve to death."

"Amen," Mr. Marsden mutters, and Laura Grace shoots
him a sidelong glare.

It's true, though. Laura Grace can't boil a pot of water
without burning it, much less manage an actual meal. If not
for Lou, who's been working for the Marsdens for as long as I
can remember, they probably *would* starve to death.

Laura Grace does, however, set a beautiful table. Everything, from the starched linen tablecloth to the Blue Willow china, the perfectly polished silver to the delicate crystal, is absolutely perfect and set just so for her dinner guests. An embroidered linen napkin is laid across my lap—a far cry from the supermarket-brand paper napkins we use at home.

Two colorful floral arrangements complement the decor, one set in the middle of the long mahogany table and another on the matching sideboard near the swinging door that leads toward the kitchen. Candles in elaborate silver candelabras cast a soft, flickering glow across it all, creating a warm, inviting palette.

Sunday dinner at the Marsdens' is more than a meal—it's an occasion. I'm dressed accordingly, wearing a pale green sundress with a sweater to ward off the chill of the air-conditioning.

"Well, I blame my mama, God rest her soul," Laura Grace says with a sigh. "She never taught me how to cook. You have no idea how lucky you are, Jemma—you and Nan both. Your mama's a great cook, and she made sure to teach you. You girls' husbands are surely going to thank her one day."

It's impossible to miss the pointed look she gives Ryder.

He ignores her and continues to attack his own roast. He's rolled up the sleeves of his white button-down shirt, but his tie is neat and his khakis perfectly pressed. He cuts off a slice of rare meat and brings it to his mouth. Chewing slowly, he fixes his gaze on the wall directly above my mother's head. It's clear that he, too, would rather be anywhere else right now—anywhere but here, a helpless victim of our mothers' machinations.

Laura Grace glances from him to me and back to him again. "Next year, when the two of you are off at Oxford, you better promise to drive over together each week for Sunday dinner, you hear?"

"Now, c'mon, Laura Grace," Mr. Marsden chides. "You know Ryder hasn't made his decision yet. You've got to give the boy some space to figure it out."

She waves one hand in dismissal. "I know. But a mama can hope, can't she? I'm sorry, but I just can't imagine the two of them going off in different directions."

"There's only one choice for the both of them, as far as I'm concerned," my mom says. "It's about time the Rebels get their football program back on track, and Ryder's just the boy to do it—with Jemma cheering him on."

I can't help but cringe, staring down at my plate. I mean, is this really what my mom dreams about? Is this the best she can imagine for me?

For a moment, everyone continues to eat silently. The tension in the air is so thick you could cut it with a knife, but I doubt Mama or Laura Grace even notice.

"Alabama's got a great football program," my dad finally

offers, earning a sharp glare from my mom. "Probably the best in the nation," he adds with an apologetic shrug.

I want to get up and hug him. Instead, I offer him a bright smile. He returns it from across the width of the table, his eyes sparkling mischievously.

Sometimes it's hard to believe my dad's a college professor— he does *not* look the part, not by any stretch of the imagination. He's tall and lanky, with messy light brown hair and pale green eyes. He looks way more at home in cargo pants and army-green T-shirts than he does in khakis and cardigans, more comfortable on the gun range or in his workshop than he does in his office or classroom. Think Daryl Dixon from *The Walking Dead* teaching physics. Yeah, that's Daddy. He's pretty awesome.

I take a bite of mashed potatoes, savoring their warm, gooey goodness. Lou really *is* an exceptional cook.

"Homecoming's next month," Mama says, obviously desperate to change the subject—to get it back on *her* track. "I hear they're having a reception this year at the sorority house for alumnae and their daughters. I can't wait for Jemma to see how nice the girls are and—"

"Mama," I interrupt, rolling my eyes. "Please."

"Can't you just imagine the two of them next year at the Phi Delta Carnation Ball?" Laura Grace asks, clapping her hands together.

Daddy looks confused. "The two of who?"

"Why, Ryder and Jemma, of course." Mama pats him on the hand. "You remember the Carnation Ball—it's the first Phi Delta party of the year. They have to go together, right, Laura Grace?"

She nods. "We've been waiting all our lives for this."

Mama finally glances my way and sees my scowl. "Aw, honey. We're just teasing, that's all."

This sort of teasing has been going on my entire life— second verse, same as the first. It's gotten real old, real fast.

"May I be excused?" I ask, pushing back from the table.

"You go on and finish your dinner," Laura Grace says, entirely unperturbed. "We'll stop teasing. I promise."

"It's okay. I'm done. It was delicious, thanks. I just need to get some air, that's all. I'm getting a bit of a headache."

Laura Grace nods. "It's this heat—way too hot for September." She waves a hand in my direction. "Go on, then. Ryder, why don't you go get Jemma some aspirin or something."

I glance over at Ryder, and our eyes meet. I shake my head, hoping he gets the message. "No, it's fine. I'm . . . uh . . . I've got some in my purse."

"Go with her, son," Mr. Marsden prods. "Be a gentleman, and get her a bottle of water to take outside with her."

Ugh. I give up. My escape plot is now ruined.

Wordlessly, Ryder rises from the table and stalks out of

the dining room. I follow behind, my sandals slapping noisily against the hardwood floor.

"Do you want water or not?" he asks me as soon as the door swings shut behind us.

"Sure. Fine. Whatever."

He turns to face me. "It *is* pretty hot out there."

"I near about melted on the drive over."

His lips twitch with the hint of a smile. "Your dad refused to turn on the AC, huh?"

I nod as I follow him out into the cavernous marble-tiled foyer. "You know his theory—'no point when you're just going down the road.' Must've been a thousand degrees in the car."

He tips his head toward the front door. "You wait out on the porch—I'll bring you a bottle of water."

"Thanks." I watch him go, wondering if we're going to pretend like last night's fight didn't happen. I hope that's the case, because I really don't feel like rehashing it.

I take off my sweater and make my way outside to sit in one of the white rockers that line the porch. The sun is just beginning to set, casting long, reddish orange swaths of color between the enormous oaks that line the driveway. The air is warm and thick, feeling somehow sinuous against my skin. The barest of breezes ruffles the thick canopy of leaves and lifts the hem of my sundress, but it does nothing to cool the air.

More than anything, I wish I had my video camera with me

so I could film the sun's slow descent, the deepening of the sky from pink to lavender to violet, the moon casting silver light across the scene before me.

"Here you go," Ryder says, startling me. He holds out a sweating bottle of water, and I take it gratefully, pressing it against my neck.

"Thanks." I glance away, hoping that he'll take the hint and leave me in peace. His presence makes me self-conscious now, but it wasn't always like this. As I look out at Magnolia Landing's grounds, I can't help but remember hot summer days when Ryder and I ran through sprinklers and ate Popsicles out on the lawn, when we rode our bikes up and down the long drive, when we built a tree fort in the largest of the oaks behind the house.

I wouldn't say we'd been friends when we were kids—not exactly. We had been more like siblings. We played; we fought. Mostly, we didn't think too much about our relationship—we didn't try to define it. And then adolescence hit. Just like that, everything was awkward and uncomfortable between us. By the time middle school began, I was all too aware that he *wasn't* my brother, or even my cousin.

"Mind if I sit?" Ryder asks.

I shrug. "It's your house." I keep my gaze trained straight ahead, refusing to look in his direction as he lowers himself into the chair beside me.

After a minute or two of silence but for the creaking rockers, he sighs loudly. "Can we call a truce now?"

"You're the one who started it," I snap. "Last night, I mean."

"Look, I've been thinking about what you said. You know, about eighth grade—"

"Do we have to talk about this?"

"Because we didn't really hang out in middle school, except for family stuff," he continues, ignoring my protest. "Until the end of eighth grade, maybe. Right around graduation."

My entire body goes rigid, my face flushing hotly with the memory.

It had all started during Christmas break that year. We'd gone to the beach with the Marsdens. I can't really explain it, but there'd been a new awareness between us that week— exchanged glances and lingering looks, an electrical current connecting us in some way. The two of us sort of tiptoed around each other, afraid to get too close, but also afraid to lose that hint of . . . something. And then Ryder asked me to go with him to the graduation dance. There was no way we were telling our parents. Instead, we made plans to meet up near the rock on the edge of campus on the night of the dance.

I'd headed toward the rock at the agreed-upon time, my hands trembling with nervous excitement as I smoothed down my brand-new emerald-green dress. A dozen or so feet away,

I stopped short at the sound of voices. Confused, I ducked behind a cluster of trees. Peeking out, I saw that Ryder was there, waiting, just as he said he'd be. But Mason and Ben were there, too. That hadn't been part of the plan—we were supposed to meet up alone and go into the dance together. I hesitated, not quite sure what to do.

"Wait . . . let me guess," came Mason's voice. "It's Jemma, right? You're taking her to the dance. That's why you're all prettied up."

"No way," Ben had said, his voice laced with incredulity.

"Oh my God, are you wearing a bow tie?" Mason shrieked. He was doubled over, laughing. "Seriously, man? You must really want her."

"Look, my mom made me ask her, okay?" Ryder said. "She felt all sorry for her 'cause no one else had, and, well, you know how that goes. Our moms are best friends and all that. Trust me, I do *not* want to go with her."

Mason was still laughing. "Aww, admit it, man. You want to feel up Jemma Cafferty!"

"Feel up *what*? Jemma's flat as a board. Anyway, I just said I'd dance with her once or twice, that's all. No big deal."

"Well, why are we standing out here, then?" Ben said.

Mason slapped Ryder on the back. "Yeah, man. Let's go have some *fun*."

They took off then, the three of them. I saw Ryder glance

back over his shoulder once before following them into the gym, and that was that.

As soon as they were gone, I ran over to the basketball courts and hid in the shadows, crying my eyes out. Once I'd finally managed to dry my tears, I made my way over to the gym and peeked in. There was Ryder, right in the middle of the dance floor, dancing with Katie McGee—who was decidedly not as flat as a board. Mason and Ben were there too, dancing with some of Katie's friends. They were all laughing and smiling, having a great time. I'd turned and fled then, fresh tears dampening my cheeks. I went back to the little cluster of trees by the rock and stayed there till it was time for Daddy to come and pick me up.

I never told a soul what happened. Lucy and Morgan assumed I'd gotten sick or something and hadn't come, and Mama and Daddy thought I'd gone and had a great time. The truth was way too embarrassing—that Ryder had humiliated me, made a complete and total fool out of me.

Never again.

"So, are you going to tell me what I did to piss you off that year? Because I'm coming up totally blank."

I turn on him. "Seriously? You're coming up blank?"

"Why don't you help me out here?"

I just stare at him uncomprehendingly.

"C'mon, Jemma," he taunts. "Use your words."

I rise, my hands curled into fists by my sides. "Oh, I'll use my words all right, douchebucket. Remember the eighth-grade dance? Is that ringing any bells for you?"

He scratches his head, looking thoughtful for a moment. And then . . ."You mean the graduation dance? If I remember correctly, you didn't even show up."

"Is that what you think? That I didn't show up?" I almost want to laugh at the absurdity of it—Ryder trying to act like the injured party, as if *I'd* stood *him* up.

"You got a better explanation?" he asks.

"I shouldn't have to explain it to you. Jerk," I add under my breath. And then, "I'm going for a walk."

He rises, towering over me now. "So you're just going to storm off? Really, Jem?"

"Yes," I say, nodding furiously. "That's *exactly* what I'm going to do. How clever of you to figure it out."

I can feel Ryder's eyes boring a hole in my back as I flounce down the stairs and hurry down the drive with as much dignity as I can muster.

ACT I
Scene 5

I close my locker and lean against it, waiting for Lucy and Morgan to catch up. Seventh period just ended—a class I share with Ryder, unfortunately—and I've got cheerleading practice in fifteen minutes. I don't know why, but I'm not in the mood. The gym is hot. Loud. I'm fighting a headache, probably because I didn't get much sleep last night.

"Hey, Jem."

I look up to see Patrick headed my way, a lopsided grin on his face. Great. Just what I need right now. My mind flashes back to Saturday night, to Patrick pressing me up against a tree, kissing me softly.

"What's up?" I ask him.

"Same old." He leans against the locker beside mine. "Hey, I was wondering if you want to go out Friday night after the game. Maybe get a pizza or something."

"You mean . . . just the two of us?" I ask dumbly.

"Yeah. I mean, I was thinking . . . Saturday was nice. You know?"

My mind is racing, casting about for an excuse. But then I see Ryder out of the corner of my eye, at his own locker. I remember the way he chided me about blowing off Patrick, as if I'm some kind of tease—which I'm not. Besides, Patrick's right—kissing him *was* unexpectedly nice.

"Sure," I say. "Why not?"

"Cool," he says, affecting total nonchalance. "Well, I've got to get to practice. Later, okay?"

I just nod, shocked to realize that I've just agreed to go on a date with Patrick. What am I going to tell my parents? With his driving record, there's no way in hell they'll let me go anywhere with him behind the wheel. I guess I'll just have to meet him wherever we decide to go. Actually, that's not such a bad idea. It'll somehow make it seem less like an official date and more like two friends hanging out.

I watch him walk off, a swagger in his step now. Or maybe it was always there. Who knows? Either way, I'm about to be late to practice. Luckily, Lucy and Morgan finally show, passing Patrick as he rounds the corner.

"Hey, you ready to head over to the gym?" Morgan asks.

"Ready as ever," I say glumly, leaning against my locker.

"Uh-oh. Why that face?" Lucy glances back over her shoulder. "Did Patrick say something to you?"

I take a deep breath before answering. "He asked me out. I said yes."

"You *what*?" Morgan shrieks.

"I know, right?" I push off the locker. "I don't know. I just figure . . . after Saturday night, I kind of owe it to him."

Lucy shakes her head. "You don't owe that boy anything."

Morgan nods. "Besides, your mama will have a hissy fit. I mean, two DUIs? If it weren't for his daddy—"

"I know. But still . . ."

"But still what?" Lucy asks. "Okay, so you kissed him. No big deal—we all make mistakes. But you can't actually go out with him."

"Why not?" I shoot back. "He's not that bad, once you get him alone."

"You hear yourself? Not that bad?" Morgan shakes her head. "You've got to set your standards higher than that."

"Yeah, just wait till next year. College boys!" Lucy waggles her brows. "Why bother with the slim pickings we've got here? Not worth the trouble, if you ask me."

Morgan shrugs. "Well, what about prom?"

Lucy is undeterred. "Prom is eight months away! Anyway—"

"Yo, Morgan!"

All three of us turn toward her brother, Mason, who stands half a hall length away.

"I'm cutting out of practice early and taking the car," he calls out. "Can you get a ride home?"

She waves one hand in his direction. "Sure. Whatever."

"Thanks. Hey, good work, Jemma! I heard you and Patrick are going out on Friday."

What the heck? I'd said yes only about three minutes ago. Talk about news traveling fast.

"Let's see . . . Patrick tells Mason. Mason tells Ryder. Ryder tells Ben." Lucy ticks it off on her fingers. "Before you know it—"

"Yeah, thanks, Luce. I get it. The whole world knows by sunset. Great."

"Hey, you're the one who agreed to go out with him," Lucy answers with a shrug. "You know how it is—small town, small school. When Jemma Cafferty goes on a date, it's going to be news. Seriously, when's the last time you actually went out with someone—when it wasn't a group thing, I mean? Tenth grade?"

I just shrug. She's right, of course. Drew Thompson, sophomore year. It lasted all of two months before kind of fizzling out. Since then, it's just been me and my friends hanging out with the usual guys, without any hint of pairing up.

Lucy reaches for my hand. "Anyway, we really *are* going to be late. C'mon, let's go."

Practice is exhausting, just as I imagined it would be. Somehow, I manage to slip during a stunt and whack the side of my head on the mat, which doesn't help any. When I finally make it home, my head is aching and I'm feeling a little queasy. Lucy tried to get me to stop at her mom's office on the way home so she could check me for a concussion, but I'd been in such a rush that I'd refused. Now I'm wondering if maybe I should have listened to her.

When I pull up and park my little Fiat at a quarter to five, I'm surprised to see my mom's car in the driveway. The library doesn't close for fifteen more minutes, and Mama's like clock-work, always arriving home at 5:25 on the dot. I mean, it's not like we've got traffic in Magnolia Branch. So yeah, the sight of her car makes me slightly uneasy. Something's up.

As soon as I step inside the house, I hear voices coming from the kitchen. I drop my bag and hurry down the hall, pausing in the kitchen doorway. Mama's on the phone, leaning against the counter, her eyes red and swollen. Daddy sits at the table across from her, raking a hand through his hair.

"What's going on?" I whisper to him.

"Shh," he says, waving me off.

"A cholesterol granuloma," Mama tells Daddy, enunciating carefully. "Write that down, Brad. Wait. What did you say, Nan? The petrous apex." She motions toward my dad again. "Write that down too."

"Can you spell it?" he asks her.

She does. And then, "Honey, I want you home. I don't care, this is way more important than school right now. We need to get a second opinion, do some research. And you . . . you need to take it easy. Get some rest."

"Let me talk to her," Daddy says, reaching for the phone. Mama hands it to him. "Nan, honey, we'd all feel better right now if you were here, not four hours away. I can get someone to cover my classes this week and—yes, I know. Are you sure? Wait. What, honey? Slow down."

Even across the room, I can hear Nan's raised voice coming through the phone as Daddy listens, his brow furrowed.

"Fine," he says with a sigh. "What time's your game? Okay, then we'll expect you by dinner on Saturday. Here. Mama wants to say good-bye."

He returns the phone to my mom.

"What's going on?" I repeat, my heart thumping noisily against my ribs. "Daddy?"

He swallows hard. "Just give me a minute, okay, half-pint?" His voice is thick, and I swear I see tears gathering in the corners of his eyes. "Why don't you go on upstairs and wash up? Let me talk to your mom, and then I'll be right up."

My pulse skyrocketing, I do as he asks. My head is still pounding and my mouth is dry—too dry—as I make my way upstairs to my room. I head straight to the bathroom I share with Nan and fill a paper cup with water from the tap, gulping it down noisily. The face staring back at me in the mirror is pale, pinched with worry.

I don't understand what they were saying—a cholesterol something and other equally unfamiliar words. They mean nothing to me. A cold knot of fear lodges in the pit of my stomach. It's obvious that something is wrong with Nan— something bad, judging by the looks on their faces. How long are they going to leave me up here alone, wondering? Worrying?

I shuffle back to my room, not quite sure what to do with myself. There's no point in starting my homework—I'm way too distracted. But I've got to do something while I wait for Daddy, or I'll go crazy. I grab my laptop and settle myself on my bed, opening up my editing software. I have to force myself to focus—to think about my film school application instead of my sister. It's the only way to stay sane right now.

I need to take a look at the footage I filmed over the summer—a mishmash of vacation, cheerleading camp, and random stuff—and see if there's anything I can use for my application project. Some sort of connecting theme, a narrative thread. Anything.

Originally, I'd thought about doing something on local history—kind of a Faulkneresque, "this is the real Yoknapatawpha County" kind of thing. But then I'd decided that that seemed a little stuffy and academic, too documentary style and not artistic enough.

On the other hand, it might make me more memorable and identifiable to the admissions committee—as in, "that girl from north Mississippi." Maybe it's not such a bad idea, after all.

But a quick glance through my video library reveals that I don't have enough relevant footage. I'll need to shoot more, several hours' worth, at different locations and times of day. I let out a sigh of frustration, realizing with a start that I'm chewing on a fingernail, a habit I kicked several years ago—or so I'd thought.

Distracted now, I cock my head and listen intently. I can just make out what sounds like muffled crying coming from downstairs. It's my mom, I realize, sobbing her heart out. My stomach lurches, and for a moment I think I'm going to be sick.

I reach a hand to my temple, trying unsuccessfully to massage away the throbbing pain. What's taking Daddy so long? And then I hear his footsteps, heavy and plodding on the stairs. I close my laptop and push it aside, making room for him beside me.

As soon as he steps into my room, I know that, whatever it is, it's bad. I can see it in the set of his jaw. He produces a Peach Nehi and holds it toward me. "Here. You look thirsty."

"Just tell me," I blurt out, taking the bottle and setting it on my nightstand. "Don't beat around the bush, okay?"

He nods. "Your sister has a benign brain tumor—a cholesterol granuloma, it's called. It's probably going to require surgery, because it's pressing on her carotid artery and on her auditory nerves. Apparently, it's already caused some hearing loss in her left ear."

"Oh my God," I say, my heart beating wildly in my chest. "Wait . . . When you say surgery, do you mean *brain* surgery?"

Daddy nods. "Cranial base surgery. The doctors there in Hattiesburg recommended a specialist in Houston."

"But I don't understand. I mean, how? How did something like this happen?"

He shrugs. "That's all I know right now, Jemma. She's been having really bad migraines, remember? She went to see a neurologist, who sent her for a routine MRI last week. She just got the results today." He takes a deep, rattling breath, his shoulders seeming to sag. "I'm going to call the neurosurgeon in Houston tomorrow and see what I can find out, maybe talk to a few doctors in Jackson, too. Nan's coming home on Saturday, and we'll go from there."

My mouth is suddenly dry again—so dry I can barely swallow. Blindly, I reach for the Nehi and take a long draft. My hands are shaking so badly when I set it down that I almost knock it over. My dad reaches for the wobbly bottle just in time, steadying it.

"Is she going to be okay?" I ask him.

He puts an arm around me, drawing me closer. "Like I said, the tumor is benign. At least, they're pretty sure it is. Your sister is strong—she'll get through this. She'll be fine."

I just nod, laying my head on his shoulder as I fight back the tears that have gathered in my eyes.

Why didn't she call me? Or text me? We've always been so close—or I thought we were. Why hadn't *I* called *her*? She's been back at school for more than a month now, and I haven't spoken to her once. Instead, I've been caught up in my own stupid problems—what song to set our pom-pom routine to, what to wear to the gala, should I or shouldn't I go out with Patrick now that I've kissed him. All meaningless things in the face of what Nan's been going through.

"It's going to be okay," Daddy says comfortingly, giving my shoulder a squeeze.

But what if it's not?

Nan's the athlete in our family, the star soccer player. The sole tofu-eating vegetarian in our family of carnivores. She all but radiates good health and vigor, and it's pretty much impossible to imagine her sick enough to require surgery.

We'd gone to Fort Walton Beach for two weeks this summer, and I can picture her there, lying on the sugar-white sand beside me, all tanned and toned, her hair twisted into a messy knot on top of her head while seagulls circled lazily overhead. I remember her propping up on one elbow to watch Ryder mess around in the clear, emerald-green water on his skimboard.

"Okay, wow," she'd said, lowering her sunglasses to look me in the eye. "I realize he's three years younger than me and our parents pretty much betrothed the two of you at birth, but if you decide you don't want him, I'm happy to take one for the team. Just saying."

I'd playfully punched her in the arm and somehow ended up chasing her down the beach, the foamy surf lapping at our ankles. I couldn't catch her, of course. She's too fast. Daddy's right—she's strong, like the petals on a magnolia bloom.

But we're talking *brain* surgery here. I shudder involuntarily at the thought, trying to push the horrifying images out of my head.

"Thanks for telling me, Daddy," I say, trying to hold it together—to be as strong as my sister.

But deep in my heart, I know that I'm not. That I never will be. Nan is the magnolia, not me.

ACT I
Scene 6

As soon as we finish supper, I slip outside and head down to the creek. I pull out a kayak from the shed by the dock and drag it down to the water's edge.

In minutes I'm paddling on the still, dark water, my kayak gliding silently through the purplish-hued twilight. Along the banks, colorful wildflowers ruffle in the breeze—wild hyacinth, swamp hibiscus, and cardinal flowers. I can hear the shuffling of muskrat and opossum in the tall grasses on either side of me. A snake slips into the water with a splash. In the distance, a lone owl hoots. These are all familiar sounds— sounds of home. As I cut my paddle through the water I feel my worries slip away, replaced by a peaceful calm.

It doesn't take me long to reach my destination, a little cove at the bend of the creek with a stretch of sandy beach. Hopping out, I lug the kayak up onto the sand, grab the towel I'd stowed inside, and head up the steep, grassy embankment.

I let out a sigh as I crest the rise, taking in the sight before me. It's ruins of some kind—a relic from the days when Magnolia Landing was a working plantation. Not much is left but a stone foundation and crumbling whitewashed bricks. Two walls still stand—at least, partially so—and a crumbling staircase rises toward the sky.

It probably used to be a storehouse of some kind, as it's not far from the original ferry-landing site that gave the plantation its name. Whatever the case, it's been taken over by nature now, tangled vines creeping across the bricks and crawling over the foundation.

But there's something about it—some sort of gothic appeal—that sparked Nan's imagination. We'd spent hours here as children, pretending that we were planters' daughters waiting for our beaux to return from the war, or abolitionists hiding out as we plotted to free slaves. Sometimes I played the part of Nan's lady's maid, braiding her long hair and decorating it with dandelions. Other times, Ryder would join us, playacting whatever male role Nan assigned him.

I find a spot on a little rise and lay down my towel before sitting on the ground and pulling out my cell from my pocket. Quickly, I type out a text: *Are you okay?*

Nan answers almost immediately. *I'm fine. See you Saturday.*

That's it—no explanation, no elaboration. I'm not sure what I expected, or why I had to come all the way out here to try to contact her. Suddenly, I feel alone. Too alone. I miss my sister; I want her here with me. Saturday is five days away—what am I supposed to do until then? I can't stop thinking about it—Nan, with a brain tumor. I can't stop worrying. Even now, my stomach is in knots.

At the sound of footsteps, I turn to find Ryder headed toward me. Somehow, I'm not surprised. He lifts one hand in greeting as he approaches wearing faded jeans and a plain white T-shirt. His hair is wet, like he's just gotten out of the shower.

As much as I hate to admit it, I'm happy to see him—glad for the company, even his.

"I figured I'd find you here," he says, his eyes filled with concern. Everything about him, from his posture to the tight set of his jaw, broadcasts a worry that matches mine.

Feud forgotten, I scoot over, making room for him on my towel. "I guess you heard?"

"Yeah. Your mom called mine." He sits down beside me, smelling of soap and aftershave. "She'll be fine, Jemma. Nan's strong," he says, almost repeating word for word what my dad had said earlier.

I reach for a blade of grass and snap it off, twirling it absently between my fingers. "This all seems so surreal. I keep hoping

I'll wake up and find out it was just a dream. Nan's always been as healthy as a horse—it just doesn't make sense."

"I know," he says with a nod. "But these kinds of things never seem to make sense. My mom said that they don't think it's cancerous, though. That this kind of tumor almost never is. So that's good, right?"

"Yeah. So I guess that means she won't have to have chemo or radiation or anything like that, but that doesn't make the surgery any less scary." I'd listened to my parents talk about it during dinner—they'd used the word "craniotomy," which sounded terrifying.

"I know, but modern medicine is pretty amazing. And just think, for the surgeons who do it every day, it's routine stuff."

"There's nothing *routine* about cutting open my sister's head." My stomach lurches at the thought, and I push it away, burying it deeply. I won't think about that right now—I can't.

"She's like a sister to me, too," Ryder says quietly. "I always envied you that, you know? A sibling. Do you have any idea how quiet it is at Magnolia Landing when you Caffertys aren't there? Dad's always in his office working, and Mom . . ." He trails off, his cheeks coloring slightly. "Well, Mom's busy planning the rest of my life. Anyway, Nan'll come through this."

"I hope you're right."

He bumps my shoulder with his side. "Hey, I'm always right. Right?"

I can't help it—a smile tugs at the corners of my mouth. "You always *think* you are, that's for sure."

He looks up at the sky, appearing thoughtful for a moment before returning his gaze to me. "Why don't you walk back to the house with me and let me drive you home."

"Nah, I've got a kayak. I left it down at the creek."

"That's okay. I'll bring it over tomorrow or something. It's getting dark. You shouldn't be out on the water alone."

"Seriously? I grew up on that creek."

"All the same, I'd feel better if you let me drive you home."

I have no idea why—he knows I'm perfectly capable of getting myself home. Still, I relent. "Fine," I say. Because, honestly, I'm not relishing the idea of paddling home in the dark, not in the mental state I'm in. "But I'm not ready to go, not just yet."

"No rush."

"Thanks." I lean back, resting on my elbows as I gaze up at the sky. A few stars are just beginning to dot the sky, faint twinkles of light on the violet-hued canvas above. I let out a long sigh. "Do you ever think about next year—about living somewhere else? I mean, even if it's just Oxford, it's going to be so different."

He just shrugs. Then, "I don't think about it too much, I guess. Senior year just started."

"I know, but still. And what about our parents? Just imagine your mom and dad all alone in that big house. I don't know. . . . It just makes me sad, I guess."

"So . . . live at home," he suggests.

"Yeah, I don't think so. Anyway, that's not what I meant. Just that . . . everything is about to change. And now this, with Nan . . ."

He swallows hard. "She's going to be fine."

"So everyone keeps saying." Despite the heat, a chill runs down my spine. I sit up, wrapping my arms around my knees.

"Look," he says, pointing toward the sky. "Right there— that's Venus. Just above and to the right of the moon. See it?"

I release my knees and brace my hands against the ground as I gaze up at the spot he's indicating—at what looks like a bright, twinkling star. "That's Venus? You sure?"

He nods. "And see that, up higher and off to the left? That's Saturn."

"Cool," I say. "You were always good with that stuff—stars and planets." He'd spent our entire childhood pointing out constellations in the night sky that I could never quite make out—things that were supposed to look like bears or dragons or what have you. To me they were just . . . stars.

For a moment we just sit there silently, our heads tipped back as we stare at the sky. A minute passes, maybe two. And then Ryder's hand grazes mine before settling on the ground, our pinkies touching.

I suck in a breath, my entire body going rigid. I'm wondering if he realizes it, if he even knows he's touching me, when just like that, he draws away.

Ryder clears his throat. "So . . . I hear you're going out with Patrick on Friday."

"And?" I ask. That brief connection that we'd shared is suddenly gone—*poof*, just like that.

"And what?" he answers with a shrug.

"Oh, I'm sure you've got an opinion on this—one you're just dying to share." Because Ryder has an opinion on *everything*.

"Well, it's just that Patrick . . ." He shakes his head. "Never mind. Forget I brought it up."

"No, go on. It's just that Patrick what?"

"Seriously, Jemma. It's none of my business."

"C'mon, Ryder, get it out of your system. What? Patrick is looking to get a piece? Is using me? Is planning on standing me up?" I can't help myself; the words just tumble out.

"I was going to say that I think he really likes you," he says, his voice flat.

I bite back my retort, forcing myself to take a deep, calming breath instead. That was *not* what I had expected him to say— not at all—and it takes me completely by surprise. Patrick really likes me? I'm not sure how I feel about that—not sure I want it to be true.

"What do you mean, he really likes me?" I ask stupidly.

"Just what I said. It's pretty simple stuff, Jemma. He *likes* you. I think he always has."

"And you know this how?"

He levels a stare at me. "Trust me on this, okay? He's got problems, sure, but he's a decent guy. Don't break his heart."

I scramble to my feet. "I agreed to go out with him—once. And I'm probably going to cancel, anyway, because after today's news, I'm really not in the mood. But the last thing I need is dating advice from you."

"How come every conversation we have ends like this— with you going off on me? You didn't use to be like this. What happened?"

He's right, and I hate myself for it—hate the way he makes me feel inside, as if I'm not good enough. I mean, let's face it—I know I'm nothing special. I'm not beauty-pageant perfect like Morgan, or fashion-model gorgeous like Lucy. Unlike Ryder and Nan, I don't have state-championship trophies lining my walls. My singing voice is only so-so, I can't draw or play a musical instrument, and if the school plays are any indicator, I can't act for shit, either.

Sure, I can shoot straight, but what good is that? And yeah, I'm an excellent student and a perfectly good cheerleader, but so what? Girls like me are a dime a dozen in the great state of Mississippi.

And all that noise our parents make—all this "you two

have to grow up and get married and unite the Marsdens and Caffertys once and for all" talk—must absolutely horrify Ryder. Because the truth is, he's all but guaranteed a charmed life—his pick of schools, of scholarships, of girls. He's probably going to end up playing in the NFL, traveling the globe and making millions of dollars, while I'll be stuck here in Magnolia Branch for the rest of my life, doing who knows what.

Tears borne of self-pity, of worry, well in my eyes, blurring my vision. A sob tears from my throat, and the tears begin to spill over. *Crap.* I bury my face in my hands, wishing more than anything that a hole would open in the ground and swallow me up. But it doesn't—and I can't stop crying, my throat constricting painfully as I try to muffle it.

"Oh, man. Are you crying? You are, aren't you? Shit." He puts an arm awkwardly around my shoulders. "C'mon, Jemma, please don't."

Somehow, I find myself leaning in to him, soaking the front of his T-shirt. He doesn't say a word. He just sits there quietly, stroking my hair as I cry it out. Five, maybe ten minutes pass before the tears dry up and my sobs are reduced to sniffles.

"I'm . . . sorry about that," I finally manage to choke out as I pull away, my cheeks burning with humiliation.

"Don't be." He trails a hand across my cheek, wiping away my tears.

I shiver in response. Without warning, he pulls me closer

into an embrace. His arms encircle me, holding me tightly as I lay my cheek against his chest, inhaling his clean scent. I can hear his heart thumping noisily against my ear, keeping time with my own.

Being this close to him is both oddly familiar and completely foreign, all at once. It's totally right and yet all wrong. My head is spinning, my mind trying to make sense of the conflicting feelings swirling inside of me, making me dizzy.

Just as abruptly, he releases me. "C'mon," he says, rising and reaching down to help me to my feet. "I should get you home now."

Wordlessly, I follow him to his truck. We remain silent throughout the short drive to my house. The windows are rolled all the way down, the night air cooling my skin and making conversation virtually impossible. When we pull up, he cuts the engine and hops out, hurrying around to open my door for me.

I step onto the driveway, trying to smooth down my wind-whipped hair. "Thanks," I murmur. "For the ride, and for . . . you know . . . everything."

Leaning against the truck with his hands thrust into his pockets, he just nods.

I know that I should walk away, but something holds me there. He leans toward me, reaching for my shoulder. For a split second, I actually think he's going to kiss me.

Instead, he gives my shoulder a little squeeze.

As I'm still puzzling this out, my mom comes barreling out the front door. "There you are! Oh, thank God. We were worried sick!"

"I—I'm fine," I stammer.

Mama shoots me a deadly glare. "Daddy's been looking all over for you! The barn, the creek . . ." She trails off, shaking her head. "Thanks for bringing her home, Ryder. I really appreciate it, hon."

"No problem, Miss Shelby," Ryder answers with a shrug, then climbs back inside his truck.

Mama turns to watch him drive off, her mouth curving into a smile. "That boy is such a gentleman."

I roll my eyes as I follow her into the house. As soon as I step inside, my cell buzzes. Stopping to lean against the door, I pull it from my pocket and glance down at the screen. It's a message from Ryder. He must have pulled over at the end of the driveway to send it. My heart does a weird little flip-flop— until I read what he's written, that is.

Don't cancel on Patrick.

ACT I
Scene 7

Y ou're not eating much," Patrick says with a frown. His tousled blond hair is still wet from his post-game shower, and he's changed into jeans and a blue-and-white-checked button-down shirt. He looks nice. Handsome, in a lean, Abercrombie & Fitch model kind of way.

"Sorry. I'm not all that hungry, I guess." I pick at the crust on my plate, ripping it into little doughy pieces.

"I'm glad you're here, though. I figured you were going to back out on me. You know, because of this stuff with your sister and all."

"No, I . . . The distraction is good for me. Helps keep my mind off it." I force myself to smile even though I'm not feeling it. I'm not feeling much of anything, really—it's like I'm numb inside.

Nan's coming home tomorrow. Just a matter of hours . . .

"It was a good game tonight," I say. "You played really well."

"Yeah, good thing, too—there were scouts crawling all over the place. Mostly there to see Ryder, of course. Dude's *so* got it made. I don't think he has any idea how lucky he is. I mean, sure, he's got talent. But mostly it's just a size thing, you know?"

I just shrug noncommittally and continue picking at my crust.

"But you looked great tonight. I got to watch you some during the third quarter after I took that hard hit."

"Thanks. I was kind of off. I almost fell during a toss."

"You mean that thing where they throw you up in the air and catch you?" he asks, even though it seems pretty self-explanatory to me. Since it's called, you know, a *toss*.

"Yeah. Listen, Patrick—"

"Uh-oh, here it comes. Look, let me lay it out on the line, Jemma. We've known each other a long time—"

"Our whole lives."

"Right. And I know it might seem like what happened on Saturday came out the blue, but I wanted to do that for a long time. Kiss you, I mean."

My mouth goes dry, and I reach for my Coke and take a sip. All I can think about is Monday night—Ryder holding me in his arms, brushing away my tears. And then later, by his car, there'd been that moment when I'd thought he was going to kiss me. Which seems pretty stupid now, considering the text I'd gotten from him just minutes later.

But what's really crazy? The fact that I'd been kinda disappointed that he hadn't. I'd lain awake half the night thinking about it, and the rest of the week hadn't been much better. I was confused. Mad at myself, more than anything.

I force my thoughts away from Ryder and back to the boy sitting across from me looking hopeful. I like him—I do. But I'm not sure I can give him what he wants from me. At least, not right now.

"All I was going to say is that it's kind of bad timing, that's all. Nan's coming home tomorrow, and I want to spend as much time with her as possible. Before her surgery," I add.

"I know." He reaches across the table for my hand, and I let him take it. "But I really want to spend time with you too."

"Can't we just . . . you know, keep it casual? Play it by ear? That's all I can promise you right now."

He shrugs. "Hey, I'll take whatever I can get."

I wince at his choice of words. Mostly because I know Patrick is an experienced guy—God knows I've listened to him talk. Ryder was right. Patrick has been known to kiss and tell on occasion, often in graphic detail. Maybe he thought it would impress me. Who knows? But I'm fairly certain I won't be *giving* him anything, least of all my virginity.

"You want some dessert?" he asks, releasing my hand to

signal for the waiter. "They've got really good cheesecake here."

"No, but you go ahead." My phone buzzes, and I glance down at the screen.

Having fun?

It's Lucy. I quickly tap out a reply. *I guess.*

Don't do anything I wouldn't do, she answers, followed by a winking smiley.

Patrick is still occupied with the waiter, so I continue the text convo. *What r u doing?* I type.

Hanging out @ Ward's. Ryder's here.

Why would I care if he's there?

Dunno. Just sayin'.

Umm, okay.

I shove my cell back into my pocket. "Sorry 'bout that. It was just Lucy."

"Ah, Luce the Deuce." He waggles his eyebrows suggestively.

"Luce the what?"

"The Deuce—that's what some of the guys call her. You know, 'cause no one ever gets past second with her."

"Seriously?" I ask, cringing. "You guys are so gross."

"I ordered you a piece of cheesecake, by the way. Cherry topping."

"Oh. Thanks." I'm pretty sure I'd said no to the offer. "So, have you decided where you want to go to school next year?"

"Depends on whether or not I get any offers to play ball. I'm not counting on Ole Miss, but maybe Delta State. How 'bout you?"

I briefly consider telling him about the NYU thing—since we'd taken that film class together and everything—but decide against it, since I don't want the whole town to know by sunrise. "I'm not sure yet," I say instead.

Just then the waiter appears bearing two dessert plates. He sets them in front of us and then busies himself refilling our water glasses before disappearing again.

"Any idea what you're going to study?" I ask as soon as we're alone again.

"You mean I'm supposed to actually study something? Besides Beer Pong 101, I mean?" He shovels a bite of cheesecake into his mouth, and I'm left wondering if he's kidding or not.

He's actually a pretty good student. Not AP track or anything like that, but he's not stupid, either.

He takes a sip of water, watching me over the rim of his cup. "Seriously, though, my dad thinks I should go prelaw. You know, follow in his footsteps and all that. Who decides this kind of thing now, anyway?"

I want to say, "Oh, you know . . . people who care about their future," but I somehow manage to bite my tongue.

I pick at my dessert, watching quietly as Patrick devours his.

"S'good, huh?" he says around a mouthful.

I just nod and continue poking. Trying not to be too obvious, I sneak a peek at my cell to check the time. It's getting late. I cross my legs. Uncross them. Fiddle with my napkin.

"You about ready to head out?" Patrick asks after a few minutes of awkward silence. "It's okay. I get it. It's been a long day. Just let me pay the check."

He reaches for his wallet just as I go for my purse. "Hey, no way," he says, shaking his head. "This is my treat. I asked *you* out, remember?"

"You sure?"

"I'm sure." He offers me a smile, his cheeks dimpling. "Sit tight; we'll get you out of here soon enough."

He's a nice guy, and I feel terrible for being so transparent. "I'm sorry I'm such a lousy date. It's just . . . like I said, bad timing, is all."

"S'okay," he says with a shrug. "You can make it up to me next time." Grinning now, he reaches into his wallet and pulls out a couple of twenties.

I stand and dig my keys out of my purse, ready to make my escape from the most awkward date ever.

He signals for the waiter. "Wait a sec and I'll walk you out."

I owe him that, at least.

"Where's Nan?" I ask my mom, glancing around the kitchen.

She opens the refrigerator and pulls out a pitcher of sweet

tea. "Out on the porch. She didn't get a lot of sleep last night, so she's napping."

I know how she feels—I didn't get a lot of sleep either. Nan hadn't pulled up into the driveway until after eight, a good two hours after my parents expected her. Needless to say, dinner had been a strained meal. We'd all just picked at our food, barely saying anything to each other. You could tell that Mama and Daddy were mad, but they wouldn't dare yell at her, not now.

After dinner, they wanted to talk to her about the research they'd done—what the neurosurgeon in Houston had to say, what the doctors in Jackson recommended, what they'd read online. Different treatment options, surgical procedures, blah, blah, blah. I'd had to slip out of the room halfway through the discussion, because frankly, it was freaking me out. I could only imagine how Nan was feeling.

"I won't wake her up," I say, and she nods, offering me a glass of tea. She looks strained. Older. These past few days have taken a toll on her, I realize—on all of us.

I lay a gentle hand on her arm. "Hey, why don't you go take a nap too?"

She sighs, her shoulders sagging. "Maybe I will."

I kiss her on the cheek and take the pitcher from her. "Go on," I say, motioning toward the door. "I'll put this away."

"Thanks, honey."

I watch her walk out, marveling at how much she looks like Nan from the back. They have the same coloring, the same long, straight, honey-blond hair, and the same athletic build.

Whereas I got my dad's coloring—reddish blond hair, pale skin—and slight build. Only somehow I got Mama's blue eyes, whereas Nan got Daddy's green ones. Genetics are funny that way.

Carefully, I set the pitcher back inside the fridge. I know how much Mama loves it. It's beautiful, round with a sort of ruffled rim—from Tiffany's. She got it as a wedding present, and it still looks as good as new.

I quickly wipe down the counter, then tiptoe out onto the sleeping porch on the west side of the house. The entire rectangular space is screened in, with two ceiling fans stirring the air from above. The wood paneling below the screens is painted white, just beginning to peel in some spots.

In the corner closest to the door, a full-size wood-frame bed hangs from the ceiling—sort of like an enormous swing. There's a white wicker bedside table against the wall and two matching wicker chairs on the far side of the porch. All the linens and cushions are white with blue ticking, and several hurricane lamps provide lighting along with white twinkle lights wrapped around the rafters.

There's a second sleeping porch on the opposite side of the house—my mom's. It's pretty much the same, except for the yellow-and-white color scheme. Still, I like this one much better. It's ours, Nan's and mine.

I find Nan stretched out on the bed, lying on her back with her legs crossed at the ankles. "Jemma, Jemma, Bo-Bemma," she calls out as I close the French doors behind me and set down my glass of tea.

"Nan, Nan, Bo-Ban," I answer, my voice breaking ever so slightly on the last syllable. I know it's silly, but it's something we've always done. "How're you feeling?"

"Fine. I'm not dying, you know. I woke up with a migraine, but my meds managed to knock it out."

"Probably the weather." I tip my head toward the dark clouds in the distance. "Storm's a'brewing."

She nods. "That always does it. My head, the barometer."

"Yeah, mine too. Sucks." It's one of those things we have in common—migraines. Which makes me wonder if a tumor is in my future too. Maybe it's just a coincidence. I hope so.

"C'mon, lie down," she says, patting the space beside her.

"Okay, but no more jokes about dying," I say as I climb up onto the bed. "It's not funny."

She ignores that. "Did you know that Great-Grandma Cafferty had the same thing in her head? At least, she probably did. It's what killed her."

"I thought she died from an aneurysm or a hemorrhage or something like that."

"Yeah, as a result of brain surgery. It was a success, but then she bled to death," she says matter-of-factly.

My stomach lurches uncomfortably. "That was ages ago. I'm sure brain surgery's come a long way since then. Don't they use lasers or something now?"

"Maybe. Guess I'll find out soon enough," she says with a shrug. "Anyway, what's up with you? Mama says you're going out with Patrick Hughes."

"I went out with him once," I say, rolling my eyes. Still, I'm glad for the change of topic. "It's no big deal. I can't believe she told you."

"Well, you know how she is. You're ruining her big plans for you and the boy next door. Speaking of, where's he going to play ball next year? Ryder, I mean."

"How the heck would I know? He doesn't discuss his plans with me. We don't talk at all unless we have to."

"Well, maybe you should think about rectifying that," she says with a grin. "You know what I mean?"

I nudge her with my foot. "Hey, I thought you were on my side."

"I dunno. . . . After seeing him this summer at the beach, maybe Mama's onto something. I mean, let's face it—the boy's hot. You could do worse. Much worse."

"Yeah, well . . . there's more to it than looks," I grumble.

"Right. There's also intelligence—check. Talent—check.

Character—check." She ticks each one off on her fingers. "As far as I can tell, he's got it all—the total package. I mean, okay, so he's the boy next door, and Mom and Laura Grace have been bugging you two about each other since forever. But seriously, what more do you want?"

I sigh heavily. "You want to know what drives me nuts about Ryder? There are no shades of gray with him. Everything's black or white, right or wrong. He's just so . . . so . . . unyielding."

"Wow, is that one of your SAT words?"

"Ha-ha, very funny. You know what I mean, though."

She shrugs. "Yeah, I know. He's always been that way. I kind of figured he'd grow out of it."

"Well, don't hold your breath. That boy's got a stick up his ass, if you ask me."

"A very attractive one at that."

"What, the stick or his ass?"

Nan laughs—a rich, booming laugh that makes me smile. I'm so glad to have her home. But then I remember why. . . .

"So, when are you going to Houston?" I ask, sobering fast.

"Probably next week. Maybe the week after. The doctor said we've got to move fast. I guess the tumor's pressing on some important stuff."

I snuggle up closer, laying my head on her shoulder. "I'm sorry this happened to you, Nan."

"Yeah, me too," she says, then falls silent. For a couple of minutes we just lie there quietly, staring at the ceiling.

"I'm sorry I didn't call or text you," she says at last. "I just . . . you know, kind of retreated into myself. I didn't want to talk to anyone."

"It's okay. I know how that goes." Because I do the same thing when I'm stressed out. I retreat. Cut myself off from everyone. I've been doing it this week, letting texts and e-mails slide. Luckily, Morgan and Lucy know me well enough to give me my space. Patrick, not so much. We'll have to work on that.

"You're going to be just fine," I say with as much conviction as I can muster.

But the truth is, I've never been more scared in all my life.

ACT I
Scene 8

Thursday is "History Bee" day in my AP European History class. Think old-fashioned spelling bee, with students standing in a line at the front of the classroom. Mr. Donaldson fires a history trivia question at you, and if you get it right you remain standing for the next round. Get it wrong, and you sit. Last man standing is declared the winner.

I have to admit, it's kind of fun—way more so than listening to a lecture. Plus, the winner gets a Hershey Bar.

"The Ardennes," I say when it's my turn, desperate for that chocolate.

Mr. Donaldson cups a hand to his ear. "Could you please speak up, Jemma?"

"The Ardennes!" I shout, wishing he'd invest in some hearing aids.

"Correct. You advance to the final round."

Beside me, Lucy mimes a high five.

Thirty minutes later, she's glaring at me as I make my way back to my desk with the Hershey Bar clutched in one hand. "I'll share," I whisper as I slide into the molded plastic seat behind her.

"You suck," she tosses over her shoulder just a second before the A-lunch bell rings. "Thank God. I'm starving."

"Me too." I stuff the chocolate bar into my backpack and rise, following the crowd out toward the cafeteria.

As soon as we get our food—something that resembles fettuccine Alfredo—we join Morgan at our usual nice-weather table out on the patio. Mason and Patrick are already there, their trays piled high with multiple sandwiches and bags of chips. Ben and Ryder have B-lunch this semester, so it's a little less rowdy than usual.

Morgan slides to the center of the bench seat, making room for Lucy and me on either side of her. "So?" she asks, one blond brow raised.

Lucy wrinkles her nose in my direction. "She won again. Wench."

"Chocolate for dessert!" I say, pulling the bar from my bag with a flourish.

Morgan grabs it with a scowl, hiding it beneath the table. "Don't let the boys see."

"Don't let the boys see what?" Mason asks around a mouthful of unidentifiable sandwich.

Morgan shakes her head. "Nothing. And could you *be* any more gross?"

"Oh, I'm sure I could," he answers with a grin.

I take a tentative bite of my pasta. Surprisingly, it's not too bad.

"Hey, how's Nan doing?" Morgan asks.

I swallow hard. "She's okay. Mostly just . . . you know, resting. Trying to take it easy."

They're leaving for Houston next week—Mama, Daddy, and Nan. Even Laura Grace is going. Everyone but me. I can't miss school, they claim. They have no idea how long they'll be gone, and they need me to hold down the fort. I'm not sure if I'm more angry or hurt about it. Probably hurt. Mostly.

"You think she'd mind if Morgan and I dropped by this weekend to see her?" Lucy asks.

"Nah. I'm sure she'd love to see y'all. Come by anytime."

"Speaking of this weekend . . ." Patrick clears his throat, vying for our attention. "Josh Harrington is having a party Saturday. Crawfish boil on their property, down by the creek. You coming, Jemma?"

I shake my head. "I don't think so. It's really not a good time."

"Aww, c'mon, Jem," he wheedles. "I'll pick you up on my

way over, and we'll just stay for a little while. An hour, tops."

I glance over at Morgan, then Lucy.

"I figured I'd go," Lucy says with a shrug.

Morgan nods. "Yeah, me too. Not much else going on."

I exhale sharply. "Fine. But just for a little bit. And I'll meet you there," I direct at Patrick.

"The DUI thing, huh?" Mason asks, smiling wryly.

"Pretty much." My cheeks flame hotly. "Sorry, Patrick."

He eyes me sharply from across the table. "Seriously? That was months ago."

"Yeah, but . . . you know how parents are," I offer lamely. The truth is, I wouldn't get in a car with him behind the wheel even if my parents *didn't* know. I'm not that stupid.

"Fine," he mutters. "Whatever."

"Hey, I've got an idea," Morgan says. "Lucy and I should meet up at your house, Jemma. We can say hi to Nan, and then we can ride over together."

"Yeah, I'll stop by Ward's and get some burgers on my way over," Lucy offers.

"Wait, you wanna eat burgers *before* a crawfish boil?" Morgan asks.

"Heck yeah. Crawfish are too much work for not enough food. Better to go with a full belly."

Reluctantly, I nod. "Sounds like a plan." It's not that I don't want to hang out with them—I do. It's just that I feel guilty about leaving Nan. Of course, she's spent most of her time alone in her room, listening to music and writing in her journal. I've tried to give her some space, but still . . . it's comforting knowing that she's there, just on the other side of the wall that separates our rooms.

Besides, it somehow seems wrong to go out and have fun while your sister sits at home with a brain tumor, you know?

After school, I head straight to the barn. Daddy's done teaching early on Thursdays, so he's already there in his workshop, stripping the paint off an antique cabinet. A Hoosier cabinet, I think it's called.

"Hey," he calls out over the blaring music. "You got a date with Delilah?"

"Yup. That kind of day." Ever since lunch, my head's been a mess. I mean, I said I'd meet Patrick at the party on Saturday. Does that make it a date? Are we actually *dating*? After all, I've kissed him twice now—first at the historical society gala and then again on Friday night, when he'd walked me to my car after dinner. Both had been nice kisses. Keyword "nice"—as in, not earth-moving. No fireworks or anything like that. And besides that one film class we'd taken together, we pretty much have nothing in common. So what's the point, really?

Am I dating him just to have someone to go out with? Or is the attraction real? Honestly, I'm not sure. Maybe it's the whole bad-boy thing—which I realize is beyond stupid. Besides, he's not *that* bad of a boy. But he is the total opposite of Ryder, which means that going out with him is the complete opposite of what my family wants me to do. Maybe that's it, then—a minor rebellion on my part.

Daddy sets down his sander. "Want to talk about it?"

"Not really," I say. "I thought I'd take some targets outside today. Down by the creek. Want to come with me?"

"Sure. Just let me put my things away. Can you get my Ruger out of the safe for me?"

"Okay. I'll get you a headset and goggles, too. Meet you outside in five?"

He's smiling now. "You got it, half-pint."

Ten minutes later, we're down by the water, setting up the targets.

"Hey, did you and Mama ever get a chance to look at the film school stuff I gave you?" I ask as we get everything moved into position. "You know, the NYU catalog and application materials?"

His hand drops away from the target he's straightening, and he turns to face me with drawn brows. "Honey, how can you even think about going off to New York now? With everything that's going on with your sister?"

I swallow hard. "But . . . I wouldn't be going anywhere till next year. She's . . . I mean, she'll be fine by then, right?"

He shakes his head. "I think you need to stick with the original plan, okay? State schools."

Silently, I nod. I can't argue with him, not now. But I'm not ready to concede, either. I mean, what harm is there in applying? I sigh uneasily. Everything just seems so tumultuous and uncertain right now. Senior year isn't supposed to feel like this. Or is it? It's definitely not what I expected; that's for sure. Somehow I expected all the pieces to start falling into place, the hazy vision of my future to begin to come into focus. Not this—confusion and doubt.

"You ready?" Daddy asks, and my attention snaps back into focus.

I tighten my grip on Delilah and take my place opposite my target. My dad moves beside me. I slip on my goggles and headset before taking a deep, calming breath—in through my nose, out through my mouth.

Arms fully extended, I raise the pistol, my gaze trained on the spot I'm aiming for—a red circle the size of a quarter more than two dozen yards away. I take one more deep breath and manage to find my center, all extraneous thoughts gone from my head. It's just Delilah and me now. When I squeeze the trigger, everything feels somehow *right*.

Too bad it won't last.

ACT I
Scene 9

The fight started just minutes before we show up at the party on Saturday night. It's immediately obvious that Tanner is getting the best of Mason, who already has a black eye and a bloodied lip by the time Lucy, Morgan, and I make our way across the grassy field and push through the gawking crowd.

"What's going on?" I ask no one in particular, shouting to be heard over the ruckus.

"They were arguing about football, what else?" Jessica Addington says.

"You know, about the game with West Lafayette," Rosie adds, stepping up beside me. "Ryder said something that made Tanner mad, and he totally lost his shit and tried to get Ryder to fight. Ryder refused and walked off. And then, I don't know,

Tanner called Ryder a pussy, and Mason flipped him off. . . ." She trails off, shaking her head.

"Next thing I know, Tanner went after Mason," Jessica finishes for her. "Stupid football rivalry—makes the boys act like idiots."

Jessica's on the cheerleading squad with us, and while I wouldn't call her one of my BFFs, we *are* friends. I'm pretty sure she's got a thing for Mason, which would explain the worry in her eyes when Tanner's fist makes contact with Mason's nose and blood gushes everywhere.

"Somebody *do* something!" she cries, glancing around wildly, her dark ponytail smacking me in the face.

"Ryder!" Rosie yells, her hands cupped around her mouth. "Where'd he go?"

I spot Patrick off to my right, moving toward the flying fists. "Tanner! That's enough, man." He tugs ineffectually at the back of his collar in an effort to draw him off Mason's prone form, but Tanner just continues throwing punches.

I have to physically restrain Morgan from going to her twin's rescue. Tanner's totally out of control, and I don't want her to get hurt. I tighten my grip on her arm, my fingernails digging into her skin.

Finally, Ryder breaks through the crowd and steps into the fray. In a matter of seconds, he manages to pull Tanner off Mason and throw him to the ground a few feet away. He stands over him, his hands clenched into fists. "What the hell's your problem, man?"

Tanner's half Ryder's size—he was crazy to pick a fight with him to begin with. Maybe he's thought better of it now, because he just lies there spent, panting.

Now that Tanner's been subdued, Morgan rushes toward her brother, kneeling beside him as she helps him to sit. Jessica hurries to his other side, handing him a wad of tissues.

"Asshole!" Mason calls out as he presses the tissues to his nose.

"You want more of this?" Tanner growls, but Ryder grabs him by one arm and drags him to his feet, pulling him away from the crowd. Ben follows behind.

Patrick appears beside me. "Hey, Jem." He drapes an arm across my shoulders. "I was starting to wonder if you were going to show. You almost missed the excitement."

"Is everyone going to just stand around and gawk, or is someone getting Mason some ice?" Lucy calls out.

Jessica rises and jogs over to the cooler under the pavilion and fills a bag with ice. "Here you go," she says breathlessly when she returns.

I shrug out from under Patrick's arm and join the crowd gathered around Mason. He looks terrible. One eye is swollen shut and his nose—or maybe it's his lip?—is gushing blood.

"Your cousin's a real douchebag," Morgan directs at me with a scowl.

I hold up both hands in mock surrender. "Hey, don't blame me! He's just a second cousin, anyway."

Mason struggles to stand, but Morgan and Jessica press him back to the ground. "I'm fine," he says, though he looks anything but.

"Just put the ice on your eye," Jessica says. "Or maybe your nose. Wow, you're really bleeding. Anyone got a rag or something like that?"

We all look around helplessly.

"Maybe in my car," Rosie says, rising. "I'll go see." She hurries toward the line of cars parked off in the distance.

Just then, Ryder reappears. "Here," he says, unbuttoning his plaid shirt to reveal a white T-shirt beneath it. In seconds, he's stripped off both shirts. He wads up the T-shirt and hands it to Morgan.

Morgan takes it with a nod. "Thanks. What'd you do with Tanner?"

"Ben's driving him home."

I chance a glance in his direction and swallow hard, my mouth suddenly dry. Because let's face it, the sight of Ryder wearing nothing but jeans that ride low on his hips is pretty impressive. I mean, obviously I've seen him in less at the beach and whatnot, but there's something about those faded jeans and the way the waistband dips low on his abdomen. . . .

Patrick must have noticed me staring, because he tightens his grip around my shoulders. "Hey, you wanna go for a walk?"

"Sure," I say lazily. But as he leads me away, I can't help glancing back over my shoulder at Ryder, who's shrugging back into his plaid shirt, his fingers flying over the buttons.

I let out a sigh and turn back toward Patrick. "Where're we headed?"

"Right here is good," he says, pressing me against the split-rail fence. As his head dips down toward mine I lay my palms flat against his chest.

"Wait." I push against him, wanting to create some space between our bodies. The crowd isn't more than fifty yards away, and I feel exposed.

"What?" he asks, a hint of impatience in his voice. "You need a beer or something?"

"No, I'm fine."

"I missed you, Jem," he says, one hand sliding up my thigh, beneath the hem of my vintage red polka-dot halter dress.

I smack his hand away. "You saw me yesterday at school and later at the game."

"You know what I mean." His mouth moves toward mine, his breath warm against my cheek.

My mind is whirling, my heart thumping against my ribs.

There's something . . . I don't know . . . a little *dangerous* about Patrick. I want to run, but I'm somehow frozen in place like a deer in the crosshairs.

His lips find mine, and I suck in my breath sharply as his tongue skims over my teeth. I want to *feel* something, to have the earth move beneath my feet. But there's no butterflies fluttering in my stomach, no lightning skittering across my skin. Instead, I've overly aware of the mechanics of it all—lips, tongue, hands. He deepens the kiss, and I feel myself pulling away mentally even as I participate physically.

My mind begins to wander. I'm thirsty now, and I wonder what my friends are doing back over by the creek. We weren't planning on staying more than an hour or so, and it's probably been half that already. I want to check the time, but my cell is back with my purse. The tall grass tickles my ankles, and I shift my weight from foot to foot, resisting the urge to reach down and scratch.

He draws away, peering down at me sharply. "What's wrong?"

I have to think of some excuse, and fast. "It's just . . . You think Mason's okay?"

"He's fine. Seriously, you're worrying about that shit right now?"

I take a deep breath before speaking. "Well, we just left him lying there bleeding."

"With half a dozen people tending to him, including his sister."

"Yeah, but I came with Morgan. If she decides to take Mason home—"

"Then I'll drive you. Okay? C'mon, Jemma. Relax."

I nod, glancing over at the crowd. The music is cranking now, and everyone's moved over to the covered pavilion where the piles of crawfish, corn, and potatoes have been dumped into plastic kiddie pools lined with newspaper.

Everyone except Ryder, that is. He's standing away from everyone else, his hands thrust into his pockets. I'm not positive, but I think he's looking right in my direction, watching Patrick and me.

Goose bumps rise on my skin, and I shiver.

"You cold?" Patrick asks.

I nod, even though I'm not. Still, it's as good an excuse as any. "I left my sweater under the pavilion with my bag."

"Okay, okay. We'll go back. Looks like the food's out, anyway." He reaches for my hand, and I let him lead me back to the party.

Mason's sitting on a picnic table beneath the pavilion, the bag of melted ice discarded on the table beside him. Jessica, Morgan, and Lucy surround him, chattering noisily over the music's din. I find my sweater and then hurry over to my friends.

"He keeps talking about this new quarterback they've got like he's the best thing since sliced bread," Mason is saying, obviously rehashing the fight. "I mean, dude, give me a break. Ryder's the best in the state. I've had enough of his trash talk."

Rosie steps up to the table, her cheeks flushed. "Hey, have any of y'all seen Ryder?"

"He's here somewhere," Morgan says, glancing over her shoulder toward the spot where I'd seen him standing not fifteen minutes ago. It's empty now.

"Yeah," Mason says. "I'm his ride home. Hey, didn't you say you needed a lift too, Jess?" Mason attempts a grin in Jessica's direction, but between his swollen eye and busted lip, it looks more like a grimace.

"There's no way I'm letting you drive," Morgan says resolutely. "You might have a head injury or something, you moron. Lucy can take my car, and I'll drive yours. It's okay, Jess—I don't mind dropping you off."

"Fine," Mason mutters. "Whatever."

Rosie plops herself down on the bench beside me. "Crap, I needed to ask Ryder something. Anyone know why he left so early? Did he take anyone with him?"

"No idea," Morgan says, shaking his head.

I wonder what she wants with Ryder—and if those rumors I'd heard about the two of them hooking up are true. Not that it's any of my business, but still.

The thing is, Rosie's pretty—*really* pretty. Sure, she's dumb as a rock, but a lot of guys don't care about that. She could have her pick of cute boys, but instead she continues to pine away for Ryder. Quite obviously, I might add.

Sometimes I think about pulling her aside and telling her to have a little self-respect, but what's the point? She wouldn't listen. She doesn't like me very much, cousin or not. Besides, if the rumors about them hooking up are true, well . . . maybe there *is* something going on between them. How the heck would I know? And more important, why should I care?

Patrick reaches for my hand. "You wanna go dance?"

I shake off the thoughts of Ryder and Rosie. "Sure. C'mon, Luce." I thump her on the shoulder.

"What am I, chopped liver?" Morgan asks with a frown.

"I thought you were too busy playing nursemaid."

"Nah, I think Jess can take it from here." She rises, tossing aside Ryder's now-bloodied T-shirt. "You'll take good care of him, right?"

Without waiting for Jessica's reply, she follows us out onto the packed earth behind the pavilion that's serving as a dance floor.

When I glance back, I see that Ryder has reappeared, standing beside Rosie. He leans down to say something in her ear, and she nods.

Patrick moves closer to me, blocking my view. He's one of

those guys who seems to think that jumping in place while pumping one's fists in the air somehow constitutes dancing. I only catch glimpses of Ryder leading Rosie to the dance floor between bobs of Patrick's head.

Curious, I turn my body slightly, angling away from him, trying to get a better view of Ryder and Rosie without being too obvious about it. Somehow, Ryder's eyes seem to meet mine across the crowd. I freeze, seemingly forgetting how to dance as I watch Rosie wrap her arms around Ryder's neck. His gaze leaves mine as his arms encircle Rosie's waist. She presses her cheek against his chest, and they start swaying back and forth, slow dancing.

To a fast song. *Ugh.*

When Patrick reaches for my hand and pulls me up against him, I let him. Anything to take my mind off what I just witnessed.

ACT I
Scene 10

O kay, the fridge is fully stocked, and I left a couple casseroles in the freezer for you." My mom glances down at the list she's left on the kitchen counter and sighs. "Are you sure you don't want to go stay with Lucy? Dr. Parrish said they'd be happy to have you. I could just give her a call and—"

"And who'll feed the dogs and cats? C'mon, Mama, I'll be fine."

"We could board them. I can call the kennel now and see if they—"

"Just stop." I can't help but roll my eyes. "We're not boarding the dogs. Stop worrying and go before you miss your flight."

She glances down at her watch. "Daddy's picking up Laura Grace right now."

Laura Grace has a degree in nursing even though she hasn't worked as an RN since before Ryder was born. But she insists that she can advocate for them at the hospital in Houston—you know, talk to the nurses and relay information, stuff like that. I think more than anything, she just wants to be there to provide moral support for my mom.

"Actually," Mama says, "maybe I should see if Ryder'll come over here and stay with you."

"No way. Forget it. I told you. I'll be fine."

"I just hate the thought of you here all by yourself. Besides, Rob's leaving for Jackson in a few days, and Ryder'll be alone. He could come stay in the guest room."

She can't be serious. "What the heck, Mama? Why don't we just share a bed?"

"Aww, honey, you know I don't mean it like that," she says. "But that reminds me. . . . No boys in the house while we're away. *Especially* Patrick Hughes." She stares at me sharply, one blond brow arched. "I had to listen to Cheryl Jackson yesterday going on and on about the two of you, about how surprised she was that I'm letting you see him."

"Ugh! Why do you listen to that woman? I swear, you don't to have to worry about Patrick. Seriously, I know the rules. Anyway, between school and cheerleading and play tryouts—"

"You're trying out for the play?"

"I figured I would. I usually do." It's something that Morgan and Lucy and I have always done together. Lucy always gets a good part, while Morgan and I are relegated to standing around onstage like scenery. Still, it's fun.

Mama nods. "Just don't overextend yourself. Now's not the time for your grades to slip."

"I know. I know. Sheesh."

The sound of tires in the driveway announces my dad's return. I let out my breath in a rush, both eager for them to leave and terrified about it, all at once.

My mom wraps me in a hug. "Oh, honey. Are you sure you'll be okay?"

"I'll be fine," I repeat, a lump forming in my throat. "Just . . . take care of Nan, okay?"

She releases me and steps back, wiping her eyes with the back of one hand. "Lou said she'd drop by and check on you every once in a while, but if you need anything, you know you can call me or Daddy anytime—day or night."

I just nod.

"And if there's a problem here at the house, call Ryder right away. He'll come over and—"

"But you said no boys," I argue stubbornly.

She gives me a pointed look. "*Except* for Ryder. Nan!" she calls out. "C'mon, Daddy's back. It's time to go."

"Coming!" Nan clatters down the stairs, her suitcase in tow. Looking at her, you'd never know she's headed to the hospital to deal with a brain tumor. She looks all bright and cheery and healthy, her hair pulled back into a ponytail.

Tears well in my eyes, and I fight to keep them from falling.

Nan shoots me a stern look. "Do *not* start crying, Jemma. Seriously, if you do, I'm going to lose my shit."

"Watch your language," Mama admonishes from the doorway where she's wrestling her bag out.

Nan rolls her eyes. "Just come over here and give me a hug, okay? No good-byes. I mean it."

I have to rise up on tiptoe to hug her. Her quick, staccato heartbeat belies her calm demeanor as she squeezes me tightly, then releases me. "Now, you listen to me," she says as soon as Mama's through the door and out of earshot. "I'll kill you if you don't apply to NYU, if that's what you really want to do."

We'd had a long talk on Saturday morning, and I'd told her everything—about Patrick, about film school and Mama's and Daddy's reluctance to let me apply.

"Don't you worry about me," she continues. "Be the person you want to be, Jemma. Don't let Mama and Daddy make all your decisions for you, okay?"

I nod, my throat aching as I continue to fight back tears.

"Pinkie swear?" She holds out one hand, pinkie extended.

I loop my little finger around hers and squeeze. "Pinkie swear."

I follow her out onto the front porch and lean against the

railing, watching them load their luggage into the back of the rental SUV. I'd offered to drive them to the airport in Memphis, but Daddy didn't want me driving back alone. He'd ultimately decided that renting a car made the most sense. After all, they have no idea how long they'll be gone. No point in leaving one of our cars in the airport lot, racking up fees.

Sadie and Beau lope up the porch stairs and sit on either side of me, their tongues lolling as I reach down and stroke their fur.

"Okay, I think that's it." Daddy slams shut the back hatch and hurries over to me. He bends down and gives me a quick hug and a peck on the cheek. "Love you, half-pint. We're just a phone call away."

"I know," I say, sniffling now. "Love you too."

Laura Grace waves from the backseat beside Nan. "You take care, sugar! Call that boy of mine if you need anything, you hear?"

"I will." I wave back as Daddy gets in the driver's side and closes the door.

The engine starts up, and off they go in a cloud of dust. I just stand there watching until the car disappears over the rise. "Well, I guess it's just you and me now," I say to the dogs. "Plus the cats," I add as Kirk struts up to the porch in a way that would make his namesake proud. "Where's the rest of your crew?"

Kirk just meows, stopping to arch his back.

Not a care in the world. Must be nice.

With nothing left to do, I head back inside and retrieve my video camera. The sun will be setting in an hour or so, and I figure I might as well film some sunset footage for my application project. Maybe I'll drive over to the old covered bridge and film there. If nothing else, it'll take my mind off the fact that my entire family is headed off to Houston without me, and that Nan—

Stop. I can't let myself go there. I take a deep, calming breath as I reach for my keys and head back out, herding the dogs inside before I lock up. As soon as I step outside, Ryder's Durango pulls up. He cuts the engine and jumps out carrying a small floral quilted bag.

"Did they leave yet?" he asks, sounding breathless.

"Yeah, you just missed them."

"Damn. Mom left this on her bed—I'm pretty sure she meant to pack it."

It looks like her makeup bag. "Uh-oh. Maybe you could FedEx it to her?"

"I guess. Do you know where they're staying?"

"With the Prescotts," I say. Lana Prescott is one of Mama's and Laura Grace's sorority sisters. "They've got a guesthouse or pool house or something like that. Anyway, Mama left the address on the kitchen counter. You want to come inside and get it?"

"Yeah, if you don't mind."

I open the front door and he follows me inside. Which, of course, makes the dogs go crazy.

"Hey, you two keeping Jemma here company?" he asks, bending down to scratch them both behind their ears.

Ryder loves dogs, but Laura Grace won't let him have one—not even a yappy little lap dog. She swears she's allergic, but I think she's actually afraid of them. Beau and Sadie are as sweet as anything, but we have to lock them up when she comes over.

"Here you go," I call out from the kitchen. "On the bottom of the last page."

He steps into the room and takes the sheaf of paper from me. "Wow. Three pages, huh? That seems a little . . . excessive."

"Yeah, well. You know how my mom is."

He takes out his cell and starts entering the address. "I was surprised to see you at Josh's party on Saturday," he says, his eyes glued to the screen.

"I don't know why. Everyone was there."

"Yeah, but you know . . . with Nan home and all, I just figured that you'd want to spend time with her."

"I *have* been spending time with Nan, thank you very much," I snap in annoyance. How dare he insinuate that I'd abandoned my sister? She's the one who made me go, who swore that it would make her somehow anxious to know I was "missing out"—her words, not mine.

"You and Patrick looked awfully cozy," Ryder says, setting Mama's note back on the counter.

So I was right—he *had* been watching us.

"So?"

"So, nothing." He shrugs. "Just making an observation."

"Yeah, you *never* just make an observation. Oh, and you and Rosie looked pretty cozy, too. I sure hope you're not leading her on. You *know* she likes you."

A muscle in his jaw works furiously as he shoves his cell phone back into his pocket. "That's the kind of guy you think I am? Seriously, Jem?"

I swallow hard, unable to reply. Because the truth is, I don't know.

"I'll see you later," he says, his voice cold and clipped. He turns and stalks out.

For some unknown reason, I follow him—down the hall, out the front door. "Don't walk out on me," I holler as he rounds the Durango and opens the driver's-side door. "If you have something to say to me, then say it."

He gets in and slams the car door shut, but I throw it open again. "C'mon," I taunt, motioning with one hand.

I'm totally losing it now—white spots dancing before my eyes, tears streaking down my cheeks. I can barely catch my breath, like I'm about to hyperventilate.

This isn't about Ryder, I realize. It's about Nan. The sudden realization hits me hard. What if I never see her again?

My knees buckle, and I start to go down. Somehow, Ryder manages to catch me just before I hit the ground. "Shit, Jemma! What's the matter with you?" He drags me to my feet and presses me against the side of his truck. "Take a deep breath. Jesus!"

I do what he says. By the third, I've slowed my heart rate to something nearing normal. Only, my cheeks are burning with mortification now. This is the second time I've broken down in front of Ryder. He must think I've lost my mind—that I've totally gone off the deep end.

"Just go," I say, my voice shaking.

He rakes both hands through his hair. "Are you kidding me? I can't leave you alone like this."

"Go," I repeat, more forcefully this time. "Just get in your car and leave, okay?"

"C'mon, Jemma. You know I can't."

"I swear I'm okay." I straighten my spine and lift my chin, trying my best to look calm, collected, and reasonably sane. "Seriously, Ryder. I just need to be alone right now."

"Fine," he says, shaking his head. "If you say so."

I step away from the car, feeling queasy now as he slips inside and starts the engine.

But before he pulls out, he rolls down his window and meets my gaze. His dark eyes look intense, full of conflict. For a split second, I wonder what's going on inside his head—if he's judging me. If he has any idea what I'm going through. If he even cares.

"She's going to be okay, Jemma," he says, then slides his sunglasses on and drives away.

I guess he *does* get it, after all.

ACT I
Scene 11

Five days later, I sit at my desk staring at my laptop as I wait for my video-editing software to load. I've managed to get a lot of new footage—good stuff, too. Pretty much all the county's historical sites, plus Magnolia Branch's important landmarks. I'm still not exactly sure what I'm going to do with it all—how I'll frame the film's narrative—but the project has turned out to be an excellent source of distraction these past few days.

Because the news from Houston hasn't been good. Nan's tumor has grown at an alarming rate since her last set of scans. They've scheduled her for surgery—a craniotomy, which means cutting open her head—early next week.

As if that isn't enough, there's an enormous late-season hurricane brewing in the Gulf. They're not quite sure of its projected path, but there's a chance it'll hit the Mississippi coast as a category one or two and then move slowly inland, right over Magnolia Branch.

Of course, my parents are totally freaking out. There's no way to reschedule Nan's surgery. It has to be done now, before any more damage is done. At first, Daddy was thinking about flying home for a couple of days, but with the uncertainty of the storm's path, it's just too risky.

Instead, he's been e-mailing me page after page of storm-prep guides, just in case. I've already gone to Wally World and stocked up on essentials like toilet paper, bottled water, and batteries, plus nonperishables like canned soup and SpaghettiOs. But now he wants me to go back and get stuff like plastic tarps and sandbags and oil for the hurricane lamps. It's like full-scale panic mode around here, even though the storm is still several days out. I'll have to brave the mayhem again tomorrow after cheerleading practice to pick up everything else on Daddy's list. Maybe I'll drag Lucy and Morgan with me.

Anyway, I'm trying not to obsess about the storm too much. I mean, I *do* have the urge to watch the Weather Channel twenty-four-seven, but that's pretty normal for me. What can I say? I *like* watching the Weather Channel. And okay, maybe I have a teeny-tiny crush on Jim Cantore. Doesn't everyone?

My stomach grumbles, reminding me that it's way past my

usual dinnertime. Lou dropped off a pan of lasagna a couple of hours ago—it's probably cold by now. I should go pop it in the oven, along with the half a baguette left over from yesterday. I already have a cucumber from Mama's garden sliced and soaked in vinegar, chilling in the fridge.

I glance back at my computer screen and sigh. Seriously, what's the point in finishing my application portfolio for NYU? It's not like my parents are going to let me go even if I *do* get in. I'm just setting myself up for disappointment. I might as well accept my fate—state school, Phi Delta, and debutante balls. And then I'll probably land right back here in Magnolia Branch. Heck, I'll probably even inherit this house once my parents decide to follow in *their* parents' footsteps and retire down on the coast. I know Nan doesn't want it; she doesn't want to be stuck here forever.

There's no way they'll ever sell it—and honestly, I wouldn't want them to. It's a part of our heritage. I love this house and everything in it. It's not that I don't want to live out my days here. It's just that I want the opportunity to . . . I don't know . . . spread my wings and fly a bit before I come back home to roost, you know? If I end up back in Magnolia Branch, I want it to be because I've *chosen* to be here. Is that really too much to ask?

The doorbell rings, startling me. I hurry downstairs, wondering who in the world would stop by unannounced at this hour. Not that it's that late, but it *is* a school night.

The dogs are going crazy, circling the front door. It takes me a minute or two to herd them away and get them corralled before I make my way back to the front hall.

"Jemma!" comes a muffled voice, followed by pounding fists. "C'mon, open up. I gotta take a leak!"

I unlock the door and throw it open with a scowl. "What are you doing here, Patrick?"

"Well, hey there, Jem," he slurs, leaning against the door-frame. Clearly, he's been drinking. The beer fumes are making me woozy. "Um, mind if I use your bathroom?"

I stand aside, gesturing for him to come inside. "Fine, but be quick about it."

I mean, my parents said no boys—especially Patrick. By nature, I'm a rule follower, not a rule breaker. He's got to go.

A couple minutes later, he stumbles out of the bathroom. "Tha's better," he says. His elbow clips Mama's vase on the hall table, knocking it to the floor, where it shatters into a million bits. *Great.* Mama loves that vase.

"Oops," is all he says. And then he starts laughing hysterically, like it's the funniest thing he's ever seen.

"Okay, it's time for you to go now." I reach for his shoulders and steer him toward the door.

"Nah, I just got here, Jem. The night's still young. Let's have some fun." He traps me against the wall with his body, leering at me with an odd, cold look in his eyes.

I duck out from under his arms. "Seriously, Patrick, you've got to go. No guys in the house while my parents are gone—I told you that. I'm going to be in enough trouble as it is about that vase."

"What they don't know can't hurt 'em, right?" He leans in for a kiss, but I sidestep away. His forehead bangs against the wall, and he remains there, leaning against it for several seconds, trying to steady himself. "C'mon, Jemma," he says at last, reaching feebly for my hand. "This is the perfect opportunity. I can spend the night, and your parents will never know."

"You're a real piece of work, you know that? You come over here drunk off your ass; you break Mama's vase and don't even offer to clean up the mess. And then you expect me to *sleep* with you?" I shake my head. "I'm really not in the mood for your bullshit, Patrick. Go, before Ryder sees your car in the driveway or something."

"Oh, you expectin' Ryder?" he slurs. "He gonna ride in on his white horse like a knight and save you? Is that what your hopin' for? Maybe tha's why you been holdin' out on me. You wanna give it to *him* instead."

His eyes are glassy, slightly unfocused. It's obvious I can't let him drive home like this.

Shit.

Ignoring his drunken little tirade, I reach for his hand and drag him into the living room, pushing him toward the velvet sofa. "C'mon, Patrick, you need to lie down. I'm going to call someone to come pick you up." His legs buckle the minute they hit the cushions, and he crumples into a heap—half on the floor, half on the sofa. He starts to make a retching noise, and I hurriedly slip off my hoodie and shove it under his face. "I swear, if you puke on my sofa, I'm going to freaking *kill* you."

Mercifully, he doesn't. Instead, he starts making a quiet, snuffling noise. Like he's passed out cold. I run upstairs and grab my cell from my bedroom, trying to decide who to call. Obviously, Ryder makes the most sense, since he lives just up the road and can be here in a matter of minutes.

But what if he mentions it to his mom? I mean, I can tell him not to, but then it makes me look guilty, like I'm trying to hide something. It's not my fault that Patrick showed up on my doorstep unannounced.

I run through the other options in my head. Calling Ben or Mason is about the same as calling Ryder. They're his best friends. They talk. I could try Tanner. He *is* my cousin, so I could invoke some sort of family loyalty oath of silence or something. Only problem is, Tanner lives on the far side of town—about as far away from here as anyone can be and still live in Magnolia Branch. Which means leaving a passed-out, about-to-puke Patrick on my couch for a good twenty minutes, waiting for a ride.

Nope. Not gonna happen. With a sigh of resignation, I dial Ryder's number.

Exactly seven minutes later, he knocks on the door. Ryder to the rescue. I resist the urge to look around for his white horse.

"Okay, where is he?" he asks with a frown. His hair is wet, his T-shirt clinging damply to his skin. I'd either caught him in the shower or in the pool. Probably the pool, since he smells vaguely of chlorine.

I hook a thumb toward the living room. "In there. Passed out on the couch."

He looks at me sharply. "*You* haven't been drinking, have you?"

He's lucky I don't slap him. "I was sitting upstairs in my room, minding my own business, when he showed up at the door. What do you *think*? Asshat," I add under my breath.

His brow furrows. "What was that?"

"Nothing. C'mon. Get him out of there before he makes a mess."

"What about his car?"

I shrug. "I'll drive it school tomorrow and get a ride home from Lucy or something."

"I'll drive you home," he offers. Correction: he asserts—arrogantly, as if he's used to giving orders. "We need to go get those tarps and sandbags anyway."

"How did you . . . ?" I trail off as the answer dawns on me. "My dad e-mailed you, didn't he?"

"Called me, actually. We'll go after school tomorrow. After practice," he amends.

"Yeah. Fine, whatever." Truthfully, I wasn't looking forward to lugging sandbags by myself. I wasn't even sure how I was going to fit them in my little Fiat. Problem solved.

Now to solve my *other* problem—the one lying on my couch.

ACT I
Scene 12

It takes me a while to locate Ryder once cheerleading practice ends. Eventually, I find him on the big grassy field beside the parking lot, tossing a football with Mason and Ben.

"I thought we were meeting by the field house," I call out as I make my way over.

He doesn't even turn around. "Nah, I'm pretty sure I said the parking lot."

"You definitely said the field house," I argue. Why can't he *ever* just admit that he's wrong?

"Geez, field house, parking lot. What difference does it make?" Mason asks. "Give it a rest, why don't you."

I shoot him a glare. "Oh, hey, Mason. Remember when your hair was long and everyone thought you were a girl?"

Ryder chuckles as he releases a perfect spiral in Mason's direction. "She's got you there."

"Hey, whose side are you on, anyway?" Mason catches the ball and cradles it against his chest, then launches it toward Ben. I just stand there watching as they continue to toss it back and forth between the three of them. Haven't they had enough football for one day?

I pull out my cell to check the time. "We should probably get going."

"I guess," Ryder says with an exaggerated sigh, like I'm putting him out or something. Which is particularly annoying since he's the one who insisted on going with me.

Ben jogs up beside me, the football tucked beneath his arm. "Where are you two off to? Whoa, you're sweaty."

I fold my arms across my damp chest. "Hey, southern girls don't sweat. We glow."

Ben snorts at that. "Says who?"

"Says Ryder's mom," I say with a grin. It's one of Laura Grace's favorite sayings—one that always makes Ryder wince.

"The hardware store," Ryder answers, snatching the ball back from Ben. "Gotta pick up some things for the storm—sandbags and stuff like that. Y'all want to come?"

"Nah, I think I'll pass." Mason wrinkles his nose. "Pretty sure I don't want to be cooped up in the truck with Jemma *glowing* like she is right now."

"Everybody thought you and Morgan were identical twin girls," I say with a smirk. "Remember, Mason? Isn't that just *so* cute?"

"I'll go," Ben chimes in. "If you're getting sandbags, you'll need some help carrying them out to the truck."

"Thanks, Ben. See, *someone's* a gentleman."

"Don't look now, Ryder, but your one-woman fan club is over there." Mason tips his head toward the school building in the distance. "I think she's scented you out. Quick. You better run."

I glance over my shoulder to find Rosie standing on the sidewalk by the building's double doors, looking around hopefully.

"Hey!" Mason calls out, waving both arms above his head. "He's over here."

Ryder's cheeks turn beet-red. He just stares at the ground, his jaw working furiously.

"C'mon, man," Ben says, throwing an elbow into Mason's side. "Don't be a dick." He grabs the football and heads toward Ryder's Durango. "We better get going. The hardware store probably closes at six."

Silently, Ryder and I hurry after him and hop inside the truck—Ben up front, me in the backseat. We don't look back to see if Rosie's following.

The thing is, I've always suspected that *Ben* has feelings for

Rosie. He's never acted on it. What's the point, what with the way she's crushing on Ryder? I doubt she's even noticed Ben's existence, which is her loss because he's really a great guy.

"Hey!" Rosie calls out, waving madly. "Ryder! Wait!"

I fix him with an accusing stare in the rearview mirror as he starts the engine and backs out of the parking space.

It's pretty clear to me that he *has* been leading her on, considering he was all over her at Josh's party and now he's totally blowing her off. Of course, he'd gotten all mad and hotly denied it when I'd accused him of it the other day. But that's Ryder for you.

I twist in my seat to watch as Rosie drops her arms to her sides, disappointment written all over her face. God, I hope she has a ride home. I quickly scan the mostly empty lot, looking for her car, and breathe a sigh of relief when I spot it over by the gym.

"So," Ben says, tapping his fingers against his thighs, "Ryder's going to watch out for you during the storm, I guess. Keep an eye on your place and everything?"

"I promised her dad I would," Ryder says.

Because God knows that's the only reason he'd do something nice for me. I can't help but roll my eyes.

"Well, it's not like I'm right down the road like Ryder is, but if you need anything, just let me know, okay? I don't mind coming out there."

"Thanks, Ben," I say, patting his shoulder. "That's sweet."

And then Ryder leans over and turns on the radio, blasting a country music station loud enough to make conversation impossible.

I guess that means we're done talking, which is fine by me.

TROPICAL STORM UPDATE flashes menacingly across the television screen, and I reach for the remote, turning up the volume several notches. Tropical Storm Paloma has been officially upgraded to hurricane status, the local meteorologist announces—just a little too gleefully, if you ask me. It's currently a category one, but they expect it to strengthen to a two before making landfall.

Oh, joy.

The US model is predicting landfall just west of Pensacola, Florida, while the European model predicts Gulfport, Mississippi. Seems like a toss-up, except that they're sending Jim Cantore to Gulfport, and everyone knows what that means.

The Mississippi coast is doomed.

The concern isn't really the storm's strength—even a two isn't all that bad, really—but its sheer size and slow-moving track. Even now, a few days out, the sky has darkened to a foul shade of gray, and we're nearly six hours from the coast. And the satellite image they're showing on the screen is pretty damn scary-looking. It's just massive.

The phone calls from my parents have gotten frantic. First they said I should pack up and head over to Magnolia Landing. The Marsdens' house is structurally more sound, they insist, and set farther away from the creek and thus less prone to flooding. We have a much better chance of riding it out safely over there.

But that would mean packing up the cats and dogs—neither of which Laura Grace wants in her house, meaning they'd be stuck in the garage—and leaving this place unattended and vulnerable. So instead, Ryder's supposed to come over here and ride out the storm with me. *If* it hits us—though that "if" is starting to look more like a "when."

And it's not just the hurricane—or what's left of it by the time it reaches us—that we have to worry about. Storms like this one often spawn tornadoes. I'm already preparing the storage room under the stairs as my storm shelter, just in case. It's long and narrow, with plenty of room. I've stocked it with sleeping bags, pillows, and battery-operated lanterns, plus assorted snacks and a case of bottled water. If the tornado sirens go off, I'm ready.

"Residents as far north as the Tennessee border should be prepared for hurricane-strength winds," the announcer drones on. "Secure anything loose, such as garbage cans and outdoor furniture, so that they don't become projectiles. Prepare for possible power outages and contamination of the water supply.

Make sure to stock up on necessary prescription medications and other medical supplies."

I hit the mute button on the TV remote, unable to listen to any more of the gloom and doom. My cell beeps, and I reach for it. There's a text from Lucy.

Looks like they might cancel school on Monday. Woot!

Information like this coming from Lucy is generally pretty reliable, since she happens to live right next door to Mrs. Crawford, the principal of Magnolia Branch High.

Yay, I can sit home and watch more Weather Channel! I text back.

This is an intervention—step away from the TV! NOW!

I laugh aloud at that. It's such a typical Lucy-like thing to say.

My mom's worried about you. Wants you to pack up and come over here.

Can't. But Ryder's coming over if the storm gets bad.

Lucy's next text is just a line of googly eyes.

Not funny, I type, even though it kind of is.

You two can plan your wedding menu. Choose your linens. Stuff like that, she texts, followed by a smiley face.

I gaze at my phone with a frown. *Also not funny.*

New topic—you going to Morgan's pageant tomorrow?

It's still on? I was kind of expecting them to cancel it, what with the storm bearing down.

Yup, afraid so.

Luckily it's a local, countywide pageant—the preliminary for the state's Junior Miss Pageant, I think—which means it's just over in Oxford at the Ford Center.

Then yeah, I answer. *Want me to drive?*

It's a full five minutes before Lucy replies. I figure she's gotten busy doing something, so I unmute the TV again. Probably a bad idea. Now they're talking about the possibility of the storm hitting during peak tides, causing widespread flooding. They're showing some old Katrina footage, which is unnecessary—because trust me, we *all* know what happened with Katrina.

I yawn and check the time. It's late. It's been a long day—school and then the football game. I should go to bed soon.

Finally, my phone chimes again. *Sure. Pick me up around noon?*

See you then, I type and then make a mental note to call the county duck club about Sunday's skeet tournament. I'm assuming they'll reschedule it, but you just never know. It's a competition that I've entered—and won—every year since I was thirteen.

And here's the thing—it *really* pisses them off. All these hunting boys and their daddies show up decked out in camo gear, determined to beat the girl who has the audacity to challenge their masculinity.

And, okay, I'll admit it. . . . I like to needle 'em just a bit. I purposely wear the girliest outfit possible—little flowery sundresses with cowboy boots, most years. Drives 'em nuts. If they're going to get beaten by a girl, they'd rather it be some tomboy wearing overalls and a flannel shirt, you know? Stupid sexist pigs.

I glance back at my phone, realizing that I haven't heard from Nan in a couple of days. Sure, I get updates from my parents on a regular basis, but that's not the same. Mostly, Nan's been upbeat. She likes her surgeons, she says—a neurosurgeon and a neuro-otologist, whatever the heck that last one is. She's trying to relax and take it easy. They've passed the time by visiting museums and taking little day trips—to Johnson Space Center, to Galveston. Still, I know she must be scared, more so as the surgery approaches.

I turn off the TV and round up the dogs to send them out for their late-night business. And then once I'm ready for bed, I'll text Nan and see if she's still up.

School wasn't canceled on Monday after all. Instead, they're releasing us at noon. Even now, a full hour before we're due to get out, it's obvious that they might have made a bad decision.

The weekend was mostly uneventful. Morgan won her pageant—no surprise there—and my skeet tournament was canceled, just as I predicted. The weather continued to deteriorate, the winds picking up alarmingly late last night. I got pretty much no sleep, as a result.

With a yawn, I glance over at the window, where sheets of driving rain are pounding the glass. The sky is a dark, ominous shade of gray—almost greenish. My stomach flutters nervously. I'm ready to go home and hunker down. It's not like we're accomplishing much today anyway. Right now we're just sitting in homeroom, submitting nominations for the homecoming court. Morgan's been elected our class maid every year since we were freshmen, so she's a shoo-in for queen. Nominations seem more like a formality. The big question is, who will she choose to be her escort?

Maybe her brother. Seems like as good a guess as any. She won't even speculate, because she doesn't want to jinx herself.

Anyway, everyone's supposed to write down three names on their ballot, and then the girl with the most votes gets our homeroom nomination. And then the entire class votes. The winner becomes homecoming queen, the runner-up our senior class maid.

The latter could go to anyone, though I'm putting my money—figuratively speaking, of course—on Jessica Addington, especially now that she and Mason seem to be an item. Jessica's already pretty popular, but having her name linked to Mason's has significantly upped her cred.

Only problem is, Mason can't escort them both.

I add Jess's name to my ballot beneath Morgan's and Lucy's and flip the page over on my desk just as a crash of thunder rattles the window. Mrs. Blakely, my homeroom teacher, glances over at the PA speaker with a scowl.

"They really need to send everyone home," she mutters. "This is getting ridiculous."

But if we can make it to noon, we get credit for the day and won't have to make it up at the end of the year. I'm assuming that's why they're holding us hostage even while the conditions continue to worsen at an alarming rate.

As if on cue, the PA system crackles to life.

"Attention, students and faculty," comes the principal's voice. "In light of the current weather situation, we will be moving up dismissal to eleven fifteen a.m."

That's just five minutes from now, according to the clock on the wall.

"Please wrap up all homeroom business immediately. Thank you, and get home safely."

"Okay, you heard the woman," Mrs. Blakely says. "Turn in your ballots and you're free to go."

Everyone rises and shuffles to the front of the room wearing anxious expressions. How are we supposed to get home safely in *this*?

I feel particularly bad for the kids who walk home. I glance over worriedly at Francie Darlington. She lives only a couple of blocks from school, but she's going to get drenched. I hurry to catch up with her as she makes her way out into the hall.

"Hey, Francie!" I call out. "Wait up. You want a ride?"

She turns, her face lighting up with a smile. "Yes! Thank you. It's crazy out there."

"I know, right? We're going to get soaked just walking to the car. Here, let me stop at my locker first." I tip my head toward the row of orange metal rectangles lining the wall.

"I've got to stop at mine, too. How 'bout I meet you over by the water fountain in five minutes?"

I nod. "Sounds good."

Francie and I aren't exactly friends—we run in totally different social circles. But she's nice. Smart. We used to take ballet together, back when we were in elementary school. Now she's the kind of girl who wears a lot of black and listens to Evanescence and Black Veil Brides and occasionally dyes her hair with stripes of vivid color. I've always admired her ability to just be herself.

We part ways, and I hurry over to my locker and fumble with the combination several times before it opens. I don't even know what to take with me—I have no idea if we'll have school tomorrow, or the next day, even. Deciding that it's best to be safe and cover all bases, I dump every textbook into my backpack. The bag's so full I can't even zip it all the way.

"Hey, you need help with that?"

I turn to find Patrick standing there, leaning against the row of lockers. "Nah, I'm good." I heft the bag up on my shoulder, trying not to groan under the weight of it.

"I just wanted to apologize again for the other night." He reaches up to brush the hair out of my eyes, his fingers lingering on my face. "Guess I had one too many."

"You think?" I say sharply. The worst part is, the next morning as I was driving his car to school, I passed Lou on her way to the Marsdens' just as I was pulling out onto Magnolia Landing Drive. And here's the thing—there are only two houses on our road, theirs and ours. One way in and one way out, and I'm pretty sure Lou would recognize Patrick's car. I mean, how many kids in Magnolia Branch drive a candy-apple-red BMW convertible? So from her perspective, it must have looked like Patrick leaving my house early in the morning after a night of unchaperoned debauchery. If she mentions it to Laura Grace, I'm screwed.

I've pretty much decided that he isn't worth all this trouble. Yeah, he's cute, and there's something exciting about that bad-boy edge he's got going on. But . . . it isn't enough. I've been giving him the cold shoulder for the past few days, hoping he'll get the message. But it turns out that Patrick isn't very good at taking hints.

"C'mon. I said I was sorry." He falls into step beside me with a shrug. "I don't know what else you want from me."

"I don't want *anything* from you, Patrick. Look, can we talk later? I've got to go. I'm giving Francie a ride home."

He pulls a face. "Why're you doing that?"

"Because I like Francie, that's why."

"Since when?"

"Since always, and I don't want her to drown out there." I stop and turn to stare at him. "Are we done here?"

"Guess so," he says with a shrug.

The crowd has thinned out now, everyone in a rush to get home before the weather gets any worse. "I'll see you later, okay? Drive safely."

"Yeah, you too," he mutters.

I shake my head in annoyance as he stalks off. How is it that *he's* mad at *me*?

With a sigh, I hurry over to the water fountain, where Francie is already waiting. "You ready?" I ask her.

"Yep. Thanks again, Jemma. I really appreciate this." Her smile is genuine, and I'm glad that I offered. I'd really like to get to know her better, I decide.

"Hey, it's no problem. God, it looks awful out there." We approach the glass double doors and pause, staring in disbelief at the scene that greets us. Students are splashing through ankle-deep water in the parking lot, dodging cars sending up huge wakes of spray. The rain seems to be blowing directly sideways now.

"I've got an umbrella," Francie offers, producing it. "Not sure how much it'll help, though."

"Probably not much. I say we make a run for it. I'm there on the front row. The blue Fiat."

"I see it," she says with a nod.

I take a deep breath and reach for the door handle. "On the count of three?"

And that's when the first tornado siren goes off.

ACT II

*A greater power than we can contradict
Hath thwarted our intents.*

—William Shakespeare, *Romeo and Juliet*

ACT II
Scene 1

O h, this is just great," I say with a sigh as the red emergency lights begin to flash menacingly. "What now?"

Beside me, Francie shrugs. "Um, I guess we take cover?"

Again, the PA system crackles to life. "All students and staff, please proceed directly to the A corridor and remain there until further notice. I repeat, the A corridor. This is not a drill—this is a tornado warning."

For a moment I just stand there, frozen in place. Francie reaches for my hand and drags me away from the door as everyone who hadn't yet left the parking lot comes dashing back inside. We all make a run for corridor A, which is right smack in the center of the school, near the media center.

We've lived through enough tornado drills to know exactly

what to do when we get there—even if we feel silly doing it. Our backs pressed against the wall, we sit on the scabbed tile floor and cover our heads. There's about seventy-five of us, I'd say. Conversation is kept to a minimum, because let's face it, it's a pretty scary situation. I mean, you pretty much know you'll be okay—but what if you're not?

Luckily, it doesn't last long. Maybe five minutes later, the voice on the PA system tells us that the warning has expired. They won't let us leave yet, though, so we sit there for another ten or fifteen minutes before they tell us it's safe to go.

"Well, that was intense," Francie says as she rises and brushes off the back of her shorts.

"I know, right? I'm still shaking." I hold out one trembling hand as evidence.

The drive home is a nightmare. I literally can't see two feet in front of me, even with the wipers on their highest speed. It's even worse after I drop off Francie—mostly because I'm all alone. It takes me nearly a half hour to make what should be a ten-minute trip, and by the time I pull up in front of my house, my hands are cramped from my death grip on the steering wheel.

It's not until I step out of the car, my legs feeling like they're made of Jell-O, that I notice Ryder's Durango parked in front of me.

"Where the hell have you been?" he calls out from the front

porch, just as I make a mad dash to join him there. His face is red, his brow furrowed over stormy eyes. "They let us out an hour ago!"

I am *really* not in the mood for his crap. "Yeah, so?"

"So I was worried sick. A tornado touched down over by the Roberts' place."

"I know! I mean, I didn't know it touched down, but I was still at school when the sirens went off." I drop my ridiculously heavy backpack and shake the rain from my hair. "Is everyone okay over there?"

He runs a visibly trembling hand through his hair. "Yeah, it just tore up their fence or something. Jesus, Jemma!"

"What is *wrong* with you? Why are you even here?"

"I'm supposed to stay over here, remember?"

"What . . . now?" I look past him and notice an army-green duffel bag by the front door. He's got a key—he could've just let himself in.

"I figured now's as good a time as any. We need to put sandbags in front of the back door before it gets any worse out, and then we've got to do something about the barn. It's awful close to the creek, and the water's rising fast."

"Well, what do you propose we do?"

"Don't you keep your guns out there? We should move them inside. And your dad has some expensive tools in his workshop—we should get those, too."

I let out a sigh. He's got a point. "Can I at least go inside first? Put my stuff away?"

"Sure." He moves to the edge of the porch and gazes up at the sky. "It looks like we might get a break in a few minutes, once this band moves through. Might as well wait for it."

I dig out my keys and unlock the door. I can hear the dogs howling their heads off the minute I step inside. "I've gotta let Beau and Sadie out," I say over my shoulder as I head toward the kitchen. "Take your stuff to the guest room and get settled, why don't you?"

That's my attempt at reestablishing the fact that *I'm* in charge here, not him. This is *my* house. My stuff. My life.

Beau and Sadie do their business in record time and hightail it back inside, dripping wet. I find a dish towel hanging by the sink and do my best to dry them off, making a mental note to leave some old towels in the front mudroom. Once we sandbag up the back door, the dogs'll have to go in and out the front, and I can't have them tracking mud all over the place.

"Hey, what happened to the vase that's usually here on the hall table?" Ryder calls out.

I wince, remembering its fate. I'd saved the broken bits in a bag, but there's no hope for it. It's destroyed. It figures he'd notice. What is he, Colonel Mustard? *In the conservatory,* I want to say. *With the candlestick.*

"Patrick happened to it," I answer instead, joining him

there in the hall. "You know, the other night. On his way back from the bathroom." I have no idea why I'm offering so many details. It's not like it's any of his business. I should have told him that we were having wild sex here in the hall and accidentally knocked it over. Would have served him right for being so nosy.

"You should make him pay for it," Ryder offers.

"Yeah, maybe. You all moved in?"

"I was thinking . . . it's safer downstairs, what with all the trees around here. You're liable to lose some. You should probably sleep in your parents' room, and I'll just take the couch."

"We've got five empty beds, not counting the sleeping porches, and you're going to sleep on the couch?" I shake my head in disbelief.

"Isn't the one in the family room a sofa bed?"

"Yeah, but it's awful. You can't sleep there—the springs are poking through the mattress."

"I'll be fine," he says with a shrug.

"Whatever." I glance over at the window, taking in the scary-looking sky. "You really think we need to sleep downstairs?"

He cocks a brow. "Have you been watching the Weather Channel?"

Have *I* been watching the Weather Channel? Ha! "I wonder if it'll be as bad as they're saying."

"Could be the worst to hit the coast since Katrina."

"Yeah, but we're nowhere near the coast," I argue. "It's just hard to imagine. . . ." I trail off, feeling foolish. "Anyway, you ready to go do those sandbags?"

He nods. "I'm ready. Sounds like the rain has let up some. You got a poncho or something like that you can put on?"

"What's the point? I'm already soaked." I can't wait to take a long, hot bath in my mom's Jacuzzi tub. "Just let me get my rain boots."

It takes us close to an hour to get the sandbags stacked properly against the back door. The rain comes and goes in bursts, the wind making an odd shrieking noise. The usually silent creek is rushing like rapids, and the grass is soaked and squishy beneath my boots. Everything beyond the lawn is mud now—great big puddles of mud.

"You think that'll do it?" I ask, straightening with a groan. My back is already killing me, and we haven't even tackled the barn yet.

"Looks good," Ryder says with a satisfied nod. "You want to take a break and get some lunch?"

Great, now I've got to make him lunch.

"Lou sent over some sandwiches," he adds.

Of course she did.

"Actually, she sent over a whole hamper of stuff. Potato salad, pickles—"

"Stop." I hold up one hand. "You had me at potato salad." Because Lou's is the best in all of Lafayette County—no lie. It's like she's got crack in there or something. Mama's tried to replicate it many times, to no avail. I'm salivating just thinking about it.

Of course, we're sopping wet and dripping everywhere by the time we step into the dry mudroom to pull off our boots. "This is crazy," I say, shaking my head like Sadie does when she's wet. "We can't walk through the house like this—we'll make a mess." Ryder's jeans are soaked through and caked with mud. I'm wearing shorts, but my bare legs are spattered all over. "We're going to have to strip here," I say, shaking my head. "Just leave it all in a pile. I'll toss it in the wash after lunch."

He just stares at me, wide-eyed. "What? Now?"

"Yeah, you go first," I say, amused by the blush that's creeping up his neck. "Geez, Ryder. It's not like I haven't seen you in your underpants before."

I have vague memories of Ryder running around Magnolia Landing's lawn wearing nothing but superhero undies. And after all the years of shared beach houses and hotel suites, well . . . like I said, we were more like siblings when we were little.

"If it'll make you more comfortable, I'll turn around," I offer.

"Nah, it's fine." He reaches for the hem of his T-shirt and pulls it over his head in one fluid motion.

And then I remember why this was a bad idea. My mouth goes dry at the sight of his tanned, sculpted chest, his narrow waist, and jutting hip bones. Oh, man. What was I thinking?

I swallow hard as he unbuttons his jeans and slides down the zipper. *Boxers or briefs?* That's all I'm thinking as he peels down the wet denim—slowly, as if he's enjoying this little striptease. He steps out of them gracefully and tosses them into a heap beside his shirt before straightening to his full height, facing me.

Oh. My. God.

I exhale sharply. The answer is boxer briefs, heather-gray ones. And right now they're clinging to him wetly, leaving absolutely nothing to the imagination. He looks like a god. A six-foot-four, football-playing god, and I am staring at him with my mouth hanging open like some kind of pathetic freak.

Snap out of it.

"Sorry," I say, averting my gaze. My cheeks are burning now. I probably look like a clown. That's what happens when a fair-skinned redhead like me blushes. "If you . . . um . . . want to shower. I mean, you know—"

"I'll just go put on something dry for now. We really need to eat and then get that stuff out of the barn."

I just nod, biting my lower lip. I can't even look at him. This is crazy.

"Your turn to strip," he says, and my gaze shoots up to meet his. He's smiling now, his dimples in full effect.

"Ugh, just go and change." I cover my eyes with one hand and flap the other toward the hall.

"I'll meet you in the kitchen in five," he says.

"Great." I let my hand drop only when I hear his footsteps move away. Then yeah, I'll admit it—I allow myself a nice long look at his backside as he walks away from me.

And let me tell you, it was *well* worth the look.

ACT II
Scene 2

God bless Lou. When I open the refrigerator, I find it stocked with premade sandwiches—chicken salad with apples and pecans, ham and cheese, and my favorite, roast beef with horseradish sauce. Two Tupperware tubs contain potato and macaroni salad, and she's thoughtfully included an assortment of pickles in mason jars. There's even a caramel cake—Ryder's favorite—covered in Saran Wrap, sitting on the counter. She must have dropped it all off this morning while I was at school.

"You want chips?" I offer as I set everything out on the kitchen table along with cups and a pitcher of sweet tea.

"Nah, this is good," Ryder answers. He goes into the pantry for napkins and paper plates, as at home in my kitchen as I am.

We're mostly silent as we eat, with only the occasional burst of quick conversation.

"When's Nan's surgery?" Ryder asks as he reaches for one of the jars of pickles. He's already eaten two sandwiches and is working on a third.

"Tomorrow," I answer around a mouthful of potato salad. "First thing in the morning."

Ryder just nods and continues to attack his food.

Nan's checking into the hospital tonight after dinner. She promised to call me once she's settled. I'm trying not to think about it too much, because whenever I do, my stomach starts feeling all weird. Like it is right now, actually.

"Your dad's staying in Jackson?" I ask him a few minutes later, even though I know the answer.

"Yeah, he's got a big case. Says he'll probably be gone a couple weeks, at least."

I can't help but frown. I mean, Jackson's just a three-hour drive from here. You'd think he could come home for a couple days—long enough to ride out the storm with his only child.

Then again, this is pretty typical of Ryder's dad. Rob Marsden is all work, work, work. He and my dad are so different that it's sometimes hard to understand why they're such good friends. Sure, Daddy loves his job, and he's good at it too. But work isn't everything to him.

Then again, they *did* grow up together, next-door neighbors and childhood playmates. They'd gone to college together, pledged the same fraternity. Their friendship is deeply rooted, steeped in tradition. Still, I wonder if they'd be such good friends now if they hadn't married BFFs who were invested in keeping the Cafferty-Marsden attachment alive and strong.

"What about Lou?" I ask. "Is she staying over at Magnolia Landing tonight?"

"Nah. She went over to stay with Jason and Evelyn." Her son and daughter-in-law. I'm glad she's not over at the Marsdens' house all by herself.

I chew slowly, listening to the sound of the rain hitting the windows around us. There's something else—a noise I didn't notice before, a low roar in the background that's hard to ignore. "Do you hear that?"

"Hear what? The rain?"

"Shh." I cock my head to one side, listening intently now.

Ryder's gaze meets mine, and I see my own concern mirrored in his eyes. He hears it too.

"What is it?" I ask, but then the answer hits me like a ton of bricks. "Oh my God, is that the *creek*?"

He nods, looking grave. "Think so. We better get this stuff put away and see what's going on out there."

We clean up the kitchen in record time and hurry to the mudroom to pull back on our rain boots.

"This is bad," Ryder says the second we step outside. The

roar is louder now and definitely coming from the direction of the creek.

We make our way around the house and down the slippery path toward the water's edge but stop long before we reach the sandy clearing. My mouth falls open at the sight that greets us, and I stand there gaping in disbelief. The picnic tables are almost completely submerged, the water from the creek pouring over the banks at an alarming rate.

"The barn!" I shout, struggling to be heard over the howl of rushing water. "We better get over there now."

"Let me get my truck."

We backtrack to the driveway, where Ryder heads for the Durango. "I'll meet you over there. If the water's rising, wait for me to go in, okay? I just want to go check on the main road."

I nod and jog over to the barn. The second I step inside, my heart sinks. The water is ankle deep. I splash over to the gun safe and spin the lock before dialing the combination and pulling open the door. I lift Delilah from her case, along with a ten-round magazine. Once she's loaded and safely locked, I holster her in the waistband of my shorts. All that's left are Daddy's two pistols and the shotgun. I find a canvas duffel bag on a shelf beside the radio and carefully stash the weapons inside.

Just as I lift the bag up on my shoulder, Ryder jogs in. "The road is out," he calls to me breathlessly. "Completely washed out just above where your driveway intersects it."

"Are you sure?" Because if what he says is true, it means we're totally cut off. There's no way out and no way in—not to my house or to the Marsdens'.

"I'm sure." There's a flicker of fear in his eyes. "I've never seen anything like it before."

My heart does a little somersault in my chest. "You think it's storm surge from whatever body of water's feeding the creek?" The Mississippi River, maybe. I have no idea.

"I don't know," he says with a shrug, then glances around, taking in our current situation. "We better get moving here. Looks like the water's rising pretty fast."

"Here. Can you take this?" I hand off the duffel bag. "Careful. It's the guns."

"Got it." He takes the heavy bag as if it weighs nothing, tossing it over his back.

I glance around helplessly. "Why don't you take it to the truck? I'm going to find something to put the rest of the stuff in, and then we can see about Daddy's workshop."

With a nod, he wades away while I search for another bag—which I find in a drawer beneath the radio. I fill it and then unplug the radio and grab that, too.

Soon we've gotten pretty much everything we can from the workshop loaded into the Durango—everything except the large pieces of furniture Daddy was working on when he left. I feel bad leaving them, especially the pretty Hoosier cabinet, but where would we put it all?

We make our way out with the last load, just some odds and ends. A sander, a jigsaw, a few CDs. The rain has let up—we must be between bands—but the sky is still a dark, heavy gray.

"You think we should try sandbagging it?" I ask, tipping my head back toward the barn.

Ryder shakes his head. "I don't think it'll do much good."

"Just in front, then? The gap's pretty big under the door. It can't hurt, right?"

"I've got a few sandbags in the Durango—probably enough for the door. I'll get 'em," he offers. "You just make sure the door is latched tight."

I want to say something along the lines of, "No, I'd thought I'd just leave it flapping in the wind," but I manage to bite my tongue. What is it with him and giving orders? I mean, I get that he's the quarterback and all, but I'm not one of his teammates.

But, hey, if he wants to thump his chest and carry the heavy sandbags, I'll let him do it. My back is aching. I stomp off toward the door and bolt shut the lower and upper portions, securing them with the padlock.

"I may have to get a few more from the house," Ryder calls out from the direction of the truck.

I turn and watch him walk toward me with a sandbag thrown over one shoulder. A blur of movement catches my eye, and I glance down to see something dark on the ground right in Ryder's path.

I jog toward it, curious. But a second later I stop dead in my tracks, my breath hitching in my chest.

It's a snake, about three or four feet long with a fat, black body and a stubby tail.

"Ryder!" I shout, just as it shoots forward toward him. *Shit.* "Stop! Don't move!"

It coils itself not six inches from where Ryder is standing. The snake's triangular head is raised, its mouth open in a threat display, showing white. It takes me only a split second to identify it: water moccasin. A cottonmouth, venomous and highly aggressive. The heavy rains must have driven it up from the creek.

As I watch in horror it strikes, missing Ryder's leg by mere inches. The snake recoils itself, preparing for another strike. If it bites an artery, Ryder could be dead in a matter of minutes.

"Don't move," I repeat, more quietly this time. I pull Delilah from my waistband, forcing my hands to steady as I release the safety.

Ryder's eyes meet mine and he nods—just a small movement, barely perceptible. But it's enough that I know he understands what I'm about to do.

He does just as I say—remains perfectly still, like he's been carved from stone. His gaze is trained on me, steady and reassuring. I can sense his fear, and yet he's somehow calm. Trusting.

I know I have one chance at this—one single shot. If I miss, we're in deep shit. A moccasin bite requires antivenin, which means a trip to the ER. And right now, our road is washed out and a slow-moving hurricane is bearing down on us.

I *can't* miss.

I take a deep, calming breath and force myself to pretend that the snake's spade-shaped head is just an inanimate target as I take aim.

One shot. One chance.

And then I pull the trigger.

ACT II
Scene 3

The shot is clean, right through the snake's head. To Ryder's credit, he doesn't even flinch. I squeeze the trigger a second time, wanting to make damn sure I've killed it.

Here's something you might not know—when you kill a snake, it continues to wriggle. Luckily, Ryder's smart enough to get out of the way at this point, because you can actually get bitten by a dead snake if you're not careful.

"You okay?" I call out, lowering my gun.

"Yeah. Shit, that was close." He flings the sandbag he was carrying to the ground.

I'm shaking now, my hands trembling as I lock the safety and shove Delilah back into the waistband of my shorts. "I think it's time to head back inside," I say. "Forget the sandbags."

"You sure?" His face is pale, slightly ashen.

"I'm sure." I glance up at the sky just as it opens up again, the light rain turning torrential in a matter of seconds.

"Let's go!" Ryder calls out, and we both dash toward the Durango.

We drive slowly back to the house, avoiding the deepest of the mud puddles.

"What do you want to do with this stuff?" Ryder asks as he pulls up beside the house and cuts the engine.

I turn and survey the load in the back. "We should take the guns in, but everything else can stay here for now."

Just then, a gust of wind buffets the truck, causing me to suck in a sharp breath.

"That was at *least* a fifty-mile-an-hour gust," Ryder says, his voice a little shaky.

"I didn't think it was supposed to get really bad till tomorrow afternoon."

"I think this is just the beginning."

Whoa. If this is just the beginning, then I'm terrified to see the worst of it.

"On the count of three, we make a run for it," Ryder says. "I'll get the guns—you just head straight for the house. Ready?"

I reach for the door handle. "Ready."

"One. Two. Three. Go!"

We both burst from the truck at lightning speed. I make a

mad dash for the front porch, slipping and sliding the whole way. I wait for Ryder in the mudroom. He runs in a few seconds later, the canvas bag thrown over his shoulder.

Again, we're dripping wet and covered in mud. Both dogs are whining, looking at us pleadingly through the mudroom door. They've got to go out, storm or no storm.

"You go on and get in the tub," Ryder offers. "I'll take 'em out real quick. It's only going to get worse."

I nod, soaked to the bone and shivering now. I've had enough for one day. I just want to get out of these clothes and sink into a hot, bubbly bath. I don't even wait for Ryder to leave with the dogs—I start stripping down to my underwear right then and there and race down the hall to my parents' room.

I'm still in the big Jacuzzi tub when the power flickers—once, twice—and then goes out, leaving me in total darkness, chin deep in lukewarm water. I don't know why, but it all hits me then—Nan's surgery tomorrow, shooting that moccasin, this stupid, never-ending storm. I start to cry, deep, gulping sobs. I know it seems childish, but I want my daddy. What if things get worse? What if the house starts to flood? Or the roof blows off? As much as I hate to admit it, I'm scared. *Really* scared.

A knock on the bathroom door startles me.

"Jemma? You okay in there?"

"I'm fine," I call out, my voice thick. My cheeks burn with

shame at being caught crying in the dark like a two-year-old.

"Do you want a candle or something? Maybe a hurricane lamp?"

"No, I'm . . ." I start to say "fine" again, but a ragged sob tears from my throat instead.

"It's going to be okay, Jem. We'll get through this."

I sink lower into the water, wanting to disappear completely. Why can't he just go away and let me have my little meltdown in private? Why, after all these years of being a jerk, does he have to suddenly be so *nice*?

"I got both dogs dried off," he continues conversationally, as if I'm not in here crying my eyes out. "They're in the kitchen eating their supper. I think Beau's pretty worked up."

I continue to bawl like a baby. I know he can hear me, that he's right outside the door, listening. Still, it takes me a good five minutes to get it all out of my system. Once the tears have slowed, I reach for my washcloth and lay it across my eyes, hoping it'll reduce the puffiness. A minute or two later, I drag it away and wring it out before laying it over the edge of the tub.

It's still dark inside the bathroom, though I can see a flicker of light coming from beneath the door. Ryder must have a flashlight, or maybe one of the battery-operated lanterns I scattered around the house, just in case. I wonder how long he's going to stand there, waiting for me.

The light flicks off, and I think maybe he's finally left me in peace. But then I hear a muffled *thump*, and I know he's still out there, probably sitting with his back against the door.

"Hey, Jem?" he says. "You saved my life, you know—out there by the barn. Most people couldn't have made that shot."

I squeeze my eyes shut, but tears leak through anyway. I hadn't wanted to kill that stupid snake, but if it had bitten Ryder and we hadn't been able to make it to the hospital in time . . .

I let the thought trail off, not wanting to examine it further.

"Thank you," he says softly. "I owe you one."

I'm trying to think of what to say in reply when jagged lightning illuminates the bathroom. The boom of thunder that follows shakes the house and rattles the windows.

"Okay, time to get out now, Jemma," Ryder calls out, his voice raised in alarm. He pounds on the door for emphasis.

I've already leapt from the tub, my heart pounding. "I'm out," I call back as I reach blindly for my towel and wrap it around myself.

"That was close. Less than a mile away, I'd say." Before he finishes the sentence, there's another crack of lightning followed by the crash of thunder. Beau starts to howl, his nails clicking against the floorboards as he comes running, looking for a place to cower.

"I'll leave this lantern here for you, okay? I'm going to go get my cell and check the Weather Channel, see what they're saying."

I hear his footsteps fade away, and then the door to my parents' room clicks shut. Hurrying out, I find the robe I'd left on my parents' bed and shimmy into it, letting my towel drop to the floor.

I can hear Beau whining from under the bed, poor guy. Funny how it's the bigger dog that gets so scared during storms, while little Sadie remains completely unfazed. Nan likes to say it's because Sadie isn't smart enough to know she should be scared, but I don't think it's that. I think it's just the terrier in her. Terriers are feisty.

Once I've tied the robe, I retrieve the towel and dry my hair as best I can. I wish I'd thought of bringing my pajamas downstairs before I'd gotten in the tub. Now I'm going to have to go up to my room and rummage around by lantern light.

It takes me a good fifteen minutes to find a clean tank top and a pair of plaid pajama shorts. I start gathering up other things—my laptop, my video camera, and my favorite picture of me and Nan, taken just this summer at the beach and displayed in a kitschy driftwood frame with seashells glued onto the corners. Better to have all the important stuff downstairs with me, where it's safe. You know, in case the roof blows off.

Which it very well might do, I decide, listening to the howling wind. It's gotten much worse since I came upstairs, rattling the glass in my windows now. I make sure the doors to my balcony are securely latched before I grab my stuff and head back downstairs.

Technically, it's not even dark out yet, but it might as well be. The sky is nearly black, with thick, rolling clouds hanging disturbingly low in the sky. The eye of the storm isn't due to hit us till sometime tomorrow, but that won't be the end of it. It'll take several hours after that for it to move completely out of the area. It's going to be a *long* couple of days.

I find Ryder in the kitchen. "Hey, it looks like we're under another tornado watch," he says, glancing up from his phone. "Where do you think we should we go if the—"

His words are cut off by the shriek of the tornado siren in the distance.

"Storage room under the stairs," I say, looking around frantically for the dogs and cats. "Now!"

ACT II
Scene 4

It takes us a dangerously long time to round up both dogs and all three cats and toss them into the storage room. When I finally climb inside after Ryder, who's carrying Sulu—the last of the cats—I'm breathing hard.

"That took way too long," Ryder says as he latches the door behind us. "We should keep them all locked in the kitchen from here on out. We have to be able to get them on a moment's notice."

"Yeah, I see that now," I grumble. Still, I'm glad he didn't argue when I told him they were all coming with us.

The tornado sirens are still wailing, the wind howling. But it's warm and cozy inside the makeshift storm shelter—and well stocked, thanks to my careful preparations.

The room is probably fifteen feet long and six feet wide, a

narrow rectangle with a ceiling that slopes down to a *V* by the door. Even at its entrance, the ceiling is too low for Ryder to stand—I have to bend my knees and duck my head slightly, and I'm a foot shorter—but it's clean and well protected, right in the center of the house and far away from exterior walls.

Two battery-operated lanterns provide ample light as I shoo the dogs down to the end of the room where I've stowed dog beds and a water dish. Sadie and Beau head straight for the beds and curl up, both of them whining pitifully now.

Kirk, Spock, and Sulu are in a small, towel-lined crate that used to be Sadie's. All three are staring at us balefully but otherwise don't seem too put out. When I set up the space, I put a large piece of plywood on top of the crate and covered it with a plastic tablecloth so it could serve double-duty as a tabletop. Pretty ingenious, if you ask me.

In the middle are two sleeping bags, along with pillows and extra blankets, and that's where Ryder and I settle.

"Don't worry. I scrubbed this place down with bleach a couple of days ago, and I made sure there were no spiders." A shiver races down my spine in spite of my assuring words, because we have some pretty nasty spiders here in Mississippi. It's not the giant, scary-looking ones you have to worry about. They're mostly harmless, except for the heart-attack factor. No, it's the little ones—the black widow and brown recluse—that are truly dangerous.

I reach for my cell phone, which I'd somehow managed to carry inside, along with my video camera. I don't even remember grabbing them, but both are sitting on the little makeshift table beside one of the lanterns. I check the time. Quarter to seven.

"That's weird. It's fully charged, but I don't have any bars."

Ryder checks his own phone. "Yeah, me either. Maybe a tower went down or something."

"I hope not." Nan's surgery is scheduled for tomorrow morning. I need to be able to contact my family.

"I wonder how long this one's going to last," Ryder says. His mouth looks pinched, his jaw tight. I hadn't noticed it before, but he looks kind of green.

"You're not going to be sick, are you?"

"No. 'Course not," he says, but I'm not convinced. "Do we have any water in here? Besides what's in the dogs' bowl, I mean."

"A whole case." I hook my thumb toward the supplies behind us. "Plus packages of peanut butter crackers, some cookies, and a box of granola bars."

"I guess being a Girl Scout all those years ago really paid off, huh?"

"Guess so. You hungry? We missed dinner."

"Nah, I'm good." He rips through the plastic packaging and retrieves a bottle of water, twisting off the cap before taking a long, deep drink. "Want one?" he asks once he's nearly drained his.

"Nah, I'm not thirsty." I'm not really hungry, either. I just wish the stupid siren would stop because it's starting to get on my nerves.

A crash of thunder shakes the storage room, startling us both. Another one follows on its heels, causing Beau to lift his head and howl. I scoot over to his side, scratching him behind one ear. "It's okay, buddy. We're safe in here." *I hope*, I add silently. "Look at Sadie. She's not being a scaredy-cat. Oops, sorry, guys," I toss over my shoulder toward the cats. "Just a figure of speech. How's it going over there in the USS *Enterprise*?"

"You always talk to them like that?" Ryder asks me, his voice a little shaky.

"Pretty much." I look at him sharply, noticing how pale he's gotten. A muscle in his jaw is working furiously, and there's a thin sheen of sweat on his forehead. "Are you okay?"

He doesn't get a chance to answer. Another clap of thunder reverberates throughout the small space, followed by a horrible cracking sound and then a terrifyingly loud crashing noise.

I rise to my knees, looking toward the door that leads out. "What the *hell* was that?"

Ryder reaches for me, his fingers circling my wrist in a manacling grip. "You can't go out there, Jemma!"

I struggle to release myself. "I've got to see——"

"No! There's a goddamned tornado out there. Shit!" He pulls me toward him, and I practically fall into his lap.

He's shaking, I realize. Trembling all over. "What is *wrong* with you?" I ask him.

"What's wrong with me?" His voice rises shrilly. "*You're* the one trying to go out in a tornado. You've got to wait till the sirens quit."

"I know. But crap, that sounded like something came through the roof."

I scoot away from him, putting space between our bodies. I can smell him—soap and shampoo and the clean, crisp-smelling cologne he always wears. I can smell something else, too—fear. He's terrified.

Of the storm?

"Okay, what's going on?"

He swallows hard, his Adam's apple bouncing in his throat. "What do you mean?"

"You seemed okay before, but . . ." But once it'd started thundering and lightning, he'd come and sat outside the bathroom door. He'd acted like he was there to comfort *me*, but maybe he was the one who'd needed comforting. Maybe he hadn't wanted to be alone. "You seem pretty freaked out right about now."

He rakes a hand through his hair, leaving it sticking up in all directions. "I'm okay."

I shake my head and reach for his hand. It's trembling. "No, you're not. What is it, the thunder? The lightning?"

He takes a deep breath, exhaling slowly before he speaks. "You remember that documentary they showed us in sixth grade? The one about Hurricane Katrina?"

"Yeah." I shrug, remembering how we'd all piled into the media center to watch it on the big, pull-down screen. I don't recall much about the movie itself, but I'm pretty sure Brad Pitt had narrated it. "What about it?"

"I had nightmares for weeks. I have no idea why it affected me the way it did."

"Seriously?"

He nods. "Ever since, well . . . let's just say I don't do well in storms. Especially hurricanes."

I just stare at him in stunned silence.

"You're going to have fun with this, aren't you?"

"No, I . . . of course not. Jeez." How big of a bitch does he think I am? "I'm not going to tell a soul. I promise. Okay? What happens in the storm shelter stays in the storm shelter," I quip, trying to lighten the mood.

His whole body seems to relax then, as if I've taken a weight off him.

"Did you seriously think I was going to rag on you for this? I mean, we've been friends forever."

He quirks one brow. "Friends?"

"Well, okay, not friends, exactly. But you know what I mean. Our moms used to put us in a crib together. Back when we were babies."

He winces. "I know."

"When we were little, things were fine. But then . . . well, middle school. It was just . . . I don't know . . . awkward. And then in eighth grade, I thought maybe . . ." I shake my head, obviously unable to form a complete sentence. "Never mind."

"You thought what? C'mon, don't stop now. You're doing a good job distracting me."

"Yeah?"

"Yeah. Call it a public service. Or . . . pretend I'm just one of the pets."

"Poor babies," I say, glancing over at the cats. Kirk and Spock are curled up together in the back of the crate, keeping the bromance alive. Sulu is sitting alone in the corner, just staring at us. "He's a she, you know."

"Who?"

"Sulu. Considering she's a calico, you'd think Daddy would have figured it out. Ow!"

"What?"

"My ears just popped." I reach up to rub them, wondering what's going on. The last thing I need right now is to get sick.

A crack of thunder shakes the walls, and then everything goes eerily silent—the rain, the wind just seem to disappear.

And then we hear it—that freight-train sound that everybody warns you about.

Holy shit.

"Hold on tight!" I yell, reaching for Ryder's hand. There's really nowhere to go, but I lean into his chest, and we somehow curl around each other, bracing for impact.

ACT II
Scene 5

Ryder's heart beats madly against my ear as we cling to each other, holding on for dear life. Adrenaline races through my veins, making my breath come in short gasps. I can feel Ryder's fingers in my hair, his nails digging into my scalp as he presses me tightly against his body, his muscles bunched and rigid.

I know I'm supposed to hate him, but all I can think right now is how glad I am he's here—glad that I'm not alone. I've never been so scared in all my life, but I know it would be worse without him.

It's over in a matter of seconds. The freight-train roar quiets, the rain returning with a vengeance. I don't need Jim Cantore to tell me it's a rain-wrapped tornado. I've watched enough *Storm Chasers* to recognize it, even from my little hidey-hole under the stairs. If we had been outside, we probably wouldn't have seen it coming, not till it was too late.

Ryder releases his grip on my head, and I pull away slightly, peering up at him. His deep brown eyes are slightly wild-looking, but otherwise he looks okay. His face isn't a shade of green, at least. I lean back against him, my head resting on his shoulder now. We're still holding hands, our fingers intertwined. Somehow, it doesn't seem at all weird. It just feels . . . safe.

Neither of us says a word, not till the sirens are silenced a few minutes later.

"I guess we should give it a few minutes," I say, my voice slightly hoarse. "You know, just to make sure that's it. No point in going out just to climb right back in."

He nods. "Besides, it's perfectly comfortable in here."

"Well, I wouldn't go that far."

"Okay, let me rephrase. It's not *un*comfortable."

I swallow hard. "I hope it's not bad out there. I'm afraid of what we're going to find."

"No matter how bad it is, we're fine; the dogs and cats are fine. That's what matters, Jemma. Anything else is replaceable."

"You sound like my dad, you know that? Have you been studying at the Bradley Cafferty School of Platitudes or something?"

"Your dad's a smart guy," he says with a shrug.

"True." I take a deep breath and let it out slowly. "You think it's safe now?"

"I guess," he says, though he doesn't sound so sure of it. "For now, at least. I mean, the tornado's gone, but we've still got the hurricane to worry about, right?"

"Yeah, but we can't hole up in here all night." For one, there's no bathroom—and I've really gotta go. Two, it's a little cramped, what with the dogs and cats and . . . you know . . . the fact that Ryder isn't exactly a *small* guy.

"Let's just go see how bad the damage is," he says, releasing my hand. "Then we can figure out what do next."

"I should probably call my parents," I say, flexing my fingers. "I'm sure they're worried sick. Here, can you get that lantern?"

Rising, I shuffle over to the door and unlatch it. The dogs raise their heads, watching, but make no move to get up. I guess they feel nice and safe here too. Ryder follows me out, bent at the waist to keep from whacking his head on the ceiling.

It isn't as bad as I expected—and not nearly as bad as it could have been. A tree—or part of one—crashed into the side of the house, right through the roof of one of the sleeping porches—my mom's. It's a mess, debris everywhere. But it looks like it's only the porch affected, so that's good. The rest of the house seems fine.

It's too dark to assess the damage outside, but a flash of lightning illuminates the yard well enough to see that Ryder's Durango is still there. I assume my Fiat is still out there too, though I can't see it. My parents' cars are parked in the detached garage behind the house, so hopefully they're safe. Assuming the garage is still standing.

I guess we'll find out tomorrow, when the sun comes up.

After a quick supper of leftover sandwiches, we try to get our parents on the phone to tell them we're okay. Only, the regular house phone is out and, for some reason, we can't get through on our cells. Which is totally freaking me out because Nan's surgery is tomorrow. My cell has exactly one bar—and as soon as you dial a number, it drops the call. Ryder's is doing the same thing. Which means we're totally and completely cut off from the rest of the world, with no way of getting in touch with anyone.

Just great.

Also, it's pitch-dark out now. We have no electricity—no lights, no access to the Weather Channel. Jim Cantore might be warning us that the entire state of Mississippi is about to blow away, and we'd never even know it.

The cats are locked in the laundry room. They're not happy, but I'm not sure what else to do. If the tornado sirens go off again, we need to be able to get them quickly.

"We should probably try to get some sleep," I say, glancing over at Ryder seated opposite me, a Scrabble board between us. We've played exactly four words in an hour. Between the dim light cast by the lanterns and the distraction of the howling winds and branches slapping the windows, well . . . let's just say they aren't ideal conditions for Scrabble.

He sets aside his tiles with a scowl. "You tired?"

"Not really." I doubt I'm going to get any sleep tonight, no matter how hard I try. "But what else are we going to do?"

"Yeah, I guess you're right." He glances uneasily at the stairs.

It's easy to follow his train of thought. "You're not sleeping up there. It's way too dangerous, just like you said." There's all kinds of debris blowing around, crashing into the roof. The ground floor is definitely safer—at least, as long as you stay away from the sleeping porches.

Ryder pats the cushion beside him. "I'll get some blankets and a pillow, and I'll be fine right here."

Before the words are even out of his mouth, a particularly forceful gust of wind rattles the windows, making us both jump.

"It's getting worse out there. Wait . . ." I rise and reach for a lantern, hurrying off toward the dining room. I'd totally forgotten about the emergency radio! I'd grown so reliant on my cell phone for just about everything—music included—that the idea of regular radio hadn't even crossed my mind. But I'd set out the emergency radio when I'd first collected the emergency supplies my dad had listed. I'd even bought replacement batteries for it, though you could power it by manual crank if you had to.

There it is, sitting right on the dining room table where I've stashed extra candles, batteries, and bottles of lamp oil. We're not totally cut off after all.

I tuck it under my arm and hurry back out to a puzzled Ryder.

"Look what I have!" I set down the lantern and hold up the radio. "It's even got a special emergency weather channel."

"That's handy," Ryder says as lightning illuminates the room in strobe-light-like flashes.

Even in the dim light, I can see him flinch as he waits for the accompanying crash of thunder. It doesn't disappoint, shaking the walls dramatically. Beau lifts his head and lets out a whimper. I imagine Ryder would do the same if I weren't here to witness it.

I sigh, realizing that I can't leave him alone out here all night. That would be cruel. I know what I've got to do. "Let's go get ready for bed," I say. "You're crashing in my parents' room with me. Go on and get your stuff. As soon as we're settled, we'll turn on the radio and see what's happening, okay?"

He just nods, his mouth set in a tight line. Six foot four and scared as a puppy.

Ten minutes later, I've changed into my sleep shorts and tank top and piled pillows onto my parents' enormous king-size bed. The dogs are curled up together at the foot of the bed. I've lit a hurricane lamp on one of the bedside tables, and it's casting flickering yellowish orange light across the pristine white bedspread—the counterpane, as my mom likes to call it. There's something beautiful about it, the play of colors. It's peaceful, a stark contrast to the storm raging outside.

I reach for my camera, thankfully fully charged, and turn it on. Silently, I pan around the room, capturing it all—the deep shadows, the flickering light, the roar of the wind.

"What're you doing?"

I glance up to find Ryder there in the doorway, his duffel bag beside him. He's changed into a pair of plaid pajama pants and a heather-gray T-shirt, and he's carrying a sleeping bag.

"Just filming," I say with a shrug.

"Got this out of the storage room," he says, holding it up. "Figured I'll sleep on the floor."

I can't help but roll my eyes. "The bed's huge, Ryder. I'm pretty sure you can stay safely on your own side without getting my cooties."

"That's not . . . it's . . . ." His words trail off, and we just stare silently at each other across the broad expanse of bed—the bed I've suggested we share. As in, both of us. Together. All night long.

Have I lost my mind?

Clearing my throat uncomfortably, I flip on the radio, twisting the dial with shaking hands. A station comes in, and I recognize the voice of a local weather forecaster.

". . . came ashore just west of Gulfport around seven p.m., packing category-two winds. Many of the casino resorts on the coast are reporting damage. The bodies of two young men who disregarded the no-swim warnings along the coast have been found near Orange Beach, Alabama. So far, these are the only storm-related fatalities reported. Hopefully, the mandatory evacuation of low-lying, coastal areas will reduce the number of life-threatening injuries as the storm moves slowly northward at about fifteen miles per hour."

Ryder perches on the edge of the bed as we continue listening.

"Residents of Lafayette County should expect worsening conditions throughout the night and into the morning hours. Pay special attention to low-lying areas as we near high tide at 8:02 a.m. Storm surge pushing up the Mississippi River will continue to make local rivers and creeks breach their banks and flood local roadways. County officials have put a curfew into effect—only necessary personnel should be on the roads until further notice. Everyone should remain indoors throughout the duration of this dangerous storm and prepare to take shelter in a safe, interior room if the need should arise. With the memories of Hurricane Katrina still fresh—"

"Turn it off," Ryder says, his voice strained.

"Let's find some music," I suggest hastily, twisting the dial till I find a station playing a popular indie-rock song. "This is good. C'mon, you might as well get comfortable. It sounds like it's going to be a long night."

The wind picks up again, so strong that I swear the walls are going to blow down. Thankfully, they don't. But Ryder's face turns that odd greenish shade again.

"You okay?" I ask him.

He nods. "I'll live. Hey, it's your turn."

"My turn for what?"

"I told you my deepest, darkest secret." He tilts his head at me. "Now you've got to tell me one of yours."

"One of my secrets?"

"Yeah. C'mon, I know you've got a bunch of 'em."

"Oh, I do, huh?"

"You're too perfect not to be hiding something," he says, and my cheeks flood with heat.

Me, too *perfect*? He's got to be kidding. Only . . . he looks serious. And earnest. I look down at the camera in my hand, studying it, and then back up at up him. I can't explain it, but I suddenly want to tell him. At least, I want to tell *someone*, and he's here, a captive audience. I hesitate a second or two, then blurt it out before I lose my nerve.

"I want to go to film school." I meet his gaze, his eyes round with surprise. "In New York."

ACT II
Scene 6

"You want to do *what*?" Ryder asks, his voice laced with disbelief.

I take a deep breath before answering. "I want to go to film school next year. In New York City. Instead of Ole Miss," I clarify, in case he doesn't get it.

His gaze meets mine, and I expect to see judgment there in his eyes. I brace for the criticism, for the rebuke that's sure to follow my declaration.

Instead, his eyes seem to light with something resembling . . . admiration? "Seriously, Jem? That's awesome," he says, smiling now. His dimples flash, the fear seemingly vanished from his face.

"You really think so?" I ask hesitantly. "I mean, I know it seems a little crazy. I've never even been to New York before."

"So?" He scoots closer, so close that I can smell his now-familiar scent—soap and cologne mixed with rain. "If anyone can take care of themselves, you can." He rakes a hand through his dark hair. "Damn, Jemma, you just shot a cottonmouth clean through the head. New York will be a cakewalk after that."

A smile tugs at the corners of my mouth. "Well . . . it's not exactly the same thing. I won't be . . . you know . . . shootin' stuff up there." My tongue loosened, I launch into the whole spiel, telling him all about the program, about the campus and the cultural opportunities.

He just nods along, making approving noises, occasionally throwing out a "wow" or a "cool." When I finally stop talking, he says, "That sounds *awesome*, Jemma. Seriously. You should go for it."

I look at him skeptically, not quite expecting such over-whelming support—and from Ryder, of all people. "Well, it doesn't really matter because Mama and Daddy pretty much nixed the idea."

"They won't even let you apply?"

"At first they promised to look over the materials and think about it. At least, Daddy did. But then . . . well, after we learned about Nan's tumor . . ." I trail off with a shrug.

"They said no?"

"Not exactly," I say. "Just . . . you know . . . that it wasn't a good time, or something like that."

"When's the application due?"

"November first for early decision. I'm almost done with the application portfolio—everything but the film project."

His eyes flash with determination. "Let's do it, then."

"What, now?" In case he's forgotten, we're right in the middle of a pretty epic storm. I hate to remind him, not wanting to see the terror creep back into his face.

"Yeah. Where's your camera? We should be documenting the storm."

"The storm?" Huh, I guess he *didn't* forget, after all. "You don't think that's a little . . . I dunno . . . boring?"

"What else did you have in mind?"

"I was going to do something on the county—tying in the whole Faulkner thing, you know? I already shot most of the footage, but I never quite figured out the narrative. Here, you wanna see what I've got so far?"

"Sure," he says.

I flip out my camera's screen, switch it into playback mode, and cue up the footage before hitting play. Ryder leans in, our shoulders touching as we watch the images sweep across the screen—the picturesque town square, the library building, the historical society headquarters, the courthouse, two covered bridges, the old Ames House, Flint Creek from several vantage points, a few different shots of Magnolia Landing and its surrounding property.

"That's real nice," Ryder says when I hit the stop button and shut the screen.

Nice? Isn't "nice" just the polite way of saying "lame"? "Anyway, it doesn't matter now," I say with a shrug. "My parents said no, remember?"

"There's got to be something else—a more compelling layer." He strokes his chin, looking thoughtful. "Strength," he says after a beat. "In the face of a crisis. That should be your theme. You document the storm, with a narrative tied into strength and courage. I bet you can even work in some Faulkner quotes, if you want to. And you can still use that footage, with some before-and-after shots. Here, hand me your camera."

A little bewildered by his enthusiasm, I hand it over. I mean, I know I should be annoyed that he's sort of hijacked my project, but truthfully, I didn't really have a firm idea where I was going with it, anyway. He's doing me a favor.

Rising, he walks over to the window, where rain and debris are pelting the glass, and hits a button. The camera beeps, indicating that he's filming. "It's about nine p.m. here in Magnolia Branch, Mississippi," he narrates, the camera aimed at the dark sky beyond the glass. "Hurricane Paloma came ashore near Gulfport just a couple hours ago. We've been feeling the effects all day, even though we're six hours to the north. The tornado sirens keep going off, and the road to this house is completely washed out. Earlier today, I almost got bit by a water moccasin, but Jemma here managed to kill it with a single shot to the head. She saved my life."

He turns the camera on me. I wave it off, but he ignores me. "Jemma's one of the strongest, most courageous people I know."

I am? Since when?

"Deadly snakes, dangerous storms," he continues. "She takes it all in stride. For now we're just hunkering down and getting ready to ride it out. I'll check in later and let y'all know how we're holding up as the conditions deteriorate. Ryder out."

I can't help but snicker. "Oh my God, did you really just say 'Ryder out'?"

He winces. "Is that too dorky?"

"Nah, it's funny." You really can't go wrong with *Star Trek* references—at least, according to Daddy. "But it's too dark in here to film. You won't be able to see anything—it'll all be in shadows."

"That's the point. Showing 'em exactly what we're experiencing here. You know, from our perspective."

"I guess," I concede. "It's not a bad idea, actually."

His mouth widens into a grin. "We should set a timer. Do an update every couple of hours or something. What do you think?"

I let out a sigh of frustration. "I think my parents won't let me go, so what's the point?"

"It can't hurt to apply," he says with a shrug. "Right? Besides, they might change their minds once you get accepted."

"*If* I get accepted."

"I'm willing to bet you will."

"Wow, you've got a lot of confidence in someone you don't even like."

A crash of thunder delays his reply. When it comes, it's unexpectedly quiet. "What makes you think I don't like you?"

Feeling suddenly vulnerable, I drag a pillow into my lap. "Gee, I don't know. Maybe because you've said so? Like, a million times."

He shakes his head. "I've never said I don't like you."

"I'm pretty sure you have. Remember that fight we had a couple of weeks ago? At Mama's party?"

"You said *you* hated *me*," he argues.

My cell phone rings, making us both jump. "It's working!" I cry, reaching for it as it peals out Daddy's ringtone. Jimmy Buffett, of course. I motion for Ryder to switch off the radio.

"Daddy? Hello?" I hit speaker and hold the phone up in front of my mouth.

"Half-pint? You there?" He's breaking up, his voice cutting in and out. I can barely make out what he's saying.

"Yeah, I'm here," I say. "Can you hear me?"

"Are you okay, hon? We heard . . . tornadoes . . . been trying . . . service out."

"We're fine," I yell, as if that's going to help. "Ryder's here, and we're okay. How's Nan?"

"Nan . . . okay . . . morning . . ."

"Daddy? You're breaking up."

"Careful . . . tomorrow . . ."

I shake my head, unable to make out what he's saying. And then the phone beeps, indicating the call's been dropped.

"Well, at least they know we're okay," Ryder says.

"*If* he heard me. Stupid phone."

"We'll try again in the morning."

I shake my head. "I don't think it's going to be any better then."

"Hey, where's your optimism?"

I flop back on the bed, staring up at the ceiling. "I'm so tired. This day sucks."

"You wanna try and get some sleep?"

"Maybe," I say with a shrug. My eyelids feel heavy all of a sudden. I take a deep breath and let it out slowly. "You want to set an alarm?"

"Nah, I'm pretty sure I'll be awake. Want me to turn out the lamp?"

"Yeah, I guess. Do you mind?"

He rolls down the wick, extinguishing the flame, and the room is cast in darkness. I slip under the sheet and plump the pillow beneath my head, trying to get comfortable.

I hear Ryder moving around on the far side of the bed.

"You're not going anywhere, are you?" I ask him.

"Not unless you want me to."

"I'm good," I say, turning onto my side.

We both fall silent, listening to the storm raging around us. It's getting worse. The wind is a high-pitched whistle, constant now. Debris crashes into the house at regular intervals, tree branches slapping against the windows. It's going to be ugly out there in the morning, that's for sure.

I think about Lucy and Morgan—wonder what they're doing right now, how they're holding up. They've got their families, at least. I hope they're all safe, their homes not affected by the tornado that blew through earlier. More than anything, I wish I could call or text them and check in.

But I can't. I'm totally cut off from everyone—everyone but Ryder.

An ear-splitting crash outside makes me jump, my breath catching in my throat. "What was *that*?"

"I think that was a tree coming down." Ryder's voice is a little shaky. "Maybe we should go back into the storage room."

"Just . . . turn the radio back on. If we need to take shelter, they'll tell us."

He does, and we listen quietly for a good half hour. There's nothing new, really. Just the storm slowing down as it tracks up the state, barreling toward us. Sounds like it will have weakened considerably by then, but we'll still get tropical storm–force winds. And the slower track means a higher chance of flooding, especially around high tide in the morning. We've got a long way to go before it's over.

Ryder turns off the radio and reaches for my camera, pointing it at me in the dark. It beeps, and a red light indicates that he's filming. "Are you scared, Jemma?"

I prop my head up on one elbow. "Yeah, I'm scared," I say, carefully weighing my words. "But . . . we'll be okay. This house has weathered plenty of storms through the years. It'll keep us safe."

"I hope you're right."

"Yeah, me too."

I hear him swallow hard. "I'm glad I'm here with you."

"I'm glad you are too," I say automatically. But then . . . I realize with a start that it's true. I *am* glad he's here. I feel safe with him. More relaxed than I would be otherwise. He thinks *I'm* distracting *him*, making him forget his fears. But the truth is, he's helping me just as much. Maybe more. I'm pretty sure I'd be a blubbering mess right about now if I were alone.

"Thanks, Ryder," I say, my voice thick.

"For what?"

"Everything." I squeeze my eyes shut. "Turn off the camera, okay?"

He does, setting it aside before stretching out on the far

side of the bed, facing me. Our gazes meet, and my stomach flutters nervously. There's something there in his dark eyes, something I've never seen before. Vulnerability . . . mixed with a kind of dark, melty chocolate expression that I don't recognize.

Our hands are lying there on the bed between us, nearly touching. I lift my pinkie, brushing it against his. Chills race down my spine at the contact, my heart pounding against my ribs.

I hear his breath catch. Slowly, his hand moves over mine, his fingertips brushing my knuckles until his entire hand covers mine. His skin is hot, the pressure reassuring. A minute passes, maybe two. It's almost like he's waiting, watching to see if I pull my hand away.

I don't.

In one quick movement, he slides his hand under mine and threads our fingers together.

We lie like that for several minutes, arms outstretched, hands joined, eyes wide open. The storm continues to rage around us, but it's like we're locked in this safe, calm place where nothing can touch us.

My breathing slows; my limbs grow heavy. My lids flutter shut. I try to resist, but it's futile. I'm exhausted.

I drift off to sleep with a smile on my lips, Ryder holding me fast.

ACT II
Scene 7

I awake with a start, shaking the cobwebs of sleep from my mind. It's pitch-dark out, the wind howling. It takes me a couple seconds to get my bearings, to realize I'm in my parents' bed, Ryder beside me, on his side, facing me. Our hands are still joined, though our fingers are slack now.

"Hey, you," he says sleepily. "That one was loud, huh?"

"What was?"

"Thunder. Rattled the windows pretty bad."

"What time is it?"

"Middle of the night, I'd say."

I *could* check my phone, but that would require sitting up and letting go of his hand. Right now, I don't want to do that. I'm too comfortable. "Have you gotten any sleep at all?" I ask him, my mouth dry and cottony.

"I think I drifted off for a little bit. Till . . . you know . . . the thunder started up again."

"Oh. Sorry."

"It should calm down some when the eye moves through."

"If there's still an eye by the time it gets here. The center of circulation usually starts breaking up once it goes inland." Yeah, all those hours watching the Weather Channel occasionally come in handy.

He gives my hand a gentle squeeze. "Wow, maybe you should consider studying meteorology. You know, if the whole film-school thing doesn't work out for you."

"I could double major," I shoot back.

"I bet you could."

"What are you going to study?" I ask, curious now. "I mean, besides football. You've got to major in something, don't you?"

He doesn't answer right away. I wonder what's going through his head—why he's hesitating.

"Astrophysics," he says at last.

"Yeah, right." I roll my eyes. "Fine, if you don't want to tell me . . ."

"I'm serious. Astrophysics for undergrad. And then maybe . . . astronomy."

"What, you mean in graduate school?"

He just nods.

"You're serious? You're going to major in something that

tough? I mean, most football players major in something like phys ed or underwater basket weaving, don't they?"

"Greg McElroy majored in business marketing," he says with a shrug, ignoring my jab.

"Yeah, but . . . astrophysics? What's the point, if you're just going to play pro football after you graduate anyway?"

"Who says I want to play pro football?" he asks, releasing my hand.

"Are you kidding me?" I sit up, staring at him in disbelief. He's the best quarterback in the state of Mississippi. I mean, football is what he does. . . . It's his life. Why *wouldn't* he play pro ball?

He rolls over onto his back, staring at the ceiling, his arms folded behind his head. "Right, I'm just some dumb jock."

"Oh, please. Everyone knows you're the smartest kid in our class. You always have been. I'd give anything for it to come as easily to me as it does to you."

He sits up abruptly, facing me. "You think it's *easy* for me? I work my ass off. You have no idea what I'm working toward. Or what I'm up against," he adds, shaking his head.

"Probably not," I concede. "Anyway, if anyone can major in astrophysics and play SEC ball at the same time, *you* can. But you might want to lose the attitude."

He drops his head into his hands. "I'm sorry, Jem. It's just . . . everyone has all these expectations. My parents, the football coach—"

"You think I don't get that? Trust me. I get it better than just about anyone."

He lets out a sigh. "I guess our families have pretty much planned out our lives for us, haven't they?"

"They *think* they have, that's for sure," I say, just before a loud, shattering crash makes me gasp.

Ryder's already up, reaching for one of the lanterns. "That came from the living room," he says. "You better get your camera. Whatever it is, we should film it."

I nod, grabbing it before following him out. Sadie jumps down and tries to go with me, but I herd her back into the bedroom.

"Shit!" Ryder calls out from the living room. "I'm going to need some help here."

I run toward his voice, terrified by the alarm I hear in it. "What is it?"

"A tree limb crashed through the window. Stop right there! Don't come any closer. There's glass everywhere. You got a tarp somewhere? And duct tape?"

I freeze, gaping at the sight. "Yeah, it's all in the dining room."

"Okay, get it and put on some rain boots or something to protect your feet. We've gotta try and tarp up the window." He pushes the furniture away from the window, the wind whistling loudly through the broken pane of glass as rain lashes against the hardwood floors.

I pan around with the camera, hoping I'm getting some usable footage in the dim lighting. The lens seems to provide a filter, making me feel somehow detached from what I'm seeing: jagged, broken glass; a tree branch half in my living room; my mom's favorite drapes pulled from the rod, flapping noisily against the battered window frame.

I've seen enough.

"I'll be right back," I say, flipping off the camera before searching for supplies. I find a pair of flip-flops in the laundry room and figure they'll do, then make my way to the dining room, where I grab a blue plastic tarp and a roll of silver duct tape. I hurry back to the living room, hoping there's not too much damage.

It takes us a good half hour to get the tarp taped up securely. I'm not sure it's going to withstand the wind for long, but it's better than nothing. It's only when we're done that I notice Ryder is tracking blood everywhere.

"Oh my God, Ryder! Your feet." While I've been tromping through the broken glass in flip-flops, Ryder is barefoot.

His eyes seem to widen with surprise as he glances down— as if he's just now noticing that he's hurt. "Can you get me an old towel or two? I'll get the floor cleaned up."

The floor? He's bleeding like a stuck pig, and he's worried about the *floor*?

I manage to find a stack of ratty old towels in the downstairs linen closet, and hand him two. "Here. Wrap these around your feet and go to the master bath and wait for me. I'll clean up the blood out here, and then I'll see about those cuts."

"Nah, I'm fine. I can—"

"Ryder! Just do it. Go."

He does, visibly wincing with pain.

It takes me another half hour to clean up the blood as best I can in the semidarkness. Whatever I missed can wait till the morning, when I can actually *see* what I'm doing.

When I make my way to the bathroom, Ryder's sitting on the edge of my mom's tub, picking glass from his feet and laying the bloody shards in a towel. He's got the oil lamp in there, along with two battery-operated lanterns, but it's still not enough light, not really.

I find the hydrogen peroxide and some cotton balls in the closet and lower myself to the floor. "Okay, let me see how bad it is."

"It's nothing," he says. "I think I got all the glass out."

I shake my head. "I love that you made *me* go get shoes while you just tromped around in the broken glass."

"It was too late; I'd already stepped in it before I even knew what was going on. Besides, there wasn't time."

"Yeah, right. C'mon, be still. You've gotta let me clean out the cuts." Holding one foot over the tub, I pour peroxide over the wounds, dabbing with cotton to make sure all the glass is out. "I think we've got some gauze and bandage tape some-where. At least, I hope so. Maybe in Nan's and my bathroom." Nan's always taking a cleat to the shin or getting a bad scrape from artificial turf. "Okay, this one's good. Let me have the other one." This foot's worse. I find a couple more slivers of glass and manage to pull them out before cleaning it up.

Luckily, Nan does have gauze and tape in the bathroom cabinet, along with a tube of Neosporin ointment. I retrieve it all as quickly as possible and hurry back to the relative safety of downstairs. Ryder remains stoically silent as I daub the wounds with ointment and then wrap his feet in gauze, securing the bandages with tape.

"Okay, done. How's that feel?"

"Fine. Um, I think I cut my hand, too. It's pretty deep, actually." He holds out his right hand—his football-throwing hand, I realize, my heart sinking. He's got it wrapped in one of the towels, blood soaking through.

"Oh my God, Ryder! Crap."

I start to unwrap it, but pause when an all-too-familiar sound rents through the night. The tornado sirens.

"You have *got* to be kidding me," I say. "I mean, what else?"

"I'll get the cats," Ryder says, rising with his injured hand cradled against his chest. "You round up Beau and Sadie."

I shake my head in frustration. "How are you going to get the cats? Look at you—you're a mess."

He opens the bathroom door with his good hand. "Don't worry. Just go."

I grab the Neosporin, peroxide, and gauze and dash out, stashing the supplies in the storage room before going back for the dogs. It doesn't take too long to coax Beau out—he's good that way—and Sadie's happy to follows us into the hall.

When I reach the storm shelter, Ryder's already there, two lanterns lighting the space. All three cats are tucked safely in the crate, meowing their displeasure. I follow the dogs in and latch the door behind myself, adrenaline surging through my veins.

"Here we go again," Ryder says. "Hope it's quick this time."

But fifteen minutes later, the sirens are still going. We've passed the time hunched over in strained silence, but there's no sign of imminent danger—no freight-train roar this time. I sit up straight, allowing my tensed muscles to relax a bit.

"Looks like we're going to be here awhile," I say. "Might as well settle in and get comfortable."

Ryder scoots over, glancing around the small space. "Damn. I took out one of the sleeping bags and left it in your parents' room."

"Just open up this one," I suggest, reaching for the zipper. "It's not like we're going to get much sleep anyway. What about your hand?"

"I think it's okay. You didn't happen to bring the gauze, did you?"

I produce it, holding it up. "Right here. Let's see what I can do."

I bandage it as best I can, considering the circumstances. "Okay, there you go," I say once I'm done.

"Thanks." He cradles it against his chest. "The sun'll be up in a couple hours. At least we'll be able to see what's going on then. I sure hope the tarp holds."

"I hope so too. If we're staying here, I guess you can let the cats out of the crate." I rise to my knees, reaching behind the case of water for the little disposable litter box I'd had the foresight to buy. I rip off the liner covering the litter and hand it to Ryder. "Here, put this in the crate and leave the door open. They'll figure it out."

Soon, kitties are scampering across our laps, happily making their way over to join Beau and Sadie in the dog beds. Spock stops long enough to rub his chin against my knee. I stroke his soft fur, glad we're all safe and sound. I don't even want to think about all the animals—livestock, pets, strays— left out to battle the elements. The very idea makes my heart hurt.

"You okay?" Ryder asks me.

"Yeah, why?"

"I dunno." He shrugs. "You just looked . . . sad or something."

I'm shocked at how well he can read me. "I was just thinking about anyone—any*thing*—stuck out there in this. You know, dogs, cats, horses. Cows," I add, sighing heavily.

"We've got cows!" Ryder quips, quoting that old movie about tornadoes—you know, the one with Bill Paxton.

I admit, it makes me smile.

"Sorry, I couldn't help myself," Ryder says. "But yeah, it *is* sad. I just . . . well, let's try not to think about it, okay?"

I yawn loudly, so far beyond exhaustion now that there's not even a word for it. "I really need to close my eyes for a little bit."

"You go on. I can't sleep anyway. I'll wake you up if things start getting bad."

"Thanks," I say, snuggling down on the open sleeping bag. My eyes close the moment my head touches the pillow.

I have no idea how long I doze, but when I open my eyes again, the sirens have quieted. Ryder's lying beside me, our shoulders touching.

"You awake?" he asks.

"Yeah," I mumble sleepily. "Is it morning yet?"

"Not quite. Soon."

I nod, and we both fall silent. Inexplicably, I find myself scooting closer to him, fitting myself against his side, seeking his warmth.

He puts an arm around me, drawing me closer.

I let out a contented sigh. There's something so familiar—

and yet so foreign—about his closeness. I think about those shared cribs, the communal Pack 'n Plays our mothers insisted on. Maybe that explains it—old memories, too far out of reach to be easily accessed, but there all the same.

That's why this feels so . . . *right*. It must be.

I feel Ryder's fingers in my hair, combing through it absently. His heart is thumping noisily against my ear, his chest rising and falling with each breath.

"Jem?"

I swallow hard before answering. "Yeah?"

"I've been thinking about what you said—you know, about the eighth-grade dance. I've been racking my brain, trying to figure out what you were talking about. And"—he swallows hard—"there's something I need to tell you."

Why is he bringing this up now? "You don't have to, Ryder," I say, my heart accelerating. "You were right. It was a long time ago."

"I know, but, well . . . just hear me out, okay?"

I nod, mentally bracing myself. I'm not sure I want to hear this—to open those old wounds again.

"I said some things that night, things I'm not proud of. And . . . it occurred to me that someone might have told you, and—"

"I heard you, Ryder," I say, cutting him off. "I was there, hiding in those trees by the rock. I heard everything."

He lets out his breath in a low whistle. "Shit. I am *so* sorry, Jemma. I didn't think. . . . I mean, not that it makes any difference, but I didn't know. I figured you'd had second thoughts or something and decided you didn't want to go with me."

"I wish," I mumble.

"The thing is, Jem, those things I said? I didn't mean them. I was there waiting for you, when Mason and Ben showed up and started teasing me. I didn't know what to do. I wanted to get rid of them, and then they started saying stuff. You know, about you."

"Yeah, I heard." Even now, all these years later, the memory makes me cringe.

"And I knew that if they knew the truth—if they knew how much I really liked you, it'd be even worse. I swear, in some crazy, convoluted way, I thought I was protecting you or something."

"I still can't believe Laura Grace made you ask me," I say. "Was Mama in on it too?"

He shakes his head. "No. Don't you get it? I made that up. My mom had nothing to do with it—she didn't even know. The truth is, I wanted to go with you. Something had changed between us, remember? At the beach over Christmas break?"

"I remember." I'd been hyperaware of him on that trip— self-conscious and nervous and giddy and excited all at once. I'd caught him staring at me when he thought I wasn't looking, and I'd stolen some secret glances myself.

"That was when I realized you were the prettiest girl in Magnolia Branch," he says. "Hell, maybe in all of Mississippi. Anyway, I was excited about the dance. I even snuck into town that afternoon and bought you a corsage. I had it in my pocket when I went to the rock to meet you."

I barely hear him, because I'm still stuck on the "prettiest girl" part of his speech.

"As soon as I lost the guys, I went back outside to look for you, but you weren't there. So I went inside and . . . well, Morgan and Lucy said you never showed, and I just thought . . ." He shakes his head. "I dunno what I thought. I was only thirteen, and I was ashamed about what I'd said to the guys and scared you didn't like me the way I liked you. So I guess I convinced myself that *you* had ditched *me*. That way, instead of feeling guilty, I could just write it off. And yeah, I realize how totally fucked up that sounds."

I let out my breath in a rush. "All these years, and you never told me?"

"It's just that . . . one day went by, then another. After a while, it just seemed easier to let you hate me, you know?"

"God, Ryder. All this time . . ." I shake my head, my cheeks burning now. "Do you have any idea how upset I was? How humiliated?"

"I'm sorry," he says, sounding miserable. "I was a jerk and a coward and . . . I don't know what else. Just . . . please say that you'll forgive me."

I lie there quietly, trying to make sense of it all—to understand the workings of a thirteen-year-old boy's mind. But my thoughts keep going back to something he'd said earlier. "You really thought I was the prettiest girl in Magnolia Branch?"

"I still do, Jemma," he says, his voice quiet.

ACT II
Scene 8

Ryder Marsden could not *possibly* have said what I think he just said. Nope. Not in a million years. But then he rises up on one elbow, gazing down at me, and . . .

My breath leaves my lungs in a *whoosh* as his head angles down toward mine, his breath warm on my cheek. I swear my heart stops beating for a second—seizing up in my chest before resuming its noisy rhythm. He's going to kiss me, I realize. Ryder is actually going to *kiss* me, and—

"You've got something . . ." He pauses, brushing his fingers across my cheek. "There. I got it."

Disappointment washes over me. He *wasn't* going to kiss me. He was just noticing a smudge of dirt on my face or something. I feel like a total idiot. My cheeks flare with heat as I scramble to a seated position and reach for a bottle of water.

"Thanks," I mumble, unscrewing the cap. I drink for a long time, mostly to avoid meeting Ryder's eyes. Problem is, I already have to pee. This is *not* going to help the situation.

"Think the sun's up yet?" I ask.

"Maybe. You wanna go see?" He reaches for his own bottle of water.

"Yeah, might as well. There's no chance I'm going back to sleep now."

"Let's go, then."

When we finally emerge from the storm shelter, the sun has just begun to rise, the sky a deep, gunmetal gray. The rain has dwindled down to a drizzle, the wind a low, manageable-sounding whine. I'm happy to see that the tarp has mostly held, just one corner flapping in the breeze. With both feet and one hand still wrapped in gauze bandages, Ryder goes straight to fixing it.

The dogs make a beeline for the front mudroom, whining all the way. I know just how they feel. "Only on leash," I tell them. Who knows what we're going to find out there, what dangers lurk just outside the door. I slip into a yellow rain slicker and pull on knee-high rain boots. Ryder joins me, putting on his own rain boots and waterproof jacket.

"Here, can you take Beau?" I ask, handing him the leash. I've got Sadie, who's straining at the bit, scratching the door. I lead the way, taking Sadie straight to the patch of grass beside the porch. Ryder follows suit, heading out just past me.

"Oh, shit!" he calls out.

I hurry to catch up to him, and then I see it—a downed tree lying across Ryder's Durango, the metal beneath it crumpled like an accordion. The windshield is cracked, the rearview mirror dangling.

"Uh-oh," I mutter, peering around the Durango to learn the fate of my Fiat. I flinch at the sight that greets me—several enormous limbs and leafy branches have pretty much buried my car. But it doesn't look as bad as the Durango. At least, the actual damage looks pretty minor. I think the height of the Durango protected my little car, taking the weight of most of the tree.

Still, this isn't good. In fact, everything toward the west looks bad. The tops of trees are ripped off in a path straight down toward the creek. And the roof of the barn should be visible off in the distance, but instead there's just a big, gaping hole where it should be.

Crap.

"The barn," I say, lifting up my hood to cover my head as the rain picks up again.

Ryder nods. "I know. Let's finish up with the dogs and then we'll go check it out."

Beau and Sadie are quick with their business, eager to get out of the rain and back inside where it's dry.

"I'm sorry about your car," I say as we head past it a few minutes later. I know how much he loves it. It was a sixteenth birthday present from his parents. They'd secretly bought it a couple days before the big day and hid it here, driving it over to Magnolia Landing early in the morning on his birthday and leaving it in the driveway for him to find when he went outside to go to school. Anyway, it doesn't look like he'll be driving it any time soon.

Ryder doesn't respond. He's too busy looking around at the damage that surrounds us. It's much worse than I expected. In addition to the smashed sleeping porch and the broken living room window, part of the roof is missing over on the far side of the house, the top of the chimney blown clean away.

There's debris everywhere, blocking our path at every turn. Limbs, branches, roof shingles . . . what looks like sheet metal. I have no idea where *that* came from. Pieces of what used to be our fence are scattered about in splintered bits.

It takes us forever to pick our way over and around it all as we head down the path toward the barn. We walk in silence, our heads bent against the battering rain. What should be a five-minute stroll takes us close to a half hour. I keep my eyes glued to the ground, on the lookout for more water moccasins driven up from the creek. The last thing we need is—

"Uh, Jemma?"

"Huh?" I glance up, blinking hard. I look around, disoriented. "What the . . . ?"

Because it's gone, the barn. *Gone.* The spot where it stood is now a pile of unidentifiable rubble. My eyes burn, my vision blurring as tears well in my eyes.

My shooting range. Daddy's workshop and all those beautiful pieces of furniture. They're gone, just like that.

"Damn," Ryder says.

I just stand there and gape, forcing back the tears.

"You can see the path the tornado took, right through there." Ryder waves an arm in a wide arc, indicating the trail of destruction.

It's immediately obvious that Magnolia Landing lies directly in the path. Ryder's thinking the same thing. I can see it in his eyes.

The wind picks up, blowing my hood off my head. I shove it back in place as I reach for my camera, remembering then that I'm supposed to be filming. Doing my best to shield the lens from the rain with my hand, I quickly pan across the scene of destruction, again feeling that same disconnect as before. Hastily, I shut down the camera and stuff it in my pocket.

Ryder just stands there, his hands on his hips as he gazes off in the distance.

"It might be okay," I say haltingly. "Magnolia Landing, I

mean. The house is half a mile away—tornadoes don't usually stay on the ground for long."

He nods but remains silent. I know he's imagining his home leveled like the barn—a pile of white stones and tumbled columns.

"Don't think about it." I take a step toward him and lay a hand on his arm. "Not till we know for sure."

A gust of wind nearly knocks me off my feet. "We should get back inside," I say, glancing up at the sky. Dark clouds obscure the horizon. I figure we're probably in what's left of the center right now, but it won't last long. There's still a lot of storm to go. We can't get careless, not now.

We head back at a plodding pace. When we reach our destroyed cars, I pull out my camera, suddenly needing the buffer of the lens to face it all—the cars, the roof, the smashed sleeping porch.

But that's not what I'm thinking about, not really. Instead, I'm thinking about the fact that my sister is having brain surgery any minute now, and there's not a *damn* thing I can do about it.

"C'mon, Jem," Ryder calls out from the safety of the front porch. "You're getting drenched out there."

Feeling utterly helpless, I follow him inside.

ACT II

Scene 9

After a quick breakfast of dry cereal and Pop-Tarts, we pull out our cell phones and check futilely for a signal. I'm not sure why we bother. There are *no* bars now—not a single one. Ryder figures the storm—maybe the tornado—took out the cell tower. Which means there's no telling when it'll be working again. So we're *still* cut off from the rest of the world.

The morning drags on endlessly. I play nursemaid, removing the bandages on Ryder's feet and hand. His feet don't look too bad, but the cut on his hand is scaring me. Truth is, it probably needed stitches last night, but it's too late now. I don't even want to think about what this means for next weekend's football game—*if* there's a game next weekend.

Right now I feel like we're in the middle of the Apocalypse.

I keep waiting for zombies to appear or something. One thing's for sure—if they do, Delilah and I are ready.

In the meantime, Ryder and I play two games of Scrabble. I win both, but I'm not sure that he didn't throw the second one. By lunchtime, we're both a little stir-crazy. The worst of it has clearly passed, but it's still pouring, with occasional gusts of wind strong enough to rattle the windows. Ryder manages to retape the tarp over the window while I scrub the floor clean of all traces of blood.

With nothing else to do after lunch, we decide to take a nap. This time, when Ryder and I climb into my parents' enormous bed, we put as much space between us as possible. We curl up on opposite sides, awkward now. So much has changed between us in the last twenty-four hours. I'm not even sure what to think about him anymore.

I want to figure it out, but I'm tired. So tired. It doesn't take me long to drift off. When I do, I dream about Ryder.

I'm walking down a narrow aisle, dragging what feels like heavy weights behind me. It's a dress, I realize—a wedding dress— so heavy that I can barely walk, barely breathe. I desperately want to stop, to sink to the ground in a puddle of white tulle, but someone's pushing me, coaxing me on.

I look up to find Ryder there at the end of the aisle, waiting for me with a scowl on his face. He's wearing a tuxedo—a white dinner jacket with a wilted red rose in his lapel. As I approach he shakes his head, shooting a warning glare in my direction.

Behind me, I hear applause. I turn to find Captain Jeremiah D. Marsden and Corporal Lewiston G. Cafferty there watching, clapping. Both wear their gray Civil War uniforms, tattered and torn, flat forage caps perched on their heads.

I turn back toward Ryder and find our parents flanking him now. They're smiling—grinning, really—their eyes gleaming almost maniacally. Ryder's dad has his fingers clamped tightly on his son's shoulder, holding him in place, keeping him from bolting.

"We did it!" Mama says to Laura Grace, who nods enthusiastically. They reach for me, beckoning me to join them there at the altar.

I try to back away, but I can't. The dress is too heavy, the pressure from behind too strong.

I bolt awake, sitting up with a start. My heart is pounding, my palms damp as I clutch the bedsheets in tight fists. I shake my head, trying to clear it. *Just a dream,* I tell myself. But I'm rattled. I mean, c'mon . . . it doesn't take a degree in psychology to figure out *that* dream.

I glance over at the far side of the bed, but it's empty. After a quick trip to the bathroom to splash cold water on my face, I head to the kitchen. My stomach's grumbling, and I'm suddenly craving a piece of Lou's caramel cake.

But I stop short at the sight of a piece of paper on the kitchen table with my name scrawled across the top.

Couldn't sleep, it says in Ryder's cramped script. *Walked over to Magnolia Landing to make sure everything's okay. Be back soon.*

I stare at the note blankly, sure he's lost his mind. It's not safe out there. The water's knee-deep and full of debris. And what if he comes across another moccasin? What then?

He's going to *walk* a half mile across a flooded field and through woods strewn with downed trees? With cut feet and a bandaged hand?

What the *hell*?

I briefly consider going after him, but dismiss the idea just as quickly. I have no idea what time he left. I slept for a couple hours—he could be back any minute now. Plus, there's two possible routes he could have taken, either following the creek or the road. And since both are flooded . . .

I shake my head in annoyance. I'm seriously pissed that he didn't even bother consulting me before setting out. Couldn't he have waited? Conditions'll surely be better by tomorrow. Besides, even if Magnolia Landing *is* a pile of rubble, there's not a single thing he can do about it, not now.

And what am I supposed to do? Just sit here like a good little girl, waiting for him? Worrying about him? Making his dinner?

Yeah right.

I glance over at the caramel cake sitting on a plate on the counter and notice that he somehow managed to put half of it away before he left. I pull the plate toward me and grab a fork before digging in, not even bothering to cut a piece. That's what he gets for setting off on this . . . this . . . stupid freaking *suicide mission* without telling me.

I take a bite, savoring it. *So good.* I need to ask Lou for the recipe someday. As for Ryder Marsden, I hope a tree falls on him. I hope his cuts get infected. I hope a water moccasin gets him good. That'll serve him right, the self-centered jerk. I mean, what is this? I bare my soul to him last night, telling him all about the film-school thing. And then he confesses the truth about the dance back in eighth grade; he says that he thought—*thinks*—I'm the prettiest girl in all of Magnolia Branch.

And *then* he gets all standoffish on me, taking off while I'm sleeping. What the hell? He *needs* me out there—me and Delilah both. In case he's forgotten, I saved his life yesterday.

I've made a mess of the cake. I push the plate away with a sigh, licking frosting from the corner of my mouth. I need to kill some time, but how? A bath, I decide. Now, while it's still light out.

The hot water holds out just long enough to fill my mom's enormous tub. There's no electricity to power the jets, but that's okay. The lavender bath salts are plenty relaxing, making me sleepy, despite the nap.

I'm half expecting to hear Ryder come clomping through the front door any minute now. But he doesn't—not while I'm in the tub and not after I'm out, dried off, and changed into clean clothes. With no power and thus no hair dryer, I work my hair into two braids. When I'm done, I take a good look at myself in the mirror. I'm not wearing a stitch of makeup, and with my hair in braids, well, I could easily pass for thirteen. The freckles across the bridge of my nose don't help any. Somehow, Nan managed to escape the freckles, but not me.

Oh man . . . *Nan*. I've been doing such a good job of *not* thinking about her. But it's there, in the back of my mind, hovering like a dark, ominous cloud. I grab my cell to check the time. She should be out of surgery by now, or close to it.

Please let her be okay.

I set my useless cell aside with a sigh—still no bars. I would give *anything* for a working phone right now. I've got to figure out a way to kill some time, or I'll go crazy.

I take the dogs out to do their business and then decide to put on work gloves and see what I can salvage in the sleeping porch. I stop working when twilight comes, the sky a pale lavender, the rain reduced to a light patter now. It's too dark for me to see what I'm doing. I have no idea how much time has passed, but I've managed to clear the floor of debris and pull out all the pillows and cushions, setting them aside in the family room to dry.

I peel off my gloves, dropping them in the laundry room before rounding up the dogs and cats and feeding them their dinner. Once that's done, I help myself to a tall glass of lukewarm tea, draining it quickly and then pouring myself another. I glance out the window above the sink, watching the sky deepen to violet as the sun sinks below the horizon.

Where the *hell* is Ryder? It's almost dark out, and he's nowhere to be seen. He's been gone for hours now—way too long. My heart accelerates, my stomach lurching uncomfortably. He should be back by now. Unless something's happened to him, that is.

A half hour later, I'm starting to panic. An hour later, I'm near frantic, pacing back and forth by the front door. Every few minutes, I pause, gazing out at the inky darkness, hoping beyond hope to see him. Each time, I'm disappointed.

Ten more minutes pass before I decide to go after him. He must be in some sort of trouble—it's the only explanation. I run through the list of possibilities in my mind: A snake bit him. Floodwaters swept him away. A tree fell on him, crushing his spine.

I've already pulled on my rain boots and jacket when I see it—a flickering light cutting through the darkness, moving toward the house. All the breath leaves my lungs in a rush.

I run out onto the front porch, trying to slow my racing heart as I peer out into the night. The light gets closer and closer, causing hope to blossom in my chest.

"Hey!" a familiar voice calls out, and I nearly weep with relief.

He's back. Thank God.

But the relief is immediately replaced with anger. "Where the *hell* have you been?" I ask, my voice shaking.

He clicks off the flashlight and makes his way up the porch steps. "Didn't you see my note?"

"Are you kidding me?" I sputter. "Do you have any idea how many hours you've been gone?"

"Yeah, sorry about that. The house was fine, but the pool was a mess. A tree fell through the screen, and the roof was ripped off the pool house."

"You're sorry? That's all you have to say?" I take two steps toward him, fury thrumming through my veins. "Do you have any idea how worried I was? God, Ryder! I thought you were lying in a ditch somewhere. I thought you were hurt, or . . . or . . ." I trail off, shaking my head. "I was about to go looking for you, out in the pitch-dark!"

He reaches for my hand, but I slap him away.

"Don't touch me! I swear, I can't even *look* at you right now." I turn and reach for the door. But before I can fling it open, Ryder pulls me toward him, his hands circling my wrists.

"Look, I'm sorry, Jemma. It took me forever to get there, what with all the flooding and everything. And then I was trying to clean stuff up and . . . well, I guess the time just got away from me."

I try to pull away, but he tightens his grip. "I didn't mean to scare you," he says.

"Well, you *did* scare me." I manage to pull one hand loose, and I use it to whack him in the chest. "Idiot!"

"I'm fine, okay? I'm here."

"I wish you weren't!" I yell, fired up now. "I wish you *were* lying in a ditch somewhere!" I stumble backward, my heel catching on the porch's floorboards.

"You don't mean that," Ryder says, sounding hurt.

He's right; I don't. But I don't care if I hurt his feelings. I'm too angry to care. Angry and relieved and pissed off and . . . and, God, I'm so glad he's okay. I thump his chest one more time in frustration, and then somehow my lips are on his— hungry and demanding and punishing all at once.

I hear him gasp in surprise. His mouth is hot, feverish even, as he kisses me back. The ground seems to tilt beneath my feet. I stagger back toward the door, dragging him with me without breaking the kiss. Ryder's tongue slips between my lips, skimming over my teeth before plunging inside. And . . .

Oh. My. God. No one's ever kissed me like this. *No* one. His hands and his tongue and his scent and his body are pressed against mine. . . . It's making me light-headed, dizzy. Electricity seems to skitter across my skin, raising gooseflesh in its wake. I cling to him, grabbing fistfuls of his T-shirt as he kisses me harder, deeper. I was meant to do this, I realize. I was *made* to kiss Ryder Marsden. Everything about it is *right*, like the last piece of a puzzle falling into place.

Somehow, we manage to open the front door and stumble blindly inside, past the mudroom, where we shed our boots and jackets. We pause right there in the front hall, our hands seemingly everywhere at once. I tug at his T-shirt, wanting it off, wanting to feel his skin against my fingertips. His hands skim up my sides beneath my tank top, to the edges of my bra. Shivers rack my entire body, making my knees go weak. Thank God for the wall behind me, because that's pretty much all that's holding me up right now.

With a groan, he abandons my mouth to trail his lips down my neck, to my shoulder, across my collarbone to the hollow between my breasts. I tangle my fingers in the hair at the nape of his neck, clutching him to me—thinking that I should make him stop, terrified that he will.

This is insane. *I'm* insane.

But you know what? That's just fine with me. Because right now, "sane" seems *way* overrated.

ACT II

Scene 10

Jemma?" Ryder murmurs, his mouth hot against my skin. "Is this okay?"

I tilt my head back against the wall, catching my breath. "Yeah," I say, panting. "It's definitely okay. Okay?"

His forehead is resting on my shoulder now, his hands skimming my hips. "You sure? I don't want to . . . I mean, I know things are kinda weird right now, but—"

"Just kiss me, Ryder."

So he does.

Does he ever.

And, of course, that's when the dang-blasted tornado siren decides to go off again.

Seriously?

Ryder steps back from me, looking a little disoriented. It

takes us both a few seconds to get our bearings. "Storage room," he says. "I'll get the cats; you get the dogs?"

I just nod, tugging my tank top back into place. Somehow it'd gotten pushed up, bunched around my bra. And Ryder . . . At some point he must have taken off his T-shirt, because he's shirtless now, his jeans riding low on his hips.

Focus, Jemma. The dogs. I've got to get the dogs.

Ryder has already taken off in the direction of the kitchen to get the cats. I force myself into action, pushing all extraneous thoughts from my head as I grab a lantern and search for Beau and Sadie.

I find them both in my parents' room. The siren sent Beau under the bed, and Sadie's lying on it, at the foot. I tuck her under one arm and slap my thigh, whistling for Beau. "C'mon, boy. Back to the closet. Let's go!"

He crawls out and follows me obediently, his tail tucked between his legs. This time, I beat Ryder to the shelter. As soon as I set down my lantern and shoo the dogs down to their end of the room, I stick my head out the door and call for him. "Ryder? What's taking you so long?"

"I'm on my way!" he yells back.

It feels like forever before he pushes open the door and ducks inside. Then I see why it took him so long. He's somehow got the three cats tucked under one arm and the cake plate clutched in the other hand. No spare for a flashlight or lantern—so he accomplished this all in the dark.

"Here," he says, handing off the cake to me before releasing Kirk, Spock, and Sulu into the crate and latching the door.

"Seriously, Ryder? You brought the cake?"

He shrugs. "I was hungry."

Hmm, I guess all that kissing worked up his appetite. For cake. I'm not sure if I should be offended or not. On the plus side, he doesn't look like he's about to puke. So we're making progress as far as his fear of storms goes. I guess that's something.

"Did you happen to bring a fork?" I ask, setting the plate on the makeshift tabletop.

He produces two from his pocket, holding them up triumphantly. So we eat cake while the sirens blare. Actually, it doesn't sound that bad out there. Still, the fact that we're so calm—that *Ryder's* so calm—should tell you how routine this is getting. As long as we don't hear that awful freight-train sound, we're good.

"What happened to the cake?" he asks between bites. "It looks like someone mutilated it while I was gone."

"Sorry," I mutter. "Guess I did some stress bingeing. You realize you're not wearing a shirt, right?"

He glances down and shrugs, his cheeks flushing ever so slightly. "Sorry 'bout that."

It might seem silly that he's apologizing, but at Magnolia

Landing, you don't come to the table unless you're fully dressed. It's one of Laura Grace's most unbendable rules—you dress for meals, even breakfast. Not that this counts as a meal, and I'm not sure you could call this plywood-on-top-of-a-crate thing a "table." But still . . .

By the time the sirens shut off, we've completely cleaned the plate, even scraping off the hardened frosting with our fingers. "That was quick," I say, setting aside the now-empty plate.

Ryder nods. "I guess we should give it a minute or two. You know, make sure it's not coming back on."

So we wait. Silently. Ryder can't even meet my eyes, and all I want to do is stare at his lips. This is crazy. I mean, what do we do now—now that the sirens are off and the cake is gone?

Apparently, the answer is pretend like nothing happened. At least, that's what we do when we leave the storm shelter five minutes later. Ryder retrieves his T-shirt from the front hall and puts it on. We walk the dogs. We make peanut butter and jelly sandwiches for supper.

While we eat, we listen to the radio. That's when we learn that our entire county is under a boil-water alert, thanks to a power outage at the water treatment facility. We've been drinking bottled water all along, but now we'll have to brush our teeth with it too. Great.

We also learn that a tornado touched down on campus over

at the university. No injuries have been reported, but a couple buildings are heavily damaged.

And, apparently, our road isn't the only one washed out. There's been widespread flash-flooding. The mandatory curfew is still in effect, so we couldn't go anywhere even if our cars weren't crushed.

After we finish our sandwiches, we play another game of Scrabble. This time, Ryder wins. Honestly, my head's just not in it. Besides, it's late. I'm tired.

"You ready for bed?" Ryder asks, as if he's read my mind.

I push aside the game board. "Yeah. You?"

"Definitely." He stretches, reaching toward the ceiling— exposing a swath of tanned skin between the hem of his shirt and the waistband of his jeans. "Sounds like the storm will have moved out by morning. We're going to have a lot of cleanup to do."

I nod. "I guess we should take the dogs out again first."

We do—quickly. It's still raining, just a drizzle now. But I feel like I'm going to start sprouting fuzzy green moss any minute now. Everything feels damp—my skin, my clothes, the furniture. It's permeated everything. I mean, Mississippi's pretty humid in general, but right now I'm afraid I'll never feel dry again.

I grab one of the lanterns we've left in the mudroom and head toward my parents' room, expecting Ryder to follow.

But he pauses at the bottom of the stairs. "I guess I should . . .

you know. The guestroom. Should be safe upstairs now."

I just stare at him, trying to decide if he's serious. But then he reaches for the banister, and I realize he is. "You don't have to," I say, my cheeks flushing hotly. "I mean . . . I'm fine with you down here. With me."

I can't believe I just said that. But, jeez, everything's so awkward now.

"You sure?" he asks, taking a step toward me.

I shift my weight from one foot to the other. "Yeah, I'm . . . you know, getting used to having you around. Anyway," I say breezily, "we might get some more severe stuff tonight. Probably shouldn't take any chances."

Oh my God, I'm practically begging him to stay with me. What is *wrong* with me?

"You're probably right," Ryder says, relenting.

I try to think of something clever to say, but come up blank. So I turn and stalk off to my parents' room instead.

Ryder finds me in the bathroom, brushing my teeth with bottled water. He stands in the doorway, leaning against the wooden frame, watching me. Our gazes meet in the mirror— which, of course, makes gooseflesh rise on my skin. I spit in the sink and take a swig of water to rinse.

"Jem?"

I turn, the marble countertop digging into my back. He moves toward me, closing the distance between us. I sway slightly on my feet as he reaches for me, his dark eyes filled with heat. His gaze sweeps across my face, warming my skin, making my breath catch in my throat.

Oh man. "Yeah?"

"I have to ask you something," he says.

"Ask—ask me what?" I stammer.

He hesitates before answering. "What's the deal with you and Patrick Hughes?"

It takes me several seconds to find my voice. "What do you mean?"

"I mean . . . Patrick is my friend and all. I just . . . I figured I should ask what's going on with you two before I . . . well, before we do something we might regret."

I blink several times, trying to figure out what he's talking about. And then it hits me. "Oh my God. Are you saying that . . . I cheated on him? With you?"

"I just wanted to make sure. If y'all are serious, well . . ." He trails off with a shrug.

"We're . . . I don't even know. We've only gone out a couple of times." I shake my head. "God, Ryder, why'd you even have to bring him up?"

I haven't even *thought* about Patrick, not once since I saw him last. I definitely wasn't thinking about him when Ryder and I were making out. And I'm pretty sure I was about to break off whatever we had going, anyway.

But now . . . now I feel guilty, like some kind of slut or something. I'm so angry with myself—angry and ashamed. And Ryder . . . I can only imagine what he thinks about me now. "Maybe you should sleep upstairs," I say.

"Okay." His voice is soft, placating. "If that's what you want."

I nod. "It's probably for the best."

But it isn't what I want, not really. And . . . okay, I know it sounds stupid, but I want him to realize that. I want him to try to convince me otherwise. I want him to tell me he's sorry that he brought it up, that he understands things are a little fuzzy with me and Patrick, that it doesn't matter anyway. That he wants to be *here*, with me.

But he doesn't. Of course he doesn't.

ACT II
Scene 11

I blink several times, turning to shield my eyes from the blinding sun streaming in through the windows. With a groan, I drag a pillow over my eyes. I'm vaguely aware of something wet on my ankle, and I sit up sharply to find Sadie at my feet, licking my exposed skin sticking out from the sheets.

"How late did I sleep?" I mumble, reaching for my cell on the bedside table.

It's 10:37 a.m. Wow. My phone still has no bars, of course. And now the battery's about dead too. Oh joy.

I shove aside the tangled sheets and rise, rubbing the sleep from my eyes. I better take the dogs out. I don't even bother to get dressed—I'm still in my sleep shorts and tank top, but it's not like I'm trying to impress anyone. Specifically Ryder.

I briefly wonder where he is. I went to bed right after he left me in the bathroom last night. Not that I fell asleep right away. Oh, no. That would have been way too easy. Instead, I lay there for hours on end, listening to him move around upstairs. Right now there's no sound coming from above. Maybe he left. I *hope* he left. I'm too embarrassed to face him.

But he hasn't. When I take the dogs out, I find him clearing the debris off our cars.

"Hey," he calls out. "I think your car is fine. You've got some dents and a crack in the windshield, but nothing major." He tosses a leafy branch toward a big pile behind him.

Okay, so we're back to pretending that nothing happened. Good. I'm down with that. "What about your Durango?"

"She's pretty banged up. Gonna need some bodywork and a whole new windshield."

"She?"

He looks at me blankly. "What?"

"You called it a 'she,'" I point out.

"Oh. Right." Color creeps into his cheeks. "Dana Durango."

"You named your car Dana?"

He just shrugs.

"Oookay. You need any help?"

"Nah, I'm just about done here." He pauses, eyeing me sharply. "You sleep well?"

"Yeah, I was out like a light," I lie, refusing to give him the satisfaction. "You?"

He shrugs. "It was awfully warm up there."

"Huh," is all I say.

"Did you eat breakfast?" he asks.

"Not yet. I will as soon as I take the dogs in. What about you?"

"Nah. I was waiting for you. Just let me clean up, and I'll meet you in the kitchen."

"Sounds good." Okay, we are just *so* awkward now. This is crazy. I can't even imagine sitting across the kitchen table from him, trying to make small talk. This is painful enough as it is.

I finish up with the dogs and take them back inside, doing my best to clean off their muddy feet before I set them free. I'm going to have to mop the floors after breakfast, I realize. There's muddy paw prints from one end of the house to the other. And now that there's actually sunlight streaming in through the broken living room window, I can see that I didn't get all the blood up.

What a mess.

Hurrying into the kitchen, I dump food into the dogs' and cats' bowls and then head back to my parents' room to get my cell phone. As soon as we're done eating, I'm going to have to go sit out in the car for a little bit and charge it. I need it fully powered once the signal comes back—*if* it ever comes back.

I glance down at the screen as I retrieve it from the bedside table and hit the on button just for kicks. And . . . oh my God! The bars are back! My pulse begins to race as little notification thingies start popping up on my screen. Missed calls. Voicemail messages.

Hallelujah!

Clutching it in one hand, I sit on the bed and scroll through the list of missed calls. Twenty-seven missed calls from my parents. *Twenty-seven?* What the heck? I guess they've been trying to call me for days, not realizing the service was out. And there's two missed calls from Lucy, both in the past ten minutes. I click over to my voice mail. There's just two messages, one from my dad's cell and one from Lucy.

"Jemma," comes my dad's voice, "call me the minute you get this, okay?" That's it; nothing else. He sounds off, a little strained or something. What does that mean? Just that he's frustrated he can't reach me? Or . . . or . . . My heart takes off at a gallop, my breath coming fast as my thoughts move into a dangerous direction.

Please let Nan be okay. Please, please, please.

I take a deep, calming breath and hit play for the second message.

"Jemma, it's Luce." She sounds like she's crying. "My phone just came back on, and . . . oh my God, I heard the news. I'm so, so sorry. Call me if you need to talk, okay?"

What? What the hell does that mean? What news? Why is she sorry?

Panic surges through my veins, making me breathless.

I need to talk to my dad—*now*. My hand shaking, I press my dad's number. I feel sick, like I'm about to puke as I listen to it ring. Once, twice, three times. Then it goes to voice mail. I try my mom's number. Same thing.

Shit. Tears burn behind my eyelids. I rise on trembling legs and head for the bathroom, sure I'm going to be sick now.

Not Nan. No, no, no. She has to be okay.

"Jemma?"

Ryder's moving through the house, looking for me, calling for me. I can't answer. I can't do anything but sink to the cold tile floor in front of the toilet, my phone still clutched in one clammy hand.

He finds me there a few minutes later. "Jemma?" He peers down at me with drawn brows. "You okay?"

All I can do is shake my head. I'm numb, paralyzed with fear. This can't be happening.

"What's going on? Are you sick or something?"

I try to answer, but nothing comes out except a strangled sob.

He crouches down beside me. "Okay, you're starting to scare me. What the hell's going on, Jem?"

I take several deep, gulping breaths and then hand him my phone. "Messages," I manage to choke out. "Just listen."

He takes the cell from me and punches the screen before raising it to his ear. I squeeze my eyes shut, trying to calm my breathing as I wait for him to finish listening.

"We don't know . . . This could mean anything," he says at last. "Did you call your dad back?"

"No answer. Same with my mom. The battery's about to die, anyway."

"Let me go get my cell. I'll try my mom. You just . . . wait here. Give me a sec, okay?"

I just nod.

He's gone for a while. I try to prepare myself, to brace for the news. But there's no preparing yourself for something like this—not really. It was supposed to be routine surgery. I mean, brain surgery, yeah. But routine. The tumor wasn't life threatening. At least, that's what they said.

But then I remember what Nan told me about Great-Grandma Cafferty. The surgery to remove the tumor was a success, but then she bled to death. A brain hemorrhage. That's what killed her.

No. I repeat the word over and over in my head like a mantra, refusing to believe that Nan's anything but fine. She can't be . . . gone. I would have felt it, would have somehow known.

I haven't eaten anything in hours, but it doesn't matter. My stomach doesn't care. Bile rises in my mouth, and I start to retch.

When I'm done, I rise on shaking legs and go to the sink, leaning heavily against the marble counter as I rinse my mouth with the bottle of water I'd left there.

And then I see Ryder in the mirror, standing in the doorway behind me, his face slightly ashen. My stomach bottoms out, the ground swaying dangerously beneath my feet. I grip the counter so tightly that my knuckles go white. "No," is all I say.

"Nan's fine. She's okay."

Relief washes over me in rippling waves. I turn toward him, reaching out blindly.

He takes me in his arms, steadying me. "The surgery went off without a hitch, my mom said. Nan's having a little"—he taps his cheek—"some kind of facial paralysis now, but they think that's temporary. She'll be just fine, Jemma."

I nod, swallowing hard. *Thank God.* "But then . . . Lucy? What was she talking about?"

Ryder takes a deep breath before he answers. "It's Patrick," he says haltingly.

Patrick?

"There's been an accident. I'm so sorry, Jem."

Patrick's dead. I don't know all the details yet, but it happened on Monday, a few hours after we'd been released from school. His car had hydroplaned and skidded off the road, then flipped over a guardrail into the swollen creek. His parents hadn't even reported him missing till close to midnight that night. They hadn't realized he was gone until then.

Why Patrick would have gone out in that awful weather is anyone's guess. But when they pulled the car out of the creek, they found a case of Schaefer Light beside him—with two empty bottles. So everyone's speculating that he was out making a beer run, stocking up for the storm.

It doesn't make sense. *None* of it makes any sense.

And all I can think about are those last words I spoke to him on Monday, just hours before the accident. He'd tried to apologize, and I had pretty much shut him down. I'd been annoyed with him. Impatient.

Then . . . I'd pretty much pushed him entirely from my mind and gone and kissed Ryder without even giving Patrick a second thought. And now? I'd never have the chance to apologize. To make it up to him. To make it *right* with him.

And here's the worst part—when I first found out, I was *so* relieved that Nan was okay that that's all I could focus on. That was all that mattered to me until a couple hours later when I talked to Lucy and Morgan and realized how upset they were. How upset they thought *I* was.

Then it hit me like a ton of bricks. Patrick and I were kinda-sorta going out. Yes, I was going to break up with him, but I hadn't gotten around to it. After all, I figured there was no rush. We weren't going anywhere during the storm. But after the storm, I was going to tell him that I thought we should go back to just being friends. That had been the plan.

Everyone—all my friends, Ryder, even my parents—expected me to be devastated by the news. And I *am* devastated. I would be even if Patrick and I hadn't gone out, hadn't kissed a few times. After all, I've known him my whole life. We've been friends forever, part of the same social circle and all that. So yeah, this is definitely a blow.

But it doesn't feel like a "my boyfriend just died" kind of blow, and that makes me feel horrible. Shallow. Lower than the lowest snake in the grass.

And here's the thing—it's obvious that Ryder shares my guilt. He's been tiptoeing around me all day, unable to meet my eyes. I mean, they were friends too. Not best friends—not like him and Mason, or even him and Ben. But good enough friends that he's hurting. And that kiss we shared—okay, it was more than just a kiss—is hanging there between us, the big, honking elephant in the room.

The worst part is, I could use some comforting right about now. But from whom? Until Daddy arrives tomorrow—*if* he manages to get on a flight and *if* the flooding on the roads has receded enough for him to get through—I'm stuck here with no one but Ryder. And every time I look at him, even glance in his direction, the guilt returns with a vengeance, creating a crushing combination of sadness, grief, and remorse. It's almost more than I can bear.

I spent an hour or two behind the lens of my camera, filming the scene of destruction around here with new perspective. After all, it looks so different in the sunlight, against the backdrop of a blue sky—the damaged roof, the crushed Durango, the broken window, the demolished sleeping porch, the pile of rubble that used to be the barn. Not to mention the flooded creek banks and the tree trunks snapped in two, looking much like broken matchsticks stuck in the ground. There's something savage about it.

But then the battery died, and there's no way to charge it except to sit in the car with the ignition running. And honestly? I'm not in the mood for that. So I've got Delilah in the waistband of my shorts and a bag full of empty cans from the recycling bin. I want to shoot stuff. It's the only way I can clear my head and gain some perspective.

I spy a stretch of splintered fence down near where the barn used to be. It'll do in a pinch, I decide. It's already ruined, so a few missed shots won't hurt anything.

I've got about an hour till the sun goes down. Plenty of time. Only problem is, it's hard to shoot straight with tears rolling down your cheeks.

I empty two magazines before I become aware of that feeling of being watched. I turn to find Ryder leaning against what's left of the enormous old oak tree—stripped bare, the swing gone—watching me.

The sadness in his eyes seems to mirror my own. Yet we can't comfort each other, not now. Not anymore.

I've lost more than Patrick as a result of the storm. I've lost something else, too—something I didn't realize I had, didn't even know that I wanted. For a fleeting moment, Ryder was my friend. Maybe more. And now? He's not.

When did my life turn into a tragedy?

ACT III

It is the east, and Juliet is the sun.

—William Shakespeare, *Romeo and Juliet*

ACT III
Scene 1

Two weeks later I'm sitting in homeroom, tapping my foot impatiently as I wait for special announcements to start. Usually, I hate homeroom, mostly because none of my friends are in the same one as me. But now . . . now I'm kind of glad for the alone time. Well, as "alone" as you can be with twenty-three other kids crowded around you, restless and impatient for lunch.

But at least I don't have to talk. Since the storm, I've been doing that retreat-into-myself thing a lot. I can't help it. It's not that I don't appreciate my friends trying to comfort me—I do. I know they love me and that they're doing their best to cheer me up. But everything's just so messed up right now, you know?

Nan's home, and that's great. She's not quite herself, though.

Mama says it's the steroids. She has to take some really strong ones to keep the swelling down and all that. But they give her terrible insomnia and make her cranky. Really cranky. Like, snap at everyone for everything kind of cranky.

The storm cleanup's been really hard on her too. Imagine just having brain surgery, and then coming home to contractors banging around all day long. So, yeah . . . she's pretty testy. Unbearable, actually. And I feel totally awful for even *thinking* that, but it's true.

And then there was Patrick's funeral. It was awful. Beyond awful. I guess he told his parents that we were going out, because they made an effort to include me in everything. They even asked me if I would speak at the service. I couldn't say no.

It was excruciating. I felt like a total fraud standing up there talking about him, pretending that we were way closer than we actually were. And his mother . . . well, she completely broke down halfway through the service. Who could blame her? What parent expects to bury their child? He was way too young to die, too vibrant to be extinguished like that. Luckily, the nature of his injuries made it impossible to have an open casket. Otherwise his parents would have insisted on it. I'm not sure I could have borne it. The only people I've known who've died have been old people. To see someone so young like that, looking so lifeless and unnatural, more like a wax doll than a real person . . .

I shudder at the thought. Yet . . . now I'm left with this nagging feeling of not having closure, or something cliché like that. But it's true. Every time I step out into the hallway at school, or into the cafeteria at lunch, I expect to see him. And then I remember . . . oh, wait, he's gone. I'm never going to see him again. *Ever.* It just doesn't compute. How can he be gone when the last time I saw him—right here at school, just after homeroom—he was perfectly fine?

And Ryder . . . well, we haven't spoken since the day Daddy came home. Not one word. But sometimes I feel his eyes following me, and I know he's thinking that I'm the kind of girl who kisses one boy while she's dating another—one who's out getting himself killed for a case of beer. But that's *not* who I am—and not how it was. But how can I possibly explain it to him without seeming callous? "Oh, I was going to break up with him anyway." I mean, he's dead now. How convenient, right?

The PA system crackles to life, and everyone glances up at it expectantly. Here it is, the big announcement we've been waiting for—homecoming court. Yeah, so important in the grand scheme of things. I'm pretty sure I couldn't care less. And then, of course, I'm hit with yet another pang of guilt. I *should* care— for Morgan's sake. She wants to win queen *so* badly, though she'd never admit it. She deserves it. And, hey, life goes on, right? At least, that's what everyone keeps telling me.

So I stare at the speaker and listen with the rest of my class-mates as the names are read off.

"Freshman maid: Jodie Abernathy. Sophomore maid: Shannon Luke. Junior maid: Carissa Oakley. Senior maid: Jemma Cafferty. And your Magnolia Branch High School Homecoming Queen is . . . Morgan Taylor. Congratulations, ladies!"

My mouth curves into a smile. She did it! This means so much to her—so much more than all the crowns she's earned in the past. Because this is more than just a pageant title, awarded by random, faceless judges who don't really know her. She was voted homecoming queen by her peers, by people who know that, in addition to being pretty, she's also smart and sweet and funny. And now Lucy and I will get to help her pick out the perfect gown, which will keep us all occupied for the next two weeks, thinking about something positive instead of continuing to wallow—

"Will the homecoming court please report to the media center for a quick meeting before the beginning of A-lunch period."

And then people are saying my name, urging me to "go." Go where? I glance beseechingly over at Francie Darlington, hoping she can enlighten me.

"They called your name," she says with a smile. "You're senior maid!"

I am? That's crazy. Maybe they got confused—mixed my name up with Jessica's, or even Lucy's. That must be it.

Mrs. Blakely tips her head toward the door. "Jemma, you're excused. Congratulations!"

"Who are you going to pick as your escort?" someone calls out from the back of the room. Someone else shushes them, and I hear Patrick's name whispered. Then the room falls eerily silent.

"Jemma?" Mrs. Blakely prods. "Go on, now."

I nod and reach for my bag, feeling suddenly ill. This can't be happening. It must have been a sympathy-vote thing, I decide. But then I remember that we voted *before* the storm. More confused than ever, I rise on shaky legs and make my way toward the door, trying to ignore the curious glances cast my way. When I step out into the hall, I let out my breath in a rush.

Morgan comes barreling down the hall toward me, grinning madly. "Oh my God!" she calls out. "I can't believe it. Both of us! This is going to be *so* awesome."

"Congratulations!" I say, trying to sound enthusiastic as she wraps me in a hug.

"You too. Seriously, Jemma, I was more excited when I heard your name than I was when I heard my own."

I can't help but smile, because I know she means it. "So what's with this meeting?"

She waves one hand in dismissal. "Oh, just logistics about the presentation, that's all. Halftime at the football game and then the following night at the dance with your escort."

I can't do this.

"I'm just going to ask Mason," she continues as we make our way toward the media center, our arms linked. "Maybe you should ask one of the other guys—Ben, maybe."

"Maybe," I say with a shrug. I don't want to ask anyone, though. People are going to say how it should be Patrick, how awful it is that he's not here to escort me. I can hear the murmurs now, the whispers and the "bless her hearts."

"Hey!" a voice calls out behind us, and we turn to find Ryder standing beside the row of orange lockers outside Mr. Jepsen's classroom. I have no idea why he's out of class early, and I don't care. "I just heard the announcement— congrats."

"Thanks," Morgan chirps. "This is epic, right? *Both* of us."

Ryder nods, his gaze shifting from Morgan to me.

I duck my head, averting my eyes. This is worse than when I hated him, I realize. At least then, it wasn't awkward. I could just ignore him and go about my business. Now I feel all queasy and mad and breathless and guilty. I need to get away from him. Fast.

Mercifully, Morgan glances down at her watch. "We gotta get going. There's a meeting in the media center."

"Right," Ryder says. "But, uh . . . Jemma, could I talk to you for a second after school today? Before practice, maybe?"

My gaze snaps up to meet his. "I . . . um, I don't think that's a good idea."

"I'll be quick," he says. "Actually, maybe I'll come over to your house after dinner. That way I can say hi to Nan."

"She's . . . really not up to visitors."

"Really?" He fixes me with a stare, one brow raised in disbelief. "'Cause your mom said just the opposite."

Crap. Now what? I'm out of excuses. Besides, the last thing I want to do is pique Morgan's curiosity. "Oh, fine. Whatever."

"Great. See you then." He turns and heads back into the classroom without a backward glance.

I have no clue what he wants to talk about. Things are already uncomfortable enough between us as it is. No use making it worse by discussing things that don't need to be discussed. We made out, even though I hadn't bothered to break up with Patrick first. It was a mistake—a *big* mistake. End of story.

The memory of that night hits me full force—his shirt was off; mine was close to it. My cheeks flare with sudden heat as I recall the feel of his fingertips skimming up my sides, moving beneath my bra as he kissed me like no one's kissed me before. Ho-ly crap.

Stop.

"What was that about?" Morgan asks as we continue on our way. "He was acting kinda weird, wasn't he?"

"I didn't notice," I say with a shrug, going for nonchalance. "Anyway, we should hurry. We're probably late already."

"Maybe he wants you to ask him to escort you," she teases, hurrying her step.

I match my pace to hers, needing to take two steps for every one of hers. "Yeah, right," I say breathlessly.

"Hey, you never know." She looks at me and winks. "Weirder things have happened."

Oh, man. She has *no* idea.

ACT III

Scene 2

After dinner, I decide to go for a walk. Yes, I'm a coward. No, I don't want to talk to Ryder. So I'll conveniently be gone when he gets here, that's all.

Glancing back over my shoulder to make sure no one's watching me, I skim down the porch steps and head away from the house. It's finally starting to feel like fall, the air slightly crisp. It's a welcome change, that's for sure. I zip up my hoodie and slip my earbuds into my ears as I follow the path down toward the creek, my feet slapping the earth in rhythm to the music. It's a slow pace, but I'm not in a rush.

When I finally reach the creek, I stop short at the sight that greets me. Of the four picnic tables that used to grace the sandy banks, only one is still standing. I'd known this was the case—Daddy had told me the day after he'd gotten back from

Houston, after he'd spent the day riding around our property on an ATV, assessing the damage. But seeing it for myself is something else entirely.

Those tables had been there forever—all my life and probably most of Daddy's, too. The wood was perfectly weathered, smoothed to perfection. But the storm had damaged three of them so badly that they'd had to be completely removed. Sure, we could replace them, but it wouldn't be the same. Kind of like the barn.

I know I should feel grateful that it wasn't worse than this, that our house is still standing, the damage minimal. Hundreds of families lost their homes in Hurricane Paloma and the tornadoes that ripped through the state in its wake. We were lucky, especially considering what a close call it'd been. The twister that leveled the barn had touched down not five hundred yards from the house. Had it decided to drop down from the sky just a little bit to the west, things would've been worse—so much so that I don't even want to think about it.

I sigh as I make my way over to the one remaining table and climb up onto the tabletop, lying down on my back so that I can watch the setting sun paint wide swaths of color—orange, pink, and lavender—across the sky. It, at least, hasn't changed. The sky, I mean. It remains just as it always was—the same as when I was five, ten, twelve, fifteen.

I close my eyes and turn up my music, wanting to lose

myself in it. And I do—so much so that I start to doze off. At least, I must have, because when I open my eyes again, the sun has fully set and the first stars are twinkling in the sky above me.

I'm vaguely aware of the sound of approaching footsteps, but it takes me a second to make the connection—to remember why I'd come out here in the first place.

"Jemma?"

Damn. I sit up and pull the earbuds from my ears, swinging my legs over the side of the table.

"Figured I'd find you out here," Ryder says, drawing up beside me.

I decide to act surprised. "What are you doing here?"

His brow creases. "I told you I was coming, remember?"

"Oh. Right."

"By the way, you might want to call your parents and tell 'em where you are."

I shrug. "Did you see Nan?"

"Yeah. She looks okay, considering she just had brain surgery. She's awfully quiet, though."

"It's better when she's quiet," I mutter, remembering the way she yelled at me for not plumping her pillow *just* so after dinner. "Trust me."

"Mind if I sit?" He tips his head toward the spot on the table beside me.

"Knock yourself out." I slide down and make room for him.

He digs his cell phone out of his back pocket and climbs up onto the table beside me. "So, I was thinking about your project. You know, the movie? I know things have been rough for you lately, what with all that's happened. So . . . um, here." He tilts the screen of his phone toward me. "I . . . uh, tried to get all the places you had in your original footage. You know, the square, the bridges, the Ames House and all that. Showing what it looks like now, after the storm."

He hits play, and the first series of images roll across the screen. I watch in amazement as he clicks through several different video files, each a couple minutes in length.

"I know it's not much," he says once the last video ends. "And the quality's probably not good enough. But maybe you can use some of it."

"I can't believe you did this." I shake my head, a little stunned. "Thank you. This is awesome, Ryder. Really."

He smiles at me, looking ridiculously pleased with himself. And, okay . . . maybe my heart melts a little bit. Just a smidgen.

Heaven help me. . . .

"There's more," he says, reaching into his pocket again. This time, he produces a folded slip of paper. "I Googled Faulkner quotes—you know, looking for things about strength or courage. I only found a few that fit, but I wrote them down for you." He hands me the slip of paper. "They're all cited and everything."

Our fingers brush as I take it from him, electricity seeming to skitter across my skin at the contact. He must have felt something, too, because he jerks his hand away like he's been burned.

Our eyes meet for a split second, and then I look away. I hope he doesn't see the tears gathering on my lashes. I have to swallow a lump in my throat before I can speak. "I can't thank you enough for this, Ryder. This means . . . so much. But . . ." I trail off, gathering courage for what I'm about to say.

"Uh-oh," he says with a wince. "There's a 'but'?"

"Yeah. I'm not applying to NYU."

"What? You have to."

I let out a sigh. "I can't, Ryder. Not now."

"Why? I just saw Nan." He gestures vaguely toward the house. "She seemed okay. Your mom said—"

"You don't understand," I say, cutting him off. How can I explain? "It's just . . . everything's so messed up. There's too much . . . change . . . as it is. It doesn't feel right. Not now."

"But you're the same, Jemma. *You* haven't changed. This is what you want, remember?"

"See, that's where you're wrong. I *have* changed. And"—I shake my head—"I don't even know what I want anymore."

He opens his mouth as if he's about to say something, but closes it just as quickly. A muscle in his jaw flexes as he eyes me sharply, his brow furrowed. "I thought you were stronger than this," he says at last. "Braver." I start to protest, but he cuts me off. "When I get home, I'm going to e-mail you these video files. I don't know anything about making films, but if you need any help, well . . ." He shrugs. "You know my number."

With that, he turns and walks away.

I leap to the ground. "Ryder, wait!"

He stops and turns to face me. "Yeah?"

"I . . . about Patrick. And then . . . you and me. I feel awful about it. Things were so crazy during the storm, like it wasn't real life or something." I take a deep, gulping breath, my cheeks burning now. "I don't want you think that I'm, you know, some kind of—"

"Just stop right there." He holds out one hand. "I don't think anything like that, okay? It was . . ." He trails off, shaking his head. "Shit, Jemma. I'm not going to lie to you. It was nice. I'm glad I kissed you. I'm pretty sure I've been wanting to for . . . well, a long time now."

"You did a pretty good job hiding it, that's for sure."

"It's just that . . . well, I've had to listen to seventeen years' worth of how you're the perfect girl for me. And goddamn, Jem. My mom already controls enough in my life. What food I eat. What clothes I wear. Hell, even my underwear. You wouldn't believe the fight she put up a few years back when I wanted to switch to boxer briefs instead of regular boxers."

I swallow hard, remembering the sight of him wearing the

underwear in question. Yeah, I'm glad he won that particular battle.

"Anyway, if my parents want it for me, it must be wrong. So I convinced myself that *you* were wrong for me. You had to be." His gaze sweeps across my face, and I swear I feel it linger on my lips. "No matter what I felt every single time I looked at you."

Oh my God. I did the *exact* same thing—thinking he had to be wrong for me just because Mama insisted we were a perfect match. Now I don't know what to think. What to feel. What's real and what's a trying-to-prove-something fabrication.

But Ryder . . . he *gets* it. He's lived it too.

I let out a sigh. "Can you imagine how different things would be if our families hated each other? If they were feuding like the First Methodists and the Cavalry Baptists?"

"I bet it'd be a whole lot less complicated, to tell you the truth. Heck, we probably would've already run off together or something by now."

"Probably so," I say, a smile tugging at my lips.

"There's something else," Ryder says, shuffling his feet, looking uncomfortable. "It's about Rosie. I wasn't being honest with her, or with myself. You were right—I *was* leading her on. At Josh's party, I mean."

"But . . . but why?" I stammer.

"Truth be told, I think I was trying to make you jealous. It wasn't fair to her, and, well . . . I came clean to her and apologized. I just wanted you to know."

"Uh-oh, I bet that wasn't pretty," I say.

"Yeah, you could say that," he answers with a wince. "She was awfully mad. Not that I blame her." His lips twitch with a smile. "You're tryin' real hard not to say 'I told you so,' aren't you?"

"I admit, it's taking some serious restraint," I say. Glancing down at my cell, I notice that I've missed three calls. Two from my parents—probably wondering where the heck I am—and one from Lucy. "It's getting late. I should probably go in."

"C'mon, I'll walk you."

He holds out a hand to me. I take it, falling into step beside him—marveling at how right it feels. I glance up at him, his face illuminated by the moonlight. Something in his expression sparks a memory. Ryder at the beach, watching me when he thought I wasn't looking. Ryder at school, glancing at me from across the hall. Ryder at Magnolia Landing, sitting across the table from me at Sunday dinner, watching me eat. I always interpreted his expression as something bordering on contempt—disdain, maybe. But now . . . now he's looking at me with that exact same expression, and I realize that maybe I was wrong all along.

In so, so many ways.

ACT III
Scene 3

The stadium lights are blindingly bright as I step out onto the field and make my way to the fifty-yard line. I take my place in the semicircle with the rest of the cheerleading squad and look out at the sea of orange and blue filling the stadium. The crowd is quiet but for the shuffling of feet, the occasional sneeze or sniffle. Off to the side of the stands, the band remains seated and silent as the football team takes the field, filling in the space behind the dozen cheerleaders. There's no running out onto the field tonight, no bursting through colorful banners while the fight song plays and fans cheer enthusiastically.

Lucy and I managed to get separated somewhere between the sidelines and the field, but she makes her way back to my side, shuffling Jessica down a spot as she squeezes in next to me. Morgan's on my other side, standing in the same pose as I am—feet planted apart, hands clasped behind our backs, heads bowed.

"You okay?" she whispers, and I glance up at her and nod.

Her hair is pulled up into a high ponytail adorned with an enormous orange bow, and she's got a temporary tattoo of our mascot, the Magnolia Branch Mustang, pawing the air on one of her rosy cheeks. Her lashes are wet with gathering tears, and she reaches up to brush one away as Ryder makes his way to the front of the assembled group with Mason and Ben following behind.

The three of them move to stand in the center of the semicircle. The principal taps the microphone twice to make sure it's on and then hands it over to Ryder.

He somehow manages to look larger, more muscular, in his football uniform—tight blue pants that end at his knees, orange jersey emblazoned with the number ten. He's wearing eye black under his eyes, and his dark hair is damp and smoothed down. I can't explain it, but he feels like a stranger to me tonight. I drop my gaze to the grass, feeling numb and strangely dissociated as he clears his throat and begins to speak.

"Tonight," he says haltingly, "we play this game in memory of Patrick Hughes, whose life was cut tragically short during Hurricane Paloma." He takes a deep breath before continuing on. "Patrick was more than just a teammate—he was a friend. To me, to everyone on this team. He always gave one hundred percent out on the field—every game, every practice. He was loyal. He was proud. He was determined."

Ryder glances down at the index card he's holding, then back up at the crowd. He scratches his chin, then clears his throat once more. I shift my weight from one foot to the other as I wait for him to continue. Ben lays a gentle hand on his shoulder, and Mason meets his gaze and nods once before Ryder's able to find his voice again.

"Patrick was a good guy," he says at last. "He always had your back, no matter what. You could count on him to make a play, to push through adversity, to play through an injury. Off the field, Patrick liked to have fun—to laugh, to play. He always knew the right thing to say to cheer someone up. He had a joke for everyone who needed one.

"This team has lost a friend," he says, his voice breaking on the last word. "A brother. We miss you, Pat. Rest in peace." Ryder wipes a tear from his cheek as he hands the microphone back to the principal.

I can't help it—a quiet sob tears from my throat. It's not just me, either. Most of the squad is crying now, and the football team too. Morgan reaches for my hand, Lucy the other. I clasp theirs, squeezing tightly, holding on for dear life as the principal begins her speech.

The rest of the ceremony is mercifully short. His jersey— number seven—is officially retired. A small section of the band stands and plays a mournful tune. The entire stadium is sobbing by the time the last note fades into nothingness. And then we clear the field. It's game time.

I can barely breathe as I take my place on the sideline.

"You don't have to do this," Lucy says as we retrieve our fluffy pom-poms, preparing for the fight song routine.

"I do," I answer. I force myself to take several deep, calming breaths. "For him. For Patrick." We've dedicated this game to him—our first game since the storm, thanks to the extensive damage wrought by the wind and the rain. I owe it to him to participate, to do my job, to cheer his team to victory. I can't just sit this one out.

Lucy nods, her eyes full of understanding. "Let me know if you need to sit down, though, okay? And if you don't want to do the stunt—"

"I'm fine with the stunt." I fell three times at practice, unable to get enough height in the toss. But I won't mess up tonight—I can't.

"I'm just not sure that—" Lucy's protest is cut off by the opening bars of the fight song. I hop into position and plaster a forced smile on my face.

I can do this. I can. Baby steps. I just have to get through the first half, and then the homecoming presentation at halftime.

After that, the last two quarters will be a breeze. And then I can go home and snuggle with Beau and Sadie and pretend that everything's okay when it isn't.

"What do you mean you didn't buy a dress yet?" Lucy shrieks. "The dance is in eight hours! What were you planning to do? Stop by the mall on your way there?" She hurries over to my closet and throws open the door. "Let's see. . . . There's gotta be something in here that'll do. Hey, what about your gala dress?" She holds up the gown in question, fluttering the tulle skirt with one hand. "It'll look awesome with the tiara!"

I shake my head. "I dunno, Luce. I just . . . I don't feel right about this."

Her dark eyes widen. "Right about what? The dress? Okay, I know you just wore it a month ago, but hardly anyone from school was there to see it. Just our friends, and they don't care. The boys won't even remember."

"No, not the dress. I meant . . . the dance. Last night was bad enough." I shudder at the memory.

Things hadn't gotten any easier after the pregame ceremony. When they'd announced the court during halftime and pinned an enormous mum to my cheerleading uniform, I'd looked out at the sea of faces and saw the pity there, heard the hushed whispers that rippled through the stands.

That's the girl who was going out with Patrick. Poor thing, so brave. I wonder who's going to escort her tomorrow night.

At least, that's what I imagined they were saying. So yeah, I'm not exactly looking forward to tonight. The crowning will be ten times worse than last night's presentation. I never asked anyone to escort me. I'm going solo. Well, not really solo, because Morgan, Lucy, and I are supposed to go together. Or that had been the plan right up until two a.m. last night, when Morgan had texted to say that she and Mason had stopped for pizza after the game and run into Clint Anderson—he'd graduated from Magnolia Branch High last year and was a freshman at State now. Apparently, they'd started talking and one thing led to another, including a make-out session in the parking lot. The end result was Clint offering to take her to the dance tonight.

I don't want to go. Only I can't seem to make Mama understand. She's over-the-moon excited about the whole homecoming court thing. She said it was going to make me a "hot commodity"—her words—at Rush next year. I'd stupidly asked why it mattered since I was just going to pledge Phi Delta anyway. At least, that was "her plan," wasn't it? Yes, I'd put extra emphasis on those words. That had led to a big lecture about how I wasn't taking it seriously enough, how important it was to go to the right houses' pref parties even if I *was* a Phi Delta triple legacy.

I glanced over to where Lucy was digging in my closet,

looking for shoes to go with my dress, and sighed. "Will you hate me if I don't go with you tonight?"

She stood so abruptly that she bumped her head on the doorjamb. "Ow! What? Are you dumping me for a guy, like Morgan did? Crap, is my head bleeding?"

I take a look at her scalp. "No, you're good. And no, there's no guy. I just . . . really don't want to go. That's all."

She fixes me with a glare. "That's not funny, Jemma. You have to go."

"You sound just like my mom."

"Well, Miss Shelby is right. *This* time."

I shake my head. "I don't know, Luce. I mean, everyone's going to be watching me. If I look like I'm not having fun, they'll all be like, 'Poor Jemma Cafferty! It's so sad, what happened.' And if I *do* have fun, it'll all be, 'Shouldn't she be in mourning or something?' I can't win either way."

"Why do you care what they think? Your friends know the truth—know how much you cared about him. That's what matters."

I swallow hard, feeling like a fraud again. "But . . . that's just it," I say, choosing my words carefully. "I *didn't* care that much about him. I was going to break up with him right after the storm, Lucy. How awful is that?"

She just stares at me, her eyes wide. And she doesn't even *know* about me making out with Ryder.

I drop my head into my hands. "I'm such a terrible person."

The mattress sinks beside me as Lucy sits and wraps a comforting arm around my shoulders. "Oh, Jem. Girlfriend . . ." She sighs loudly. "I'd think a lot less of you if you *had* been in love with him. That's the honest-to-God truth. I know it's awful to speak ill of the dead and all that, but you know what? Patrick Hughes was trouble. He wasn't right for you. I couldn't for the life of me figure out what you saw in him. But . . . you know, I was trying to be supportive and all that."

"Thank you," I say, leaning in to her and resting my head on her shoulder. "I just . . . I don't know what I'm doing anymore."

"Look, you do what you need to do about tonight. Don't worry about me. Ben is going *sans* date. I'll just hang with him. Or be Morgan and Clint's third wheel. I'm fine with that. Okay?"

"You're sure?"

She nods. "Totally. But, hey, if you change your mind, those pale pink strappy heels will look hot with that dress."

She's right. They will. Not that it matters. I'm not going. It's time for a serious talk with Mama.

"I love you, Luce," I say, feeling more confident now.

"'Course you do. I'm awesome. Now, can I get an ice pack for my head?"

The talk with Mama didn't go well. She actually tossed out phrases like "social suicide" and swore that I was going to regret this decision for the "rest of my life." Yes, she actually said that. Talk about melodramatic.

After Lucy left, I called Morgan and told her that I wasn't going. I feel terrible about it—what kind of person ditches her friend the night she's going to be crowned homecoming queen?

The horrible kind, that's who. I've let down my friends—actually, my entire class, if you think about it. They *did* vote me their class maid, for some crazy reason. And, of course, I've disappointed my mom. You know, with my social suicide and all.

So I decided, hey, I'm on a roll. Might as well dig the hole even deeper. So I'm trying to edit my NYU application film while everyone else is headed over to the school gym for the dance. I still haven't decided if I'm actually going to apply or not, but the deadline's just a week away. So . . . you know. Just in case.

As promised, Ryder e-mailed me the footage he'd shot on his phone—all the "after" shots. I've matched it up with the "before" shots, making a montage. I drum my nails against my laptop, trying to decide if I want to place it before the actual storm documentation or after. I also need to choose music, something that creates the perfect atmosphere. Hmm, what if—

Thunk.

Frowning, I glance over at the French doors that lead to my balcony. *What the heck was that?* It sounded like a rock hitting the glass. I feel like I'm back in the storm, the house being pelted with debris.

Thunk.

I rise and hurry over to the glass, pulling back the sheer curtains to peer out at the setting sun. The sky is perfectly clear, not a cloud in sight. No hurricane. Just—

Thunk. I jump back in alarm, my heart pounding against my ribs.

And then I hear, "Jemma!" A loud whisper, coming from below. I open up the doors and step outside. Moving quickly to the railing, I lean against it and peer down to find Ryder standing there, staring up at me. He's dressed in a suit and tie—the same charcoal suit he wore to the gala, with a narrow silver-blue tie.

"What are you doing?" I call down to him.

He drops a handful of pebbles, scattering them into the grass by his feet. "Shh! Can I come up?"

I lower my voice to match his. "What's wrong with the front door?"

He eyes me with raised brows. "Really?"

I picture my parents downstairs. Imagine what questions they'd ask, what gleeful conclusions they'd leap to at the sight of him here, asking to see me. I shake my head and reach a hand down toward him. "Here, can you climb?"

There's a vine-covered trellis against the house beside my

balcony. If he can just get a foothold, he's tall enough to swing himself up and over the railing.

Which he does in less than two minutes. Pretty impressive, actually. Once he's got both feet on the balcony, he casually brushes himself off. Somehow, he manages to look like he just stepped off the cover of *GQ*.

I tip my head toward the window. "You wanna come in?"

"You think it's safe?"

"Just let me go lock the door," I say before hurrying back inside.

And don't think I'm not amused by the irony. Because unlike normal people, we're not sneaking around to avoid being caught and punished. Nope. On the contrary, our parents would *celebrate* if they caught us in my bedroom together. I'm talking music and streamers and champagne toasts.

As quietly as possible, I turn the key in the lock, listening for the *click*. Sorry, folks. No party tonight.

ACT III

Scene 4

No sooner have I locked the door than Mama calls up to me. "Hey, Jemma?"

Crap. I motion for Ryder to stay out on the balcony, and then I unlock the door and stick my head out. "Yeah?"

"I'm going over to Laura Grace's for a little bit. Nan's sleeping on the porch, and Daddy's out in the garage." His new, temporary workshop until we can rebuild the barn. "Call me when your sister wakes up, okay?"

I force a cheerful tone into my voice. "Okay. Tell Laura Grace I said hi."

"Okeydoke. Bye, hon."

I stand there, my head sticking out into the hall, until I hear the front door close. Then I slip back inside and relock the door, just in case. "Coast is clear," I say.

Ryder has to bend in half to step through the open French doors. "Watch your head," I warn, amazed by the sheer size of him. Somehow, my room looks smaller with him in it.

"Wow," he says, looking around. "You've redecorated."

"When was the last time you were in here?" I search my memory, browsing through images of a much smaller, shaggy-haired Ryder in my room. Eight, maybe nine?

"It's been a while, I guess." He moves over to my mirror, framed with photos that I've tacked up haphazardly on the white wicker frame. Mostly me, Morgan, and Lucy in various posed and candid shots. One of Morgan, just after being crowned Miss Teen Lafayette Country. A couple of the entire cheerleading squad at cheer camp.

I see his gaze linger on one picture in the top right corner. Curious, I move closer, till I can see the photo in question. It was taken on vacation—Fort Walton Beach, at the Goofy Golf—several years ago. Nan and I are standing under the green T-Rex with our arms thrown around each other. Ryder is beside us, leaning on a golf club. He's clearly in the middle of a growth spurt, because he looks all skinny and stretched out. I'd guess we're about twelve.

If you look through our family photo albums, you'll probably find a million pictures that include Ryder. But this is the only one of him in my room. I'd kind of forgotten about it.

But now . . . I'm glad it's here.

"Look how skinny I was," he says.

"Look how chubby *I* was," I shoot back, noting my round face.

"You were not chubby. You were cute. In that, you know, awkward years kind of way."

"Thanks. I think." I scratch my head. "Anyway, how come you're not at the dance?"

"I ran into Lucy. She told me you weren't coming."

"And?"

"And"—he glances down at his watch—"crowning doesn't start for another hour. If you—"

"Stop right there. What part of 'not going' don't you get?"

He takes a step toward me, closing the distance between us. "Look, Jemma, I messed this up in eighth grade. Let me make it right."

I shake my head. "This doesn't have anything to do with eighth grade. I can't go."

"Yes, you can."

"Shut up and listen to me, Ryder." I fold my arms across my chest, fixing him with a glare. "I said I can't go."

He drops his gaze to the floor. When he raises it again to meet mine, warring emotions are playing across his features, as plain as day. "Look, I know my timing is for shit. I should just keep my mouth shut and walk out of here right now."

He actually heads for the window. But then he stops and

turns back to face me. "Fuck it," he says. "I was a coward then, but not this time. I'm crazy about you, Jemma. *Beyond* crazy. Shit, I think I'm in love with you. I want to take you to this dance. I know it's too soon—that everyone's going to talk. You know, because of Patrick . . ." He trails off, looking miserable. "Damn." He rakes a hand through his hair and turns back to the window.

He's halfway out before I manage to rouse myself from the shock-induced stupor that has kept me frozen to one spot, unable to say a single word. I launch myself into action.

"Ryder, wait! Stop!" I grab him by the wrist and drag him back inside, pulling him up against my body. His eyes widen as I rise up on tiptoe and press my lips against his.

He loves me. Ryder Marsden *loves* me. I don't know what to say—what to think or feel or do. All I know is that I want to kiss him. Badly.

So I do. The kiss is soft, gentle. Tender. It steals my breath away and makes me want more—so much more. *Later.* There's no time, not now.

I force myself to drag my lips away from his. "I've got to get dressed. If we hurry, we can still make it in time."

I send Ryder down while I change, tasking him with finding my dad in the garage and telling him where we're going. Thank God, Mama's not home. Daddy won't ask too many questions. He'll just assume I changed my mind and that Ryder's giving me a ride. As simple as that.

Somehow, I get ready in record time. Vintage dress from the night of the gala. Pink strappy shoes. I smooth my hair into a low ponytail over one shoulder, glad I didn't straighten my hair today. For once, the messy waves work. A quick swipe of mascara, a little blush, pink gloss, and I'm good to go.

"Where's your car?" I ask as soon as I step out onto the porch and find Ryder there, waiting. His Durango's still in the shop, but he's been driving his dad's old Audi.

"I was in stealth mode," he answers with a sly smile. "Left it at the top of the road so they wouldn't know I was here." He glances down at my heels and winces. "I can see now that was a bad idea." He rubs his chin thoughtfully for a second. "Wait, I know." Before I even have a chance to react, he reaches down and scoops me up, literally sweeping me right off my feet and carrying me down the drive toward my awaiting chariot.

We make it *just* in the nick of time. They're already announcing the sophomore maid and her escort as we push our way through the crowd toward the stage. The rest of the court is lined up next to the stairs. The moment Morgan spots me, her face lights up. Frantically, she waves me over.

"Oh my God! You're here! I can't believe it. Go tell Mrs. Richmond. I told her you weren't coming." She pushes me toward the teacher standing at the edge of the stage, holding a clipboard. I guess she's in charge of arranging us in order and getting us where we're supposed to be at the right time or something.

"You're here," Mrs. Richmond says, her voice laced with surprise. She gestures for me to take my place in line in front of Morgan and Clint and then hurries up the stairs to whisper something in the principal's ear.

No one misses a beat. The junior maid is announced, and the girl in front of me makes her way up onto the stage with her escort. It's my turn next, and I realize then that I never turned in the name of my escort—because I hadn't planned on being here. I glance around wildly for Ryder, but he's nowhere to be seen, swallowed up by the sea of people in cocktail dresses and suits.

Crap. I thought he realized that escorting me on court was part of the deal, once I'd agreed to go. I guess he'd figured it'd be easier on me, what with the whole Patrick thing, if I was alone onstage. But I don't want to be alone. I want Ryder with me. By my side, supporting me.

Always.

I finally spot him in the crowd—it's not too hard, since he's a head taller than pretty much everyone else—and our eyes meet. My stomach drops to my feet—you know, that feeling you get on a roller coaster right after you crest that first hill and start plummeting toward the ground.

Oh my God, this can't be happening. I've fallen in love with Ryder Marsden, the boy I'm supposed to hate. And it has nothing to do with his confession, his declaration that *he* loves *me*. Sure, it might have forced me to examine my feelings faster than I would have on my own, but it was there all along, taking root, growing, blossoming.

Heck, it's a full-blown garden at this point.

"Our senior maid is Miss Jemma Cafferty!" comes the principal's voice. "Jemma is a varsity cheerleader, a member of the Wheelettes social sorority, the French Honor Club, the National Honor Society, and the Peer Mentors. She's escorted tonight by . . . ahem, sorry. I'm afraid there's no escort, so we'll just—"

"Ryder Marsden," I call out as I make my way across the stage. "I'm escorted by Ryder Marsden."

The collective gasp that follows my announcement is like something out of the movies. I swear, it's just like that scene in *Gone with the Wind* where Rhett offers one hundred and fifty dollars in gold to dance with Scarlett, and she walks through the scandalized bystanders to take her place beside Rhett for the Virginia reel.

Only it's the reverse. I'm standing here doing the scandalizing, and Ryder's doing the walking.

"Apparently, Jemma's escort is Ryder Marsden," the principal ad-libs into the microphone, looking a little frazzled. "Ryder is . . . um . . . the starting quarterback for the varsity football team, and, um . . . in the National Honor Society and . . ." She trails off helplessly.

"A Peer Mentor," he adds helpfully as he steps up beside me and takes my hand. The smile he flashes in my direction as Mrs. Crawford places the tiara on my head is dazzling—way more so than the tiara itself. My knees go a little weak, and I clutch him tightly as I wobble on my four-inch heels.

But here's the thing: If the crowd is whispering about me, I don't hear it. I'm aware only of Ryder beside me, my hand resting in the crook of his arm as he leads me to our spot on the stage beside the junior maid and her escort, where we wait for Morgan to be crowned queen.

Oh, there'll be hell to pay tomorrow. I have no idea what we're going to tell our parents. Right now I don't even care. Just like Scarlett O'Hara, I'm going to enjoy myself tonight and worry about the rest later.

After all, tomorrow *is* another . . . Well, you know how the saying goes.

ACT III
Scene 5

As soon as the crowning is over and Ryder and I make our way down from the stage, Lucy makes a beeline toward us, her brow knit over narrowed eyes.

"I'm going to go find the guys," Ryder says, releasing my hand.

"I thought you weren't coming," she says as Ryder brushes past her, headed toward the long refreshment tables where Mason and Ben are standing with Jessica and one of the JV cheerleaders—I think her name is Kelsey. Or maybe it's Kasey.

I force my gaze back to Lucy. "I wasn't. My plans changed at the last minute."

"Okay, 'fess up. Is there something you'd like to share with me? Like, why you're here tonight with your archenemy?"

"I needed a ride; that's all," I say with a shrug. "Ryder happened to stop by." I glance back toward the refreshment table. I can't help myself. It looks like Jessica and Mason are arguing. Jessica's face is red, and she's waving her hands around while she talks. In the meantime, Kelsey/Kasey is just standing there, looking up adoringly at Ryder.

Lucy snaps her fingers to get my attention. "Hey, earth to Jemma!"

"Sorry," I say, giving her my full attention again.

"I can't believe you asked Ryder to escort you. What, did Miss Shelby make you, or something?"

I almost laugh at that. It's like the eighth-grade dance, in reverse. Only difference is, I'm not going to throw him under the bus. "No, trust me. Mama has no idea." And that's all I'm going to say about it right now. "C'mon, let's go get something to drink. I'm dying here."

I lead a bewildered Lucy across the room toward the punch table—and okay, toward the people who happen to be standing in front of it. What can I say? I have no shame. Not tonight.

"Hey!" Ben calls out as we approach. "You looked great up there, Jemma."

"Thanks." My cheeks flush hotly as Ryder flashes me a dazzling smile. "Where'd Jessica go?" I ask Mason. She and Kelsey/Kasey have disappeared into the crowd.

"Who knows?" Mason mutters. "She's mad at me about

something." He eyes me up and down. "Isn't that the same dress you wore to your mama's party?"

"Yeah." I self-consciously smooth down the tulle skirt. "And thanks for pointing that out, Mase. Appreciate it."

Beside me, Lucy rolls her eyes. "Idiot."

Mason shoves his hands into his pockets. "Hey, I'm just keeping it real. Oh, look, there's Rosie. Better run and hide, Ryder."

We all turn to look in unison. Rosie looks gorgeous in a scarlet-colored chiffon dress, her blond curls loose around her shoulders. Her head is held high, and she appears fiercely determined as she approaches our group.

"Hey, Ben," she says, ignoring the rest of us. "You want to dance?"

Ben's cheeks turn the same scarlet as Rosie's dress. He and Ryder exchange a pointed look while Lucy and I just stand there gawking.

"Go on, man," Ryder says, nudging him. "You look great, Rosie," he adds. "Nice dress."

She smiles up at him, her blue eyes seeming to glitter beneath the disco-ball lighting. "Thanks. You don't look so bad yourself." She glances from Ryder to me and back to Ryder again. "The two of you . . . You looked good together up there."

"I know, right?" Lucy nods, and I shoot her a "what are you

doing?" glare. She ignores it. "Maybe these two should stop the hating and listen to their parents."

An awkward silence follows. Finally, Ben seems to remember why Rosie came over in the first place. "Um, you want to go dance?"

"Yeah. I love this song."

Ben nods. "Okay. Catch you guys later."

Rosie's smile seems genuine as she follows Ben to the dance floor. I hope that means she's finally figured out what a sweetheart he is.

As soon as they're gone, Lucy lets out a low whistle. "Whoa, did that just happen?"

"I think it did," I say, watching as Rosie wraps her arms around Ben's neck. She must have said something funny, because he throws his head back and laughs.

Lucy shakes her head in amazement. "I swear, it's like we're in some kind of alternate universe tonight."

"Well, in that case, how about you and me, Luce?" Mason says with a cocky grin. "Think you can handle me on the dance floor?"

"Oh, what the hell?" Lucy says with a shrug. "Why not!" She reaches for Mason's hand and drags him toward the dance floor but stops a few feet away and turns back to face Ryder and me. "Hey, you two—behave!" In seconds, she and Mason are swallowed by the crowd.

"And then there were two," Ryder says, reaching for my hand. He leans down, his lips near my ear. "Do you have any idea how badly I want to kiss you right now?" he whispers.

"Later," I say with a shiver. It's not an empty word. It's a promise.

He gives my hand a squeeze. "So . . . until then, I guess we dance."

"We dance," I say as a slow song begins to play.

Talk about good timing.

We were able to successfully downplay the whole going-to-the-dance-together thing to our parents. I guess our history of acting like we despise each other worked in our favor, because they actually believed that I changed my mind at the last minute and called Ryder to take me—just because he lives down the street. And then, since I didn't have an escort, Ryder offered to stand in.

Mama saw this as a perfect opportunity to remind me what a gentleman Ryder is—how selfless and generous and downright *perfect* he is. Only, this time, I agreed with her. Secretly, of course.

I have no idea how Ryder and I are going to manage this from here on out. We didn't talk about it last night. We didn't really talk, period. We danced. We laughed. We had fun with our friends.

We saved the kissing for later, when Ryder brought me home. He parked the Audi at the end of our road, far away from prying eyes. We leaned against the car under the bright moonlight and kissed until we were breathless, until my lips were swollen and my cheeks were flushed and I thought I was going to melt into a puddle of goo from the sheer *rightness* of it all.

And then we'd driven up to the house and he'd walked me to the front door. We were careful then, keeping our distance. I figured my mom had her nose pressed to the glass, waiting for us. She probably did, considering how quickly she'd burst into the living room when I walked in the front door, firing a barrage of questions at me before I'd even made it out of the mudroom.

And now I'm just lying in bed, purportedly napping since I'd gotten up early to go to church, but really texting with Ryder.

Did you finish editing your film? he asks.

I turn over onto my side, cradling the phone. *Yeah. It looks pretty good. I'll upload it to YouTube and send you the link, if you wanna see.*

'Course I do. Do it now.

So I do. It takes a while for the video to load. Once it's done, I type out an e-mail with the link and hit send. Then I slump back onto my bed and retrieve my phone. *Okay, check your e-mail.*

Minutes pass. I close my eyes, reliving my favorite moments from last night. Most include Ryder, but there's also the moment when Morgan was crowned queen. I've never seen her look happier, and I have to admit, she and Clint made a really cute couple. Of course, Clint goes to State and Morgan's planning on going to Ole Miss, so I'm not sure how that's going to work out.

And that thought reminds me about my own situation with Ryder. Here we are, doing . . . something. Finally. But in less than a year's time, we're heading off to college. I have no idea where he'll end up. He hasn't given me any clues as to where he's leaning toward right now. It *could* be Ole Miss, but it could just as easily be Alabama or LSU or even Tennessee.

And me . . . well, here I am, finishing up my application to NYU. I've got this one last piece to upload and then my portfolio is complete. I've already had my SAT scores sent, and truth be told, I'm pretty stoked about the possibility. The more I think about it, the more I want to go. It turns out NYU has a rifle team—yes, I've been doing my research. And okay, yeah, I prefer to shoot a pistol, but I'm pretty damn good with a rifle, too. Remember all those skeet tournament trophies I've won? Yep, with a rifle.

Turns out there's even a pistol range in Manhattan, on Twentieth Street, which isn't too far from NYU's campus. Who knows? Maybe I can find an Olympic development team or something. That would make Daddy happy. And let's face it—you can take the girl out of Mississippi, but you can't take Mississippi out of the girl.

But I'm not getting my hopes up *too* high. I know I probably won't get in. But if I do, well . . . I'm just going to have to make my parents understand. Only problem is, before, I'd factored in only the price of leaving all my friends behind. Which, trust me, seems overwhelmingly costly to begin with. But now I have to factor in leaving Ryder, too.

I don't know what to do. Ryder's being so supportive about the whole thing, so encouraging and helpful. What does that mean? That he *wants* me to go? To leave him? I'm so confused, so—

Wow, Jemma! This is awesome. Seriously. It's perfect.

I read his text with a big, goofy grin on my face.

Did you upload it to admissions yet?

Not yet, I type.

Do it. Now, before you chicken out. The deadline's just a couple days away.

My heart begins to pound, my palms damp as I type my response. *But my parents, remember?*

You can talk to Brad and Shelby about it once you get your acceptance letter. C'mon, do it. I'll wait right here. Let me know when you're done.

I take a deep breath and then nod to myself. *I can do this. It's just an application. I don't have to make any decisions now.* What the hell, right?

It takes me only a matter of minutes. Eight, to be exact.

I did it, I type.

I'm proud of you, Jem.

I swear, you'd almost think he wants to get rid of me.

There's a knock on my door. "Jemma?"

I barely have time to type *BRB* and shove my cell under the pillow before Nan walks in. "You sleeping?"

"Nah, just lying here." I sit up and stretch. "How're you feeling?"

"Could be worse." She sits on the edge of my bed with a sigh. "You've been avoiding me. What's up?"

"I'm just a little . . . distracted lately, that's all. All this . . . stuff . . . going on."

"Stuff? Care to elaborate?"

"Hey, your eye looks better," I say, hedging.

"I know, right? It's about damn time. I was getting worried about going back to school looking like a freak."

"You've got time," I tell her. "January's still two months away."

She smiles mischievously. "Want to know a secret?" She doesn't wait for my response before continuing on. "I don't think I'm going back to Southern. I'm thinking about transferring to Ole Miss instead."

"Seriously? Why would you do that?"

"I guess this tumor and the surgery and everything has given me a new perspective on things. And besides, Dean and I have been talking a lot lately."

"Dean Somers?" I ask. Dean was her on-and-off high-school boyfriend. They'd broken up during her senior year, when he was a freshman at Ole Miss and cheated on her at a frat party.

"Yeah. Dean's graduating in the spring and starting grad school, getting an apartment off campus. And, well, we were thinking . . . you know." She shrugs.

I eye her suspiciously. "You were thinking *what*?"

"That maybe I'd move in with him."

"You would *do* that?" I ask, unable to disguise the incredulity in my voice.

She chews on her lower lip before answering me. "Okay, maybe not now," she says at last. "But I want to be there in Oxford with him. One thing I've learned from all of this is that life is fragile. I mean, when Patrick went out to make that beer run, do you think he was thinking, 'This could be it for me'? I'm telling you, Jemma—you've got to decide what you want and go for it. You never know how much time you've got left. It's like that song—how does it go? 'We might not get tomorrow'?"

"I didn't know you listen to Pitbull," I say with a smile.

"I didn't know *you* did," she shoots back.

"Hey, what can I say? He's Mr. Worldwide." Behind me, my phone buzzes with a new text.

Nan looks around me suspiciously. "Why are you hiding your cell phone under your pillow?"

Busted. "Because I thought you were Mama," I answer truthfully.

"And you didn't want her to know . . . what?"

I exhale slowly, trying to decide how much to reveal to her. I reach for my phone and drag it out. "You kind of caught me and Ryder texting."

"You and Ryder? Why is that a secret? Wait—do you mean you two were *sexting*?"

"Oh my God! No. Eww!" That's just so . . . tacky.

She shrugs. "Well, then, what's the big deal?"

I realize there's only one way to make her understand what a huge, enormous, monumental deal it is—I have to tell her the truth.

So I do.

When I'm finished, Nan just smiles and says, "It's about damn time you put that boy out of his misery. He's only been in love with you since . . . well, since forever."

I roll my eyes. "No, you've got it backward. We've *hated* each other since forever."

"Love, hate," she says with a smile. "Such a fine line between the two, isn't there?"

And you know what? I realize then that she's right.

ACT III
Scene 6

Friday's football game is the last of the regular season. Afterward, we all go out for pizza. Ryder and I don't get a chance to be alone—not once. Which might be a good thing, since I'm still not sure what's going on between us exactly. Lucy and Morgan are sleeping over, so we ride back to my house together, all piled into my little Fiat.

When we pull up, I'm surprised to see Laura Grace's car there. It's late, and Laura Grace is *not* a night person. Which can mean only one thing—something's up. My stomach plummets as I consider the possibility that maybe they somehow *know*.

The house is unusually quiet when we step inside. I send Morgan and Lucy up to my room to get changed out of their cheerleading uniforms while I tiptoe around downstairs, looking for Mama and Laura Grace. It doesn't take me long to find them. They're in the kitchen, their usual hangout spot, with the door closed. And, okay . . . I know it's a terrible thing to do, but I lurk outside the door, eavesdropping. I've got to know what's going on, in case I'm about to get ambushed or something.

So, I lean my ear against the door—this is the tricky part, because it's a swinging door—and listen.

"I just can't believe Rob would do this," comes Laura Grace's sniffly voice. Clearly, she's crying. "The both of them, going behind my back."

"Just because a scout came to the game—"

"You don't understand, Shelby. This . . . this is, like, the final step in the recruitment process. The man came all the way from New York to watch him play! He's here to finalize the deal."

"And Ryder's already had his transcripts sent there? His SAT scores and everything?"

"Apparently. Which means this has been in the works for months, and no one even bothered to tell me. And then they're both like, 'Oh, by the way . . .'" Her voice breaks on a sob. "How could they do this to me?"

Mama makes comforting noises, and then I hear her sigh. "I just don't understand why Ryder would want to play for a school like Columbia when he could have his pick of SEC schools. *Real* football schools."

286

Columbia? What the *hell* are they talking about? Columbia's in New York City. Ryder's not going to school in New York City. If he were—if there was even a remote possibility—he would have told me.

Right? I mean, after I poured my guts out to him, telling him how I wanted to go to NYU, it seems like that would have been the perfect opening for him to have said, "Hey, guess what? Me too."

But he didn't. He didn't even mention it, not once. I need to talk to him. *Now.*

Moving on silent feet, I hurry back upstairs. Morgan and Lucy have changed into pj's and are lying on my bed, both of them doing something on their cell phones.

"I need you two to cover for me," I say before I've really thought it through.

Lucy sits up with a start. "Cover for you?"

"I . . . yeah." *What do I tell them?* "I need to slip out for a little bit, that's all."

"Slip out where?" Morgan asks, still typing furiously on her phone.

Oh my God. I've got to tell them. They're my best friends. How can I *not* tell them? Especially considering the fact that I need them to cover for me so that I can go yell at someone else I consider a friend for *not* telling me something. So ironic, right?

"I need to go talk to Ryder," I say as I quickly tap out a text message. *Meet me at the ruins. Fifteen minutes.* "And I know you have a million questions and that I shouldn't just run out without answering them first, but I promise that I will the second I get back, okay?"

"Well, what are we supposed to tell your mom if she comes looking for you?"

"It doesn't really matter, as long as you don't mention Ryder. Say . . . say that I'm outside. That I left something in the car," I suggest, even though I know it's a lame excuse.

"I'm confused," Morgan says, finally setting her phone aside. "Why do you need to go see Ryder? Besides, if your mom knew that's where you were going, she'd probably throw a party, not freak out. Wait . . ." Her expression shifts dramatically, her eyes widening. "Oh my God! That's *why* you don't want her to know! Because you and Ryder . . ." She glances over at Lucy, waiting for her to make the mental leap.

"Jemma and Ryder what? *What?*" Lucy looks from me to Morgan and back to me again. And then I see it—comprehension lights up her face. "Holy shit! No way! I mean, I know you went to homecoming together and everything, but I thought that was just . . . you know, as friends."

"Yeah, I figured his mom made him take you, or—" Morgan stops short, as if she's just realized what she's said. "Something," she finishes lamely.

"I'll tell you everything when I get back," I say, glancing toward my closed door. "I doubt Mama will come looking for me, but if she does, say that I went outside to get something out of the car. That I *just* left. And then text me, okay?"

They nod in unison.

My phone beeps, and I glance down at the screen.

I'm on my way.

"Crap, I'm going to have to take a kayak." I glance down with a frown, realizing I'm still in my uniform. Not the best kayaking attire, but my parents will surely hear the car.

Morgan shakes her head. "You can't kayak in the dark."

"Of course I can. Full moon." I tip my head toward the window. The curtains are drawn back, the bright moon framed in the panes of glass.

"You're crazy," Lucy says with a scowl. "There're snakes in that creek."

Don't I know it. I shudder involuntarily.

"And God knows what else. Drive, okay?" Lucy reaches for my hand and gives it a reassuring squeeze. "And then if your mom asks, we'll tell her that you had to run out to the drugstore. For . . . I dunno, tampons or something. I'll say I had a feminine emergency and that I'm real picky about what brand I use and that you don't have that kind, so . . ."

"So you went to get them for her," Morgan finishes for her.

"Because you're such a good friend," Lucy singsongs.

I consider my options. Mama and Laura Grace are so caught up in their conversation that she didn't even notice us come in. Why would she notice a car now, especially if I'm quiet? And if she does notice, well . . . Lucy's suggestion is a good one. It sounds like something Lucy would do, sending me out late at night on a drugstore run just because she didn't like my brand of tampons.

"Okay," I say with a nod. "Stick to the tampon story, but text me if she comes looking."

"Well, go on, then," Lucy says, shooing me toward the door. "You're making your mama's dreams come true, girlfriend."

"I know," I say. "And that's exactly why she's *not* going to find out about it."

I park my car around the back of Magnolia Landing, hidden in the shadows of an old oak dripping Spanish moss. It's a short walk from there to the ruins. Ryder's already there, waiting for me. He's leaning against one of the crumbling walls, staring out into the night. He doesn't even turn at the sound of my approach.

Carefully picking my way across the bumpy path, I move to stand directly in front of him. He meets my gaze but remains silent.

You know that stereotype about redheads and tempers? Well, in my case, it happens to be true. I'm not exactly sure why, but I'm so angry that my breath is coming in shallow pants, stars seeming to dance in front of my eyes.

"I was going to tell you," he says at last. "I swear I was. This wasn't how I meant for you to find out."

"Oh, yeah?" I spit out. "*When* were you going to tell me, Ryder?"

"I didn't know that scout was coming tonight," he says, skirting around the question. "As soon as I found out, I tried to find you, but the game was about to start and you were already on the field. And then . . . you were with Morgan and Lucy after."

I shake my head. "Don't you get it? You just sat there and let me go on and on about film school in New York, and not once did you even mention Columbia. I can maybe see why you wouldn't have during the storm. But after? I thought that we were . . . that you and I . . ." I trail off miserably. "I guess I was wrong." I turn and stalk off toward my car.

"You don't understand," he calls out after me. And then he's there beside me, reaching for my arm.

I shrug him off. "What don't I understand? That you're a jackass? Because trust me, I understand that just fine."

"So that's it?" He folds his arms across his chest. "You're just going to storm off like you always do? You're not even going to hear me out?"

"Fine." I fold my arms across my chest. "Let's hear it, then. This should be good."

"God, Jemma." He rolls his eyes. "Why do you have to make everything so difficult?"

"Oh, *I'm* making it difficult?" I start to walk away, but then turn back to face him again. "You know what? I am *so* done with you."

He advances on me, closing the distance between us in two long strides. "How 'bout this? *I'm* done with *you*. If you're too blind to see what's going on here, then that's your fucking problem, not mine."

"Fine!" I shout, shoving him hard against the chest with both hands.

He takes one step back, both hands held up in surrender. "Fine."

For several seconds, we stand there staring each other down. Anger radiates off the both of us in waves, crackling like electricity.

And then . . . he sort of staggers back. All his swagger, his bravado, crumbles away in a split second, just like that. "Why do we keep doing this? Yelling at each other like this?"

I let out my breath in a huff. "Because you always piss me off, that's why, acting all smug and superior."

"Yeah, and you always throw temper tantrums like some kind of spoiled brat. That's just who we are. We're not perfect." He takes a deep, rattling breath. "But we're good together, Jem."

He's right. I know he is, but . . .

"You say you love me, but you can't even be bothered to tell me that you're applying to a school in the same city as me? Not until the cat's out the bag and everyone knows? What am I supposed to think, Ryder?"

He rakes a hand through his hair. "Don't you get it? I want you to follow your dreams. To do what you want to do with your life—not what your parents want, or what Nan wants, or what I want. I didn't want to take that away from you. If you knew I was thinking about going to Columbia . . ." He shakes his head.

"Then what? I'm having a hard time following your logic here."

He sighs, his enormous shoulders seeming to sag. "I didn't want you to apply just because I'm going to be in New York. Or hell, even worse, *not* apply because I'm going to be there. I was going to tell you right after you finished your application. But I wanted to tell you in person. And then the scout shows up at the game tonight, and what was I supposed to do? My mom is freaking out; you're freaking out." He throws his hands in the air in frustration. "I've totally fucked this up."

It hits me then, the truth of the situation. He made his decision about Columbia on his own, and he wanted me to be able to do the same. Of course.

Hell, if it hadn't been for the storm bringing us together

like it did, I probably *would* have turned down NYU rather than risk going off to New York with him, and that's the truth.

I drop my gaze to the ground and take a deep breath, cursing myself for being such an idiot.

"No, you haven't," I say at last, raising my eyes to meet his confused ones.

"Haven't what?"

"Fucked it up." I take a tentative step toward him. "I get it now. God, Ryder. Why do you have to be so perfect?"

"Perfect? I've been in love with you for so long now, and I've never managed to get it right, not once."

I have to bite my lip to keep from grinning. "News flash—I think you've finally got it this time."

His smile makes my heart leap. "Do you have any idea what was going through my head when you first told me about NYU? I couldn't believe it. It was like . . . like a gift fell right into my lap. Like winning the lottery. All this time I thought going off to New York would mean leaving you behind. And now—"

"Now we both better get in," I finish for him, though it probably wasn't what he was going to say. I mean, he's a shoo-in for Columbia. Perfect grades, high SATs, *and* a superstar quarterback the likes of which the Ivy League rarely sees. He's every college admissions director's dream. But me? If I get into NYU, it'll be by the skin of my teeth. Because they want geographic diversity or something lame like that. I'm nothing special.

"Where will you go if you don't get into NYU?" he asks.

"Where else?" I say. "Ole Miss, with Lucy and Morgan."

"Then Ole Miss is my backup too. Here's the thing, Jem. I'm going wherever you're going—whether it's New York or Oxford. I'm not missing my chance this time."

"Why?" The word just tumbles out of my mouth before I can stop myself. "You're going to be some kind of college superstar, whether it's the SEC or the Ivy League. You'll probably win a freaking Heisman."

"And you just might win an Oscar," he counters.

I roll my eyes. "Yeah, right. Please."

"Why not? God, Jemma, you don't even see it. How strong and smart and tenacious you are. Everything you do, you do well. I've never seen you put your mind to something and not come out on top. You win that trophy at cheer camp every single summer—what's it called, the superstar award? Only three people at the whole camp get it or something like that, right?"

"How'd you know about that?"

"Miss Shelby told my mom. I think they put it in the yearbook, too, don't they?"

"Maybe," I say with a shrug. It's not that big of a deal. It's just a cheerleading trophy.

"And how long did it take you to win your first shooting

tournament after your dad bought you that gun? Six months, tops? From what I hear, you're the best shot in all of Magnolia Branch."

"Okay, *that's* true," I say, a smile tugging at the corners of my mouth.

He reaches for my hand. "And then there's those dresses you make, like the one you wore to homecoming. You take something old and make it new—turn it into something special. My mom says you and Lucy could make a fortune selling 'em, and I bet she's right. Don't you see? You're not just *good* at the stuff you do—you're the *best*. That's just the way you are. So I have no doubt that you're going to be some award-winning filmmaker if you put your mind to it."

My heart swells unexpectedly. "You really think that?"

He nods, his dark eyes shining. "I really do."

"Tell me again why we've hated each other all these years?"

"Because we're both stubborn as mules?" he offers.

I can't help but laugh. "Yeah, I'd say that about covers it."

"I love you, Jemma. I'll wait as long as it takes for you to feel the same. I'll wait forever if I have to."

I suck in a breath. *He doesn't know.* How would he? He's said it to me, but I've never once said it back. "Trust me, you had me at 'prettiest girl in all of Magnolia Branch,' and then you sealed the deal with that whole 'best shot' thing."

"Wait. . . . Are you saying . . . I mean—"

"Shhh." I put my finger against his lips. "Though you're really cute when you're stuttering like that."

"Hey, I don't stutter."

"Neither do I. I love you, Ryder Marsden. See?" I rise up on tiptoe and press my lips against his.

His arms encircle my waist, drawing me closer, till there's no space whatsoever between our bodies, till I can't tell where he ends and I begin. His mouth moves against mine, and he kisses me hungrily. Thoroughly. Expertly. And *so* very hotly.

This kiss is somehow different from the ones that have come before it. It's a promise that he is mine, that I am his. It's an acceptance of our fate. It's the ultimate acknowledgment of something that's been there all along, just waiting for us to discover it. To enjoy it. To celebrate it.

So we do.

We pull apart only when my phone buzzes in my jacket pocket, startling us both. I pull it out and glance down at the screen with trepidation. Just as I feared, it's from Lucy.

Mom alert! Abort mission now!

ACT III
Scene 7

I've gotta go," I say, scowling at my phone.

"Now?" Ryder asks, tipping my chin up with one hand so that our eyes meet.

"Unfortunately. It's my mom. Lucy and Morgan are covering for me, but I've got to get back. I'm supposed to be at the drugstore."

"What are we going to tell them? Our moms, I mean?"

I shake my head. "We can't tell them anything. At least, not yet. Can you imagine the pressure they'd put on us if they knew? I mean, they already drive us nuts and they think we *hate* each other."

"You're right. So . . . we keep it a secret?"

"Not exactly. I've got to tell Lucy and Morgan. Just . . . not our parents, okay? Besides, think how fun it will be, sneaking around."

His eyes light with mischief. "Good point."

"Don't go getting any naughty ideas," I tease. "C'mon, walk me to my car."

He takes my hand and falls into step beside me, glancing down at me with a wicked grin.

"What?" I ask.

"Hey, you're the one who brought up 'naughty,' not me."

I poke him playfully in the ribs.

"I've got an idea," he says. "Let's pretend we've got to do a school project together. You know, say that we've been paired up against our will. We can make a big fuss about it—complain about having to spend so much time together."

"While we secretly do lots of naughty things?" I offer.

He nods. "Exactly."

I shiver, imagining the possibilities. Suddenly, I'm looking forward to those Sunday dinners at Magnolia Landing. And to Christmas and the inevitable Cafferty-Marsden winter vacation. In fact, the rest of the school year looms ahead like a lengthy stretch of opportunities, no longer filled with uncertainty and doubt, but with the knowledge that I'm on the right path now . . . the *perfect* path.

And like Nan suggested, I'm going to grab it. Embrace it. Hold on to it tightly—just like I'm holding on to this boy beside me.

We reach my car way too quickly. I'm not ready to go, to leave him, to begin this necessary charade. I lean against my car's door with a sigh, drawing Ryder toward me. His entire body is pressed against mine, firing every cell inside me at once. My knees go weak as he kisses me softly, his lips lingering on mine, despite the urgency.

"Good night," I whisper.

"Good night," he whispers back, his breath warm against my cheek.

Oh man. It just about kills me to slip inside the car and turn the key in the ignition. I'm grinning to myself as I drive away, watching as Ryder becomes a speck in my rearview mirror before melting into the night.

When I slip inside my house five minutes later, I find them all standing around the living room—Mama, Laura Grace, Lucy, and Morgan. I force my features into a mask of frustration. "Sorry, Luce," I say. "I went to two different stores, and neither one had your brand."

"Did you try Parker Drugs?" Laura Grace asks. "They've got a better selection than the big chain stores."

"Darn it, no." I set my keys down with a *thunk*, thinking that my acting skills are surely getting tested tonight. "I didn't even think to try there."

"Well, now you know. Okay, I'm going to take off. You girls have a good time, you hear?"

I rush over to Laura Grace and give her a hug. I don't know why—maybe it's because I know exactly how she's feeling tonight.

"Aww, sugar." She pats me on the back before releasing me. "You're such a good girl."

I feel a momentary flash of guilt, but it passes quickly. She's getting what she wants. She just doesn't know it yet, that's all. "Love you, Miss Laura Grace."

Her eyes fill with tears. Clearly, it's been an emotional night for her. "I love you too, princess." She glances over at my mom.

"It'll all work out," Mama assures her. "I know it will."

"From your lips to God's ears," she says, then makes her way to the front door. "Good night, y'all." With a wave, she's gone.

"You girls want a snack?" Mama asks.

I glance over at my friends, who are both standing behind my mom, shaking their heads frantically.

"Nah, that's okay. We've got some important girl talk to catch up on." They both dash up the stairs before the words are even out of my mouth.

As I follow them up, my phone buzzes. I pause, my heart racing with anticipation. I know it's from Ryder even before I see his name on the screen, followed by three lines of text.

My bounty is as boundless as the sea,
My love as deep; the more I give to thee,
The more I have, for both are infinite.

Romeo and Juliet? I type back, smiling giddily. I should know this—we studied the play in ninth grade.

Yeah. It's Juliet's line, but it works for me.

I love you, Ryder Marsden.

Not half as much as I love you, Jemma Cafferty.

Sighing dreamily, I shove the phone back in my jacket pocket and hurry off to find my friends.

Do I *ever* have a tale to tell them.

Six weeks later

The acceptance letter came in yesterday's mail. Good timing, because Ryder got his the day before and already signed his letter of intent. It was easy to convince my parents that NYU is the right choice for me now that they know Ryder is bound for New York City too—next year's starting quarterback for the Columbia Lions. And me? I'm going to film school. If I say it enough times, maybe I'll actually start to believe it.

My dream, not my parents'. But now . . . now it's so much more.

"Can you pass the salad?" my dad asks Laura Grace.

"Here you go, honey," she says, handing him the heavy crystal bowl before directing her attention back to my mom. "Maybe they should take the train up to New York. Out of Memphis. I think they'd have to go up to Chicago and then over."

"That's a long trip," Mr. Marsden says. "They'd probably have to change trains a couple of times."

"Yes, but think how scenic it would be," Mama says. "Besides, they could get a roomette—that'd give them some space to stretch out and get some sleep. What do you think, Jemma?"

It takes me a second to realize that she's talking to me. I'm too focused on the fact that Ryder's sitting beside me—just inches away—holding my hand beneath the table. "What?" I ask, glancing around at the expectant faces. "Oh, the train. Yeah, maybe."

"They should go up a week early," Laura Grace declares. "Take some time to see the city. Maybe catch a couple of Broadway shows or ball games or something. We could go with them!"

"No," Ryder says, a little too loudly. "I just meant . . . we should probably do it on our own, me and Jemma. Learn our way around and all that. Y'all can come up for Thanksgiving break, once we get settled and everything."

Laura Grace nods. "That's a great idea. We could get rooms at the Plaza, watch the Macy's Parade. And the two of you can show *us* around."

Ryder nods. "Exactly."

Beneath the table, I give his hand a squeeze.

Laura Grace eyes my plate suspiciously. "You're just pushing your food around, aren't you? You've barely taken two bites. I thought you loved Lou's Cornish hens."

"I do. I'm sorry. All I can think about is that English project due this week." I look over at Ryder with a faux scowl.

"We're already way behind—you've always got some excuse. We should probably work on it tonight."

"Probably so," Ryder says with an exasperated-sounding sigh.

"That's the third project the two of you have been paired up on," Mama says, shaking her head. "I hope you two can behave well enough to get your work done properly. No more arguing like the last time."

We'd pretended to fight over a calculus project. Yes, a calculus *project*. Is there really any such thing?

"We're trying really hard to behave," I say, shooting Ryder a sidelong glance. "Right?"

His cheeks pinken deliciously at the innuendo. I love it when Ryder blushes. Totally adorable.

"Right," he mumbles, his gaze fixed on his lap.

Laura Grace gives us both a pointed look. "You two better learn to get along, you hear? You're going to be spending a lot of time together for the next four years."

Four years. Just the two of us—away from our meddling mamas. I have to bite my lip to force back the smile that's threatening to give us away.

"She's right," Mama says, nodding. "The only way I'm allowing Jemma to go to NYU is if she promises not to go off campus without Ryder to escort her."

Escort me? What is it, the 1950s or something? Besides, I don't think she realizes that NYU isn't a traditional campus.

There's no fences or gates or anything like that. I guess she'll find out when she comes to visit over Thanksgiving, but by then it'll be too late. That's what she gets for not looking over the application materials I gave her.

"Fine," I say, trying to sound slightly annoyed. "I promise."

Beneath the table, Ryder releases my hand and lays it open in my lap, palm up. And then I feel him tracing letters on my palm with his fingertip.

I. L. O. V. E. Y. O. U.

I can't help myself—I shiver. I shiver a lot when Ryder's around, it turns out. He seems to have that effect on me.

"Are you cold, Jemma?" Laura Grace asks me. "Ryder, go get her a sweatshirt or something. You two are done eating, anyway. Go on. Take her into the living room and light the fire."

"Nah, I'm fine," I say, just because I know the old Jemma would have argued.

"Well, go work on your project, then. It's warmer in the den."

"My room's like an oven," Ryder deadpans, and I have to stifle a laugh, pretending to cough instead.

"Take her up there, then, before she catches cold. Go. Scoot." Laura Grace waves her hands in our direction.

We rise from the table in unison, both of us trying to look as unhappy about it as possible. Silently, I follow him out. As soon as the door swings shut behind us, he reaches for my hand and pulls me close.

"Shh, listen," I say, cocking my head toward the door.

"I still can't believe it," comes Laura Grace's muffled voice. "The both of them, going off to school together, just like we always hoped they would. They'll find their way into each other's hearts eventually, just you wait and see."

I hear my mom's tinkling laughter. "I guess their plan to escape each other didn't work out so well after all, did it, now? I'm sure they never even imagined—"

"I just hope they don't kill each other," Daddy interrupts.

"They'll be fine," Mr. Marsden answers.

"Well, I guess we won this round, didn't we?" Mama says, her voice full of obvious delight.

I glance up at Ryder, dressed for Sunday dinner—khakis, plaid button-down with a T-shirt beneath. His spiky hair is sticking up haphazardly, his dimples wide as he smiles down at me with so much love in those deep, dark chocolate eyes of his that it lights up his whole face. And me? I'm so happy when I'm with him that Nan says I glow, that a bright, shining light seems to radiate off the pair of us wherever we go.

Despite their gloating, it's easy to see that they *didn't* win, our parents. Nope.

We won.

Have a craving for forbidden romance?
Read on for a taste of Kristi Cook's
Haven, Book One in the Haven trilogy.

I'll never forget that first glimpse of Winterhaven as we pulled up the long, curving drive—gray stones bathed in the lavender haze of dusk, looking like an old European university, all flying buttresses and stone spires reaching toward the sky. Leaves in every shade of the autumn spectrum—red, yellow, orange, brown—littered the ground at my feet, crunching beneath my boots as I stepped out of the car and looked around. This was it—my new home, my new life.

Typically, I had just been dumped there as unceremoniously as had the luggage at my feet. My mom hadn't even bothered to come along for the ride. Okay, technically Patsy is my stepmother, but since my real mom died when I was four and my dad married Patsy about, oh, two seconds later, she's all I've got. She was always clear about her priorities, though—my

dad, and her career, in that order. I think I made the list somewhere between the Junior League and Jimmy Choo shoes.

To give Patsy credit, though, she *had* made an effort to
spend more time with me after my dad died. I thought we were
making progress when she took an entire Saturday afternoon
off and invited me out to lunch. But that's when she dropped
the bomb—she'd been offered a job in New York, a once-in-
a-lifetime opportunity, she called it. So less than a month into
my junior year, Patsy gave me a choice: stay in Atlanta with
Gran, or move to New York with her.

There were no other options, no one else to foist me off on.
No living relatives except for Gran, my real mom's mother.
And as much as I adore Gran, I just wasn't sure that she was
up to having me move in with her and Lupe, her companion/
housekeeper. After all, Gran was old, set in her ways. I didn't
want to be a burden.

And, okay . . . I'll admit that there was more to it than that.
Way more. I can't really explain it, but once I saw that Winterhaven brochure in the pile that Patsy had dumped in my lap, I
somehow *knew* that this was the place for me. I'd been so sure
of it that I'd actually refused to apply anywhere else.

And so . . . here I was. Time to see if my instincts had
been correct. I made my way up the stairs toward the largest
of the buildings, the one marked ADMINISTRATION. Taking a
deep breath, I pushed open a set of double doors at the top of

the stairs and stepped inside, looking around a huge rotunda. On either side of me, two staircases curved up, like a swan's wings. Up above was a stained-glass-tiled dome, a huge chandelier hanging from its center. Directly below it stood a bronze statue cordoned off by red velvet ropes. WASHINGTON IRVING, the plaque read. The school's founder. Which, I had to admit, was pretty cool.

Letting out a low whistle of appreciation, I turned in slow circles, admiring the view. *Wow.* The glossy brochure hadn't done this place justice. I hoped it was costing Patsy a fortune.

At the sound of approaching footsteps, I froze, my heart thumping loudly against my ribs. A tall woman with graying auburn hair came into view, smiling as she hurried toward me, her high heels clicking noisily against the black-and-white checkerboard marble tiles.

"You must be Miss McKenna," she called out. "Welcome to Winterhaven, *chérie*. I'm Nicole Girard. Are these all of your belongings?" She nodded toward the two trunks the driver had left at my side before disappearing without a word.

"That's it," I answered, my voice a bit rusty. "I had the rest of my stuff shipped."

"Very good. Just leave them there, and I'll take you right up to the headmaster's office. Dr. Blackwell is looking forward to welcoming you."

"Great." I tried to sound enthusiastic. Glancing back one

last time at my trunks, I followed Mrs. Girard up the stairs on my left and down a long hall lined with portraits of stern-looking old men in suits. Former headmasters, I guessed.

Finally we stopped in front of a large, arched wooden door that looked like it belonged in a medieval castle. Mrs. Girard knocked three times before turning the brass handle. "Dr. Blackwell?" she called out, stepping inside with me trailing behind. "The new student has arrived."

A leather chair swiveled around, startling me so badly that I took a step back and nearly tripped over my own feet. A man sat behind the massive desk, watching me. His hair was totally silver, but his skin was surprisingly smooth except for crinkles at the corners of his eyes—eyes as silver as his hair. With his wire-rimmed spectacles and a pipe between his teeth, he looked just like I imagined a headmaster should.

"Welcome, Miss McKenna. What a pleasure to meet you."

"Th-thank you, sir," I stammered.

"And how was your journey?"

"I think I slept through most of it," I answered truthfully.

"I do hope you were able to explore the city a bit before coming here. I told your stepmother there was no rush."

"I did, thanks." I had spent two weeks helping Patsy settle into her new apartment on the Upper East Side.

"Very good." He nodded. "Thank you, Nicole. I'll ring the bell when I'm ready for you to show Miss McKenna to her room."

"Very well, sir," the woman replied, then took her leave with one last smile in my direction.

Dr. Blackwell motioned for me to take a seat opposite him, so I settled myself into the chair across from his desk.

"Well, then," he said, laying down his pipe and shuffling a stack of papers. "I have your transcripts right here. Quite impressive. Windsor Day School, advanced classes, honor roll. A fencer." He took off his glasses and looked up at me. "Hmm, on the state championship team, it says."

"Yes, sir. I'm recovering from an injury, though." Almost out of habit, I reached across to rub my right shoulder.

"Well, you'll be pleased to know that we've quite a fencing program here at Winterhaven. Our instructor is an Olympic gold medalist. I'm sure there will be a place for you on the girls team."

I shifted in my seat. At Windsor we'd had just one team— and I had been the only girl on it.

"As to your schedule, we've made some placements based upon your credits, but you'll find our class offerings a little different here from those at Windsor Day. If anything doesn't appeal to you, let us know at the end of the day tomorrow and we'll make the necessary adjustments."

"I'm sure it'll be fine." I took the page he pushed across the desk.

"Breakfast is served in the dining hall from seven till eight thirty, lunch at noon, and dinner from five to six thirty." He shuffled through some more papers on his desk. "Let's see, you'll be in the East Hall dormitory. Mrs. Girard is house-mistress there, and her word is law. I'm sure I needn't tell you that smoking and alcoholic beverages are strictly forbidden. Mrs. Girard will inform you of the remaining dormitory rules when she shows you to your room."

I must have looked panicked, because he smiled a gentle, grandfatherly smile. "I assure you, they are nothing too strict. Now then, have you any questions for me?"

"Um, a roommate?" I asked hopefully.

"Ah, yes. You do have a roommate, and she's eagerly await-ing your arrival. Miss Cecilia Bradford. I believe you'll get on famously."

I nodded, hoping he was right. I wanted to fit in. To *blend* in.

Dr. Blackwell steepled his hands beneath his chin, silently watching me for a moment. "I'm very sorry about your father's death, Miss McKenna," he said, startling me.

My stomach rolled over in my gut. Was that information there in the papers on his desk? It had happened two years ago, but it still felt like yesterday. I couldn't stand to think about it, even now. Especially now. *What doesn't break us only makes us stronger*, Gran liked to say, but it never did make me feel any better.

"Quite tragic," the headmaster added. "Not something one can easily forget, is it?"

"No," I muttered, dropping my gaze to my lap. It wasn't easy to forget, especially when people kept bringing it up.

"I imagine that tomorrow will be a day of discovery for you. You might find yourself somewhat . . . surprised by what you find here at Winterhaven. If you have any questions or simply need to talk to someone, my door is always open. Figuratively speaking, of course."

I only nodded in reply.

"Well, then." He tipped his head toward the door. "Shall I ring the bell for Mrs. Girard?"

"That'd be great," I said, standing on shaky legs.

"I hope your first night at Winterhaven is a pleasant one, Miss McKenna." He extended one hand toward me as Mrs. Girard bustled back in.

"Thank you, sir." As I took his hand, a shudder ran up my arm. His hand was cold—like ice—despite the fire crackling away in the fireplace behind him.

"Come now, Miss McKenna," Mrs. Girard said. "If we go quickly, we might catch Miss Bradford before she heads down to dinner."

With a nod, I picked up my bag and stuffed my class schedule inside, then followed her out. We seemed to walk forever, one corridor leading to the next, up one staircase and down another. How in the world was I ever going to find my way around this place?

Finally we entered what looked like an oversize, paneled study with a stone fireplace on one side, a wall-mounted television in the corner, and bookshelves taking up the opposite wall. Brown leather couches and chairs were scattered about.

"This is the East Hall lounge," Mrs. Girard explained, "where you'll have study hour after dinner each night. Other than that, it's to use as you please. Vending machines are just over there, beside the mailboxes. Girls' rooms are this way." She motioned to the right, and I followed her into yet another hall, this one lined with group photos of girls, all wearing blue velvet gowns. About halfway down the hall we stopped in front of a door with the number 217 on it, and she knocked sharply. When no one answered, she produced a key from her pocket and turned it in the lock.

"Here we are," she said.

Stepping inside, I quickly surveyed the place. The room was surprisingly big, with two white wooden beds on either side of a window. The required desk and dresser were there beside each bed, and an open doorway on one side of the room led to what looked like a little sitting area, complete with love seat, chair, and coffee table. *Not bad*, I thought. It was actually pretty nice.

Mrs. Girard cocked her head toward the bare side of the

room. "I'll send the housekeeper right up with some clean linens for your bed."

"Thank you," I said, setting my bag on the empty desk.

"I see your trunks made it up here already, and your course books are there on the shelves." With a nod, she rubbed her hands together. "Now, then. House rules. No boys on the girls' floor, and vice versa. No smoking, no alcoholic beverages. You will find snacks and beverages in the lounge and the café. The housekeepers come on Tuesdays and Fridays, so I ask that you have your clutter cleared away on those mornings. No cell phones in the lounge, or anywhere else on campus, for that matter. They must remain here in your room at all times. No music so loud as to disturb your neighbors. Lights out by eleven on school nights, midnight curfew on weekends. I suppose that's it for now. The rest can wait."

There was more? I wasn't what you'd call a party animal—not at all—but lights out at eleven seemed a little harsh, and so did the cell phone thing. I wasn't used to going anywhere without my cell.

"Oh, and the restrooms and showers are just next door, on your right." Just then the door was flung open, and a girl about my height wearing a pink robe and bunny slippers burst in, her hair wrapped in a towel.

"Oh!" She stepped back in surprise when she saw us standing there. "You're here!"

"Good evening, Miss Bradford," Mrs. Girard said. "I've brought you your new roommate."

"You must be Violet," she said brightly.

"And you must be Cecilia." Deep brown skin, dark eyes, curly hair peeking out of her towel. She was beautiful, and I felt like a pale plain Jane in comparison.

She waved one hand in dismissal. "Oh, everyone calls me Cece. You have *no* idea how glad I am you're here."

Mrs. Girard moved toward the door. "Well then, I think we're done going over the rules, Miss McKenna. Here's your key"—she laid it on my desk—"and I'll leave you two to get acquainted. You have your class schedule?"

I nodded. "Yes, ma'am."

"Very good. You'll find a campus map on the back. Have a wonderful evening, then. And don't forget, Dr. Blackwell and myself are available to answer any questions that might arise over the course of the day tomorrow."

After she left, I turned my attention to Cece. She was standing by her bed, watching me curiously. "I cleaned out the closet and made sure your half was empty," she offered.

"Thanks. The room is much nicer than I expected. Big."

"Yeah, it's not too bad, except for the shared bath. But you get used to it. And hey, at least it's right next door."

I cleared my throat, trying to think of something to say. "You've been here since freshman year?" I asked at last, knowing it sounded lame.

"Yup. Home sweet home." She removed the towel from her head, revealing dark curls that fell just past her shoulders. "So you're from Atlanta?"

"Lived there my whole life," I said with a shrug. Same neighborhood, same house—just down the block from Gran, who'd live there *her* whole life. God, we were a boring bunch.

Still, it had been comfortable. If only Patsy had left well enough alone, hadn't forced me to choose between her—the closest thing I had to a parent—and the only place I'd ever called home.

But she *had* made me choose, and I'd chosen Winterhaven. I tried to think of this as a new beginning, a fresh start. I'd reinvent myself—the new-and-improved Violet McKenna. No one here would know the names I'd been called—freak, weirdo. Half-jokingly, of course, but my friends had no idea how close to the truth they'd been, and how much that scared me. I *was* a freak, and I'd do just about anything to make sure no one here noticed it.

"Well, I've lived *here* my whole life," Cece said. "The city, I mean. My mom's family is from New Orleans, though, so we spend a lot of time down there. I think I've got some voodoo queen in my blood!"

"Now *that* sounds interesting." I sat down on my bed, watching as Cece walked over to the sitting area and started picking up magazines that were scattered about.

"Just don't let my mother hear you say that," she called back over one shoulder. "So, what is it that you do?"

"You mean, like, fencing?"

"You're a fencer?" she asked, carrying the magazines over to her desk and leaving them in a pile that looked in serious danger of toppling over. "You mean swords and all that stuff?"

"Yeah. I hear the program here is pretty good."

"Oh. Yeah, sure. But I meant . . . you know . . ." Cece trailed off, shaking her head when I said nothing. "Never mind," she said with a shrug, glancing up at the clock above her desk. "Crap, when did it get so late? I've got a student council meeting tonight."

She hurried over to her dresser, pulling open drawers and haphazardly pulling things out. Minutes later she was dressed in jeans and a pink T-shirt, a touch of gloss on her lips. Very low maintenance—I liked that.

"So, you're on student council?" I asked, just trying to make conversation.

"Yep, you're looking at the newly elected junior class president," she said with a grin, grabbing her keys off her desk and stuffing them into a pocket.

"Cool," I said.

She shrugged. "I don't know. Is it cool? I swear, sometimes I think I'm headed toward total dorkdom."

"No, it really *is* cool." Actually, everything about Cece seemed cool, which made me feel like an even bigger loser.

She paused by the door. "I feel terrible just leaving you here, fifteen minutes after you walk through the door. Want me to call some of my friends, ask them to come over and show you around?"

I shook my head. "No, I swear I'll be fine. By the time you get back, I'll have everything all unpacked and organized."

She bit her lower lip, then nodded. "Okay. I guess I'll go, then."

"Go," I answered with a laugh, shooing her out.

As soon as the door closed behind her, I looked around with a sigh, surveying the blank side of the room—my new digs, such as they were. I'd never shared a room with anyone before, much less a bathroom. It was definitely going to take some getting used to, but I had a really good feeling about Cece.

I couldn't resist the urge to go over to her desk and straighten the magazines, though. *Vogue, Entertainment Weekly, Rolling Stone.* Yeah, we were going to get along just fine.

Across the room, my cell phone made a chirping sound. Hurrying back to my own desk, I dug around in my bag till I found it. I expected a message from Patsy, checking to make sure that I'd arrived safely and all that. Instead I found a text from Whitney, my best friend since the very first day of kindergarten, when we'd trooped into our classroom and found our cubbies, conveniently alphabetized by first name, right next to each other. We'd sort of started to drift apart lately, mostly because she'd left Windsor for a performing arts school freshman year. She had new friends, new interests, and I had gotten increasingly busy with fencing. Still, she'd always been a phone call away. *She still is,* I reminded myself.

I scanned her message—asking how it was going so far—and smiled. At least *someone* cared. I sent her a quick text back, promising to e-mail her as soon as I got my laptop set up.

If I could find my laptop, that is. I glanced down at the trunks that held nearly all my earthly possessions, and sighed. Time to start unpacking.

Morning came far too quickly. Still in my pajamas, I winced at the sight of my bloodshot eyes staring back at me in the mirror.

"You're going to miss breakfast if you don't hurry and get dressed," Cece said, eyeing me from across the room as she pulled on her shoes.

"I know. I just . . . I didn't get much sleep last night. New bed and all." I'd actually lain awake most of the night, only drifting off somewhere near dawn.

"I'll wait for you," she offered.

I weighed my options. I could go down now and face the crowd—get it over with. Or I could enjoy some quiet time alone and pull myself together. Ultimately I took the coward's way out. "It's okay, you go on ahead. I just need some coffee."

"There's a coffee machine in the lounge. At least, they call it coffee. Personally, I think they're using the term a little too loosely."

I had to laugh at that. "The way I feel right now, just about anything will do. What time's first period?"

"Eight forty-five. What's your first class?"

I hadn't even glanced at my schedule yet. "Let me see." I grabbed my bag and rummaged through it till I found the sheet Dr. Blackwell had given me. "First period, Hackley Hall, Corridor A, Room 312. Culture and Society in Nineteenth-Century Britain." Wow, that *was* a sophisticated-sounding course for high school.

"That's an advanced-level class," Cece said, wrinkling her nose. "You must be a brainiac or something."

I just shrugged. I'd been called worse.

"Anyway," she continued, "Hackley Hall is where all the junior- and senior-level classes are held, and it's the building just behind us. Here, give me your schedule and I'll show you on the map."

I handed it over along with a pen and watched as she scanned my class list, turned it over and circled a big rectangle on the map, then drew a line from what must be the dorms to the circled building. "There you go," she said, handing it back to me. "After that, you're on your own. Your classes are all more advanced than mine. But I'll save you a seat in the dining hall at lunch, okay?"

"That'd be great. Will I get lost trying to find my way there?"

"Nope. Just follow the hungry crowd."

"Gotcha."

Grinning, she stuffed some notebooks into a pale pink backpack. "I just know you're going to love it here," she said, pausing by the doorway.

God, I hoped she was right.

About the Author

As a child Kristi Cook took her nose out of a book only long enough to take a ballet class (or five) each week. Not much has changed since then, except she's added motherhood to the mix and enjoys penning her own novels as much as reading everybody else's. A transplanted southern gal, Kristi lives in New York City with her husband and two daughters. Visit her online at www.kristi-cook.com.

DESTINY BROUGHT THEM TOGETHER.
NOW IT WILL TEAR THEM APART.

Witness Violet and Aidan's
forbidden love story in Kristi Cook's Haven trilogy.